A Balancing Act

by

Ilona Fridl

A Balancing Act

Cover Art by *Rae Monet, Inc. Design*

The Wild Rose Press, Inc.
PO Box 708
Adams Basin, NY 14410-0708
Visit us at www.thewildrosepress.com

Publishing History
First American Rose Edition, 2018
Print ISBN 978-1-5092-2013-7
Digital ISBN 978-1-5092-2014-4

Published in the United States of America

The young man nodded to her, but his eyes were sad. "Miss La Rue, I'm Dr. Mallory, your surgeon. I need to talk to you."

The nurse set a tray of bandages and tools on a stand by Nora's bed. She, too, looked sad. She slipped her hand around Nora's and squeezed it slightly.

Mallory absently ran his fingers through his hair. "You asked what happened." He paused. "Miss La Rue, from what I was told, you were found under the tent with your leg trapped under a horse and a tent post. Apparently, in it's death struggles, the horse ground your leg into the wooden blocks of the ring."

Nora's throat constricted and tears filled her eyes. "King is dead?" She gripped the nurse's hand.

He nodded. "That's what I was told." He took a deep breath. "Your leg was severely shattered. We had to remove it above the knee."

What he told her went through her ears, but her mind rejected it. What seemed like an eternity passed before she realized what he said. Shaking, she sat partway up, lifted the sheet and looked down at the bandaged stump that was once her right leg. "No! Oh, please, no! It can't be gone! Put it back! Put it back!" A wail came from her throat like it had been sent from the bowels of hell.

Books by Ilona Fridl
available from The Wild Rose Press, Inc.

Silver Screen Heroes
Golden North
Bronze Skies
Dangerous Times (boxed set)
Prime Catch
Iris Rainbow
That Monroe Girl
A Sacrificial Matter
A Balancing Act

~*~

Praise for Ilona Fridl's Dangerous Times Series

"*SILVER SCREEN HEROES* has it all. Suspense, romance, mystery, history....I found myself drawn into the story on several levels."

~Night Owl Romance Reviews Top Pick (4.75 Stars)

"Ilona Fridl's *GOLDEN NORTH* is truly an adventure worth joining. Take an armchair travel opportunity to go to Alaska. This wild state is a wonderful backdrop for such a great novel."

~Night Owl Reviews Top Pick (4.75 Stars)

"[*BRONZE SKIES* is] a quick and enjoyable read that drew me in from the first page to the last even without reading the first two books...There was romance, some laughter, lots of angst, and a few tears. There was family, friends, history, battles, casualties, injuries, a stalker, mystery, and suspense."

~Romancing the Book (4 Roses)

Dedication

To Kathie, you taught me how to soar.

Chapter 1

Milwaukee, Wisconsin, 1890s

An ominous rumble of thunder and a shift of wind let Lenora La Rue know her father had been right to have the roustabouts double-stake the tents. The smell of rain had wafted on the breeze all day. The show was already underway and the band blasted another Sousa march for the acrobats balancing on balls and cylinders, throwing each other around the ring.

Her horse, King Charles, shuffled nervously and snorted. The big white charger was starting to froth. She murmured to him and stroked his forehead. The horse calmed some, but she could see the white of his eye.

A young man with a clipboard held the performer entrance flap to keep it from whipping in the wind, but the rest of the canvas bucked like a wild thing. "Are you ready, Nora?"

She huffed as she grabbed the strap on the harness and mounted the broad back of her steed. "That's Miss La Rue to you. And, yes, I'm ready."

The young man paled at the rebuff, but at her music cue, he opened the flap. She rode past him without the slightest glance. She heard Lyman, the ringmaster, blow his whistle and say, "Now, here's Miss Lenora La Rue our Bareback Rider Extraordinaire!" A wave of applause and cheers exploded out of the crowd as she waved and guided her steed to the center ring. The familiar smell of sawdust, sweat, and popcorn was swirling about with the wind coming in from the entrances and under the tent.

The band launched into "Over the Waves," and with her knees she urged King into a slow canter around the edge of the wooden block ring. One hand grasped the back strap on the harness, and she went up to her knees and arched her slippered foot to touch the back of her head. Nora was vaguely aware of murmurs going through the audience, but she was concentrating on her performance cued precisely to the band. That halted when a shaft of lightning split the skies and was visible through the heavy canvas. The shock waves of thunder shook the ground.

A wall of roars and screeches came from the menagerie by the main entrance as the terrified animals in their cages panicked. A huge whoosh of air came through the openings in the tent, along with the popping sounds of the wooden stakes being pulled out of the wet ground. The massive poles holding up the tent started to groan as the audience stampeded to the exit.

King started to scream and reared up. Nora held on grimly to the back strap, the only thing that kept her from flying off. People were blocking every exit, pushing and shoving to get out. She didn't want King to trample anyone, so she used all her strength to control the big steed.

Suddenly, a noise like a speeding train came through the tent, and the whole end blew up. The tent pole she was next to teetered and came crashing down on her and King. She tried to jump free, but her foot was entangled in the side strap. Horse and pole came down, crushing her leg on the wooden block of the ring. A pain like fire engulfed her from foot to hip. King thrashed for a few moments, grinding her leg some more, then was still. She tried desperately to move the big animal, but the pole was holding them firmly down. The tent canvas was around her like a cocoon. She heard cries and screams coming from all around.

Nora eased her body down onto the sawdust-covered ground. *May as well wait until somebody finds me.* A shock of pain hit her as she adjusted her trapped leg, and then she was freezing. A strange sort of calm replaced the pain, and she drifted into blackness.

****

Dr. John Mallory stretched out on an empty hospital bed, meaning to catch a few winks after a busy day. The hospital hummed around him as nurses prepared patients for the night. A knock on the wall over the bed broke the quiet in his slightly achy head.

"On your feet, son. A runner let us know a cyclone took out the La Rue Family Circus, and injured are being brought here."

John peeked through his half-closed eyes at his father, Dr. Ben Mallory, chief of surgery. "I was at that circus yesterday with Thea." He rubbed his face. "What happened?"

"The main tent collapsed, and many people were caught in the stampede for the exits. I have all the operation rooms being set up. Wash your face and hands, son. It's going to be a long night."

In the surgery quarters, John leaned over the basin and splashed cold water on his face, shocking him awake. He rolled up his shirtsleeves and grabbed the soap. One of the nurses tied his surgical apron while he washed his hands. Several of his fellow doctors came in and did the same.

A commotion in the hallway told him the casualty wagons had arrived. Shrieks and moans flowed under the closed door, and John glanced at the others with concern. "I hope there's enough of us to help them all."

Dr. Alfred Schmidt answered in his clipped German accent, "I tink ve get yust ta vorst cases since ve vere ta closest."

Dr. Henry Chase nodded. "They're sending the others downtown."

John put his hand on the knob of the door and glanced back. "Are you ready?" Both young surgeons glanced at each other and silently nodded. With a deep sigh, John opened the door and stepped into the carnage in the hall. Seven wooden gurneys held bloodied bodies.

Dr. Ben was directing chaos. "Your first patients are prepped. John, take room number one, Alfred, two, and Henry, three."

John heard the hiss of the carbolic acid spray as he stepped inside. "Did you administer the ether, Andy?" he directed to the male nurse at the head of the table.

"Yes, sir, but I don't think he's breathing."

John's surgical assistant, Arthur, put the end of the stethoscope bell on the man's chest. "No heartbeat or air in the lungs. I think he's gone."

John had to make a quick decision whether to try to save him or let him go. If he worked on him now, he could lose some of the other patients waiting. He agonized, then said, "Bring in the next patient," through gritted teeth. The worst part of being a surgeon was the life-or-death decisions he sometimes had to make. They went against his grain; he would save everyone, if he could.

The gurney with the sheeted body was wheeled out and another came in. The assistant and the nurse shifted a body onto the table. The woman moaned.

As Andy was fixing the ether, John caught a glimpse of her face. "That's Lenora La Rue, the bareback rider!"

Arthur wheeled over the surgical instruments. "How do you know?"

"I saw the show last night. Help me with the sheet." John noticed the blood over the right leg as the men folded the sheet from her feet. John was used to seeing mangled limbs, but he gasped in spite of himself.

The tights she'd been wearing were mostly cut away except for the right knee and down to her foot. A tourniquet was around her thigh. Below it, her leg had skin, blood, and bits of bone ground into it everywhere. Arthur was studying the chart. "It says her horse and one of the main posts fell on her leg. The horse was probably thrashing and her leg was caught between it and something hard."

John thought a moment. "That probably kept her from bleeding to death. Prepare for amputation. The bone is simply too mashed up to save. We'll have to cut the bone here." He pointed to just above the knee. "We should have enough good skin to wrap."

Andy administered the ether while John picked up the scalpel to sculpt the skin. Cutting carefully, he got enough to cushion the bone stub, then picked up the saw. Arthur held back the top layer of skin while John sawed through the bone. He smoothed the end down, with his assistant's help, and folded the skin over it.

John was careful to keep the scar from being over the bone stub, so an artificial limb would work well. Fine stitches lined the long wound.

John straightened up, and Arthur handed him a clean towel to wipe his hands. "Arthur, could you bandage the stub for me? I'll wash up for the next patient." At Arthur's nod, he went to the wash basin and soaped the blood off all the way to his elbows.

****

Nora felt a soft breeze caressing her face, but she was very warm. Vague images came to her of canvas tearing, then hands and arms freeing her. Terrible pain came, with calming blackness following. The feeling of being moved from place to place. A horrible smell brought the blackness back. Violent sickness, and then some peace. All the while, shadowy shapes came and went.

She attempted to move her fingers. *Ah, yes, there they go. Good. I seem to be alive.* Her right arm responded slightly to the command to raise it. Some pain. A low moan escaped her lips.

"Nurse! Nurse! I think she's coming around!"

Mother's here. The circus didn't move on without me. She ventured opening an eyelid. Light from the window flooded in, and she squinted. "Mother?" came as squeak from her mouth.

A hand rested on her arm. "I'm here, dear, even if I am needed elsewhere."

Nora gave a low, throaty whisper, "Where am I?"

"You're at the Milwaukee Hospital."

"How long?"

"A couple of days." Her mother's answers were short and terse.

"What happened?"

Just as Nora said that, a woman in a white starched uniform and nurse's hat came into view behind her mother. A young man in a white coat was right beside the nurse.

The young man nodded to her, but his eyes were sad. "Miss La Rue, I'm Dr. Mallory, your surgeon. I need to talk to you."

The nurse set a tray of bandages and tools on a stand by Nora's bed. She, too, looked sad. She slipped her hand around Nora's and squeezed it slightly.

Mallory absently ran his fingers through his hair. "You asked what happened." He paused. "Miss La Rue, from what I was told, you were found under the tent with your leg trapped under a horse and a tent post. Apparently, in it's death struggles, the horse ground your leg into the wooden blocks of the ring."

Nora's throat constricted and tears filled her eyes. "King is dead?" She gripped the nurse's hand.

He nodded. "That's what I was told." He took a deep breath. "Your leg was severely shattered. We had to remove it above the knee."

What he told her went through her ears, but her mind rejected it. What seemed like an eternity passed before she realized what he said. Shaking, she sat partway up, lifted the sheet and looked down at the bandaged stump that was once her right leg. "No! Oh, please, no! It can't be gone! Put it back! Put it back!" A wail came from her throat like it had been sent from the bowels of hell.

The nurse sat on the edge of the bed and put her arm around her, trying to soothe her distress. "We have to change the dressing now." She eased Nora back to a lying position and held her down gently. "Go ahead, Doctor."

He started working on her leg, but the nurse blocked her view. Nora didn't think she was ready for the sight of her ruined body anyway. What was she going to do now? She had never known anything else but performing in the circus. Her short life was ended at the age of twenty-two.

Through all of this, her mother sat back, observing dispassionately. Not a warm glance or word came to comfort her stricken daughter. *What else should I expect from a woman who never wanted children? She pours all her effort onto my brother, because he will inherit the circus. Me, I'm just the result of a drunken night in bed.* Her hatred bubbled forth in a small sob.

Mallory glanced up. "I hope I didn't hurt you."

Nora shook her head. "Not too much." She looked at her mother. "Did Rico come to see me?"

Her mother regarded her coldly. "Why would he want to marry you now? I haven't seen him."

Nora's fingers clutched into claws. "Get out of here! I don't want to look at your face anymore!" Hot tears ran down her cheeks.

Mallory gestured at the nurse. "Finish up for me. I'll escort Mrs. La Rue out." He firmly took her arm and led her out of the ward.

The nurse finished with the bandage and patted Nora's shoulder. "You poor girl."

Nora angrily shook her hand off. "Leave me alone." She buried her face in her hands and cried. The nurse came back with some medicine.

"Take this. It will calm you down."

Nora took the pills, then threw the glass of water

on the floor, and it shattered.

****

John led Margarete La Rue out of the ward and down the hall, where she haughtily jerked her arm away. She turned on him. "How dare you treat me this way!"

"Woman, what's the matter with you? Don't you have a drop of human kindness? Your daughter lost a leg, and you treat her with disdain." John had never heard this from a mother before, and his heart went out to Miss La Rue.

"This was her fault; she didn't get out of the tent in time. Her carelessness cost us an expensive trained stallion."

"The horse? You're concerned about a horse?" A clearing of the throat stopped John from going further. He turned and found his father behind him.

"May I be of help?" Ben directed to Margarete.

She huffed. "This insolent young doctor was lecturing me about my daughter."

Ben gave slight nod. "I'm very sorry. I will discuss this matter with him."

She turned on her heel and strode to the stairs without another word.

Ben studied his son for a few moments. "May I see you in my office?" When they arrived in the simple austere room with the senior Mallory's diplomas hanging on the wall, Ben Mallory sat behind his desk and studied his son over steepled fingers. "John, you're not a year into your practice yet, but you must understand that you can't get so involved in your patients' lives. You will see unpleasant things between people. We're here to fix the body, not the soul."

John put his hands firmly on the desk and looked his father in the eye. "I'm of the belief that state of mind is important in healing. Unhappy people seem to take longer to regain health than happier ones."

Ben shook his head. "You've been reading too much from these crazy analysts. Just stick to what you were trained to do, or I'll have to give your patient to someone else."

John opened his mouth to further the argument but then paused. "I'll do as you say, sir. Excuse me, I have to look in on my other patients." He turned and left the office.

That evening, John got off his shift and went to his apartment to sleep the sleep of the dead. He didn't know when he'd ever been this exhausted. *Well, now I know what my father was talking about when he mentioned catastrophes.* Blackness overtook him when his head hit the pillow.

Chapter 2

Nora woke to find handsome Rico Vanzetti sitting by her bed. "Rico, you did come to me," she creaked through the narcotic haze. This was her love. Her strength. She'd loved him ever since her father hired him for the high-wire act.

Rico stood and took her hand in his. She saw in his eyes what she didn't want to see. "Nora, I must speak to you of something," he said with his slight Italian accent. "I am no good to take care of someone. The circus and traveling is all I know. When I asked for your hand, we were both whole and strong." She saw the muscles in his jaw contract. "Now I ask you to release me from our promise."

She snatched her hand from his grasp. "Get out of my sight. I don't ever want to see you again. How dare you abandon me now!" She tried to throw the pitcher of water that was on the table by her bed, but it just shattered on the floor after the retreating form.

A nurse hurried in, as Nora burst into angry tears, and tried to calm her. She was about to push the nurse away, but changed her mind. Nora needed a loving touch from someone right now, so she sagged into the nurse's arms, crying out her anger and misery.

What seemed like hours later, she heard, "Miss La Rue, I would like to talk to you."

When the nurse stood, Nora saw the young doctor,

Mallory. All the fight had gone out of her, and she felt oddly numb. All that was left was a cold blanket of sadness. "Not now. I want to be left alone."

Mallory turned to the nurse and pointed to a traveling case by the table. "Get Miss La Rue cleaned up and dressed. I'll be taking her outside for a while." He glanced at Nora. "I'll be back in a half hour."

"Yes, Doctor." The nurse nodded.

"I don't want to go anywhere," Nora retorted.

"You could use some fresh air," he said as he strode out of the ward.

The nurse opened the case and pulled out a day dress, shaking out the wrinkles. "This should do."

Nora endured the humiliating ritual of being washed by putting her mind someplace else. The nurse was gentle but firm. Soon Nora was dressed, and the nurse was finished braiding her hair by the time Mallory came in with a cushioned wheelchair. "Help me with Miss La Rue."

The nurse helped Nora turn to sit on the side of the bed. Nora's stiff muscles protested at the sudden movement, and she cried out, "Leave me!"

Mallory took her firmly by the arm. "You have to start moving if you want to get stronger." The nurse grasped Nora's other arm. "Now, Miss La Rue, push up onto your foot."

Ribbons of pain streaked through her body, but she gritted her teeth and made the muscles work. Mallory and the nurse turned her around in front of the wheelchair, and she eased onto the seat. For the first time she was fully aware of the missing limb. Lying in bed, she could tell herself it was still there. The nurse tucked a blanket around Nora's lap and legs.

Mallory positioned himself behind the chair and rolled her out into the hall. Smells of antiseptic and bleached sheets permeated the sea-green-tiled halls. He set her in front of a double door and pushed a button. With a grinding clatter on the other side, the doors opened to a cage-like door that also opened. A man with a large black mustache sat on a small stool in front of the controls.

Mallory wheeled her into the elevator. "Ground floor, Luigi."

"Yes, Doc Mallory," he said with a smile that moved his mustache. He pulled a lever that closed the doors, and the grinding started again as they were lowered. The lines on the floor and the landing came together, and the elevator stopped with a slight jerk. The doors opened to a hallway with the sun coming through the massive windows. The doctor pushed her through the large double doors and into the hazy summer breezes of coal-tinted air. They came to a green patch with an elm tree and an iron-and-wood bench in the shade.

The city was laid out before them, a sea of church steeples gleaming in the sun. Smokestacks belched out black and gray clouds that cast long shadows across buildings. Schooners were docked at the harbor in the river, their sails shifting in the breeze. Carriages and wagons of all kinds clattered down the streets. Here and there, ladies dressed in their light summer clothes carried shopping baskets to the markets.

"Miss La Rue?" Dr. Mallory had positioned the chair to face the bench and sat across from her. "I need to discuss your situation with you."

She pursed her lips. "My situation is that you

removed my leg and rendered me useless. How much more clear can that be?"

He sat back. "I don't wish to be blunt, but when you came in, your leg was a pulp of skin and bones ground to dust. I had no choice but to amputate. Now it's true, you won't be a bareback rider anymore, it's also true there are other things you can do."

"I can't walk anymore," she shot back.

He gave her a slight smile that made him look boyish. "That's where you're wrong. Artificial limbs have greatly improved in the past years. You can be on your feet in no time."

A wave of disgust came over her. She had seen the like of the aging soldiers from the War Between the States, begging out on the streets with their peg legs and metal arms. She had given them coins out of pity, never dreaming she would one day be part of their ranks. "Good. I can walk to the street corner with my tin cup of pencils."

He leaned forward, looking in her eyes intensely. "Miss La Rue, you've got to have more faith in yourself. There's more to you than begging."

She sighed. "You don't understand. I was brought up all my life for one thing. I have a very poor school education. There's nothing else I can do." Admitting that fact to herself twisted her gut. Hopelessness filled her soul. *Everyone I ever knew abandoned me. What is left? A life of misery?*

She felt a hand on hers and looked into a pair of honest brown eyes. "I think I can help you find your way."

Nora pulled back and replaced her emotional mask. "What can a young surgeon do for me? Cut and redo my soul?"

Mallory sat in thought for a moment. "I have an aunt who runs a small sanitarium in Waukesha, not far from here. She is a retired nurse and has helped many amputees. I'd like to set you up with her."

She pursed her lips. "That will cost money, I'm sure. I don't know how much I'd be allowed to keep of my share in the circus."

"I'll see if I can work something out with her, and I'll talk to your parents."

Anger bubbled to the surface. "If they aren't too busy." She paused. "Will you take me back to my bed? I'm tired."

A look of puzzlement crossed his face before his expression took on a sad downward cast. "I'm very sorry, Miss La Rue." He rose and wheeled her back to the building.

****

John paced the length of his father's office, hitting his right fist into his left palm. "I have to go to the circus grounds to talk to Mr. La Rue."

Dr. Ben Mallory sat back. "You can't. You're on duty until this evening."

"We're slow today, and I haven't seen any of Miss La Rue's family since her mother strode out of here." He stopped in front of the desk and slapped his hand on it. "Miss La Rue will be ready to be transferred out in a few days, and I have to know where they want her to go."

"I imagine they'll take her with them. I'm sure it has taken some time to clean up the grounds after the cyclone. John, I think you're getting too involved in her life. No, I can't spare you. There might be an emergency and everyone would need to be here."

John opened his mouth to say something more, but closed it again. "Yes, sir. I'll be in the lounge for a while if you need me." He went down the hall and pushed the door open to the sun-brightened austere room with its whitewashed walls. Scattered around were tables and chairs where sat doctors conversing or poring over books and forms. He went to the gas stove that always had a big coffee kettle on the back burner. Picking up a towel to hold the handle, he poured himself a cup in his ceramic mug that was kept on a peg next to the stove. Seeing Henry near the window, he set his mug on the small table. "May I join you?"

Henry waved his hand toward the empty chair. "Sit yourself down, John." He pointed out the window to the bench under the shade of the elm. "I saw you out there with that circus performer. I hear she's quite a hellion."

"Angry. Her mother doesn't care a whit for her, I haven't seen her father, and the poor excuse for an intended dropped her like a hot rivet." He tapped the table with his fingers. "I'm going to have a talk with her father, wherever he is."

"Don't you think you're—"

"Getting too involved?" John finished the sentence. "That's what my father said. Maybe so, but she's found herself in a difficult situation, and nobody else is helping her."

The sun was hanging low in the hazy summer sky when John left the hospital after his shift and headed to the livery stable a block away. He waved to the owner as he passed through the big double doors. "Evening, Lem. Could you hitch Dandy to our rig for me?"

Lem pulled the harness off a hook on the wooden

wall. "Going for an outing with Thea tonight?"

John shook his head. "I'm off to the fairgrounds on an errand. I need to talk to the owner of the circus."

Lem paused in buckling the big dappled gray horse to the rig. "Didn't you hear? The circus is loading up at the train depot. They're moving out tonight."

John cursed under his breath. "Then I'd better hurry." He grabbed his whip and climbed onto the driver's seat, gathered the reins, and gave a smart crack over the horse's back. Dandy took off at a trot, and John hoped he could get to the depot in time.

The sun was etching the western hills when he spotted the draft teams loading what was salvageable onto the flat cars. They had a hoist loading the wagons that had sustained the most damage and were unable to roll.

John pulled up next to one of the teamsters. "Hello! Can you tell me where to find Mr. La Rue?"

The man let loose with a stream of tobacco. "He's the one over there in the derby hat, pointing at the cages."

John thanked him and drove Dandy to a space out of the way, where he left the horse and carriage and hurried to La Rue. "Sir, may I talk to you?"

He turned a ruddy, harried face to glare at John. "What is it? Can't you see I'm busy?"

"Mr. La Rue, I'm Dr. John Mallory, your daughter's surgeon. I need to speak to you about her."

La Rue paused. "What about her?"

"She will be released from the hospital in a week or so. Where do you want her to go?"

He waved his hand. "Look, Mallory, I have a broken circus to try to put back together. I don't have time to take care of a cripple."

"I can't just turn her out on the street, sir."

La Rue pursed his lips. "What do you suggest, Doctor?"

"I have an aunt in Waukesha who runs a small sanitarium. She is a nurse who could take care of your daughter while she heals. Would that be to your satisfaction, sir?"

He waved his hand. "Yes, yes. Do what you can. I'll wire you the money to take care of her. Now I must get back to my job."

"Where is your home base?"

"Peru, Indiana. Just send any messages to the post office. They know where to find me."

John tipped his hat and took leave of Mr. La Rue. His disgust for the girl's family was bubbling inside him as he hopped onto the rig and turned Dandy toward Thea's home.

Twilight enveloped the city as John pulled up in front of the modest house Thea shared with her widowed mother not far from the hospital. The whitewashed picket fence's gate squeaked as he pushed through it. Thea met him on the front porch. "John, you're late. What happened?"

"I've had a harrowing week."

A voice from inside called, "Is that John? Have him come in."

They entered into a small parlor, and John greeted the graying tintype of Thea. "Good evening, Mrs. Lindstrom." He removed his hat and put it on a peg by the door. The bulb in the parlor lamp with its fringed amber velvet lampshade gave a warm golden glow.

Mrs. Lindstrom waved her hand toward the kitchen

in the back of the house. "Thea, go get some refreshments. John, sit yourself down."

John settled into the blue velvet parlor chair across from Mrs. Lindstrom, and in a few seconds Thea came back with a tray of hot tea and a plate of sugar cookies for all of them and set it on a table between their chairs. As Thea settled in her chair, she took one of the cups and saucers of tea. "John was about to tell me what has been going on this week."

He took a sip of the liquid. "I imagine you've heard of the cyclone that took out the circus?" At their acknowledgment, he went on to tell them about Nora and her family.

Mrs. Lindstrom shook her head. "That poor child. No wonder she is so angry."

Thea laid a hand on his arm. "What are you going to do?"

John set his cup down. "I'm going to get in touch with my Aunt Elinore in Waukesha to see if she has room for Miss La Rue. She has done so much for the war soldiers who have lost limbs."

"Let me know if I can help in any way."

John nodded. "Maybe you could help when we go on the interurban. I'm going to start her on crutches tomorrow, but she may still be weak. I'm sure the trip will tire her." He stifled a yawn. "I think I'd better go get some rest. Thank you for the tea and company." He rose, and Thea went with him to the porch.

The streetlights bathed the neighborhood in a soft yellow glow, and the summer air hung heavy and moist. John fingered the brim of his hat. "I'm sorry; I've neglected you badly in the past few weeks."

The corners of Thea's mouth curled. "You're a

doctor. I know your life isn't always your own."

He kissed her cheek. "I'll let you know when we take her to my aunt's." They said their goodnights, and he mounted the rig and took it home.

Chapter 3

Nora read the letter from her father, then crumpled it into a tight wad. *Why should I have expected anything different? They've left, and who knows when they will send for me.* She sent the wad of paper into the trash basket by the nightstand. The days had been getting longer in the hospital, and she gnawed over her fate. How awful it felt to be a burden on everybody, including herself. *It would be easy to break a glass...*

"Miss La Rue, you are going for a walk with me today."

Nora looked up, and there was the young doctor standing by her bed with a pair of crutches. "I'm too tired. Go away."

"Nonsense. You need to get up, or you will be in bed and a wheelchair for the rest of your life. You shouldn't want that for yourself."

One thing about this Dr. Mallory, he was persistent. She sighed. "What do you want me to do?"

"That's the spirit!" A nurse came in behind him, and he turned to her. "Get Miss La Rue in her robe and have her sit on the side of the bed." He leaned the crutches at the foot of the bed and dashed out.

When the nurse had Nora ready, he returned with a cane. "Now, Miss La Rue, pull yourself up onto your left foot." He thrust the cane into her right hand.

She hesitated. "I'm too weak to do it myself. You

have to help me."

He stepped back. "No."

The nurse glanced at him. "But, Doctor—"

"Hush, Miss Jones. She *has* to do this herself."

Nora thrust aside the hopelessness she felt and gripped both her hands on the cane. She pulled herself up a little bit, and the muscles in her lower back and thigh protested. Down she went with an "Oof!"

"Try again," Mallory encouraged.

She made a low curse in her throat and attempted to stand again, with the same result. Several more times and she was getting angry. Perspiration dotted her forehead. Gritting her teeth, she made a fast forward motion that almost propelled her into the curtain. Mallory caught her by the shoulders, steadying her as she triumphantly jammed the cane on the floor and raised herself to a standing position. Her breath caught with the effort. "I did it!" Nora beamed at him.

"You surely did, Miss La Rue." He handed her the crutches and took the cane. "Now you learn how to walk on crutches."

She placed the rests under her armpits and leaned on the crutches. "What do I do?"

"Raise your body up and swing your foot forward until it touches the floor again."

She pressed her hands on the cross pieces and pushed herself, but instead of going forward, she ended sitting on the bed again. She threw the crutches on the floor. "I can't do this!"

Mallory sank to his haunches in front of her. "What happened the first time you got on a horse?"

"My father put me on when I was about five."

"No, no. I mean when you had to get on by

yourself."

"I made several attempts and fell off the other side. What has this got to do with the situation?"

"Why didn't you give up then?"

"Because I really wanted to ride."

"Miss La Rue, I can help you walk again, but like those early attempts at riding, it's going to take time and practice. Now, do you want to do this, or do you want to stay an invalid all your life?"

Somewhere he had found the determined Nora. No, she didn't want to be a burden for the rest of her life. "Give me the cane!" Mallory handed it to her. She gritted her teeth and made her muscles work. Her left knee moved like a rusted piece of machinery, and beads of sweat stood out on her face. With a painful pull, she was up on her left leg. "I...did it!" she panted.

"Bravo, Miss La Rue!" Mallory picked up the crutches. "Now try these again."

Nora settled onto the rests and this time leaned slightly forward and pushed herself. Her foot came to rest a few inches in front; then she moved the crutches. Gingerly, she kept moving until she arrived at the foot of the bed. Fatigue began to claim her.

"Turn around and come back. That's enough for today," came Mallory's voice.

She carefully made a horseshoe turn and came back to the side of the bed. The nurse gave the crutches to Mallory and steadied Nora's arm as Nora sank onto the bed again. She put her face into her hands, unbelieving how tired she was from her short walk.

During the next few days, Nora practiced on the crutches for longer times until she could travel down the hallway and back. It felt freeing not to have to stay in that hospital bed.

Dr. Mallory came in one night after the nurse had taken the dinner tray. He pulled a chair next to her and sat down. "Miss La Rue, you are to be discharged tomorrow. I wrote to my aunt, and she will be happy to take you in. Your father told me before he left that he will wire what money you need."

She scowled. "That was certainly generous of him." She looked at Mallory. "How am I supposed to get there?"

"I and my young lady are going to escort you."

Nora experienced an unexpected pang at that. *Jealous? How could I be?* She managed a smile. "How kind you are."

"I'll have the nurse get you ready in the morning." He patted her hand and left.

Nora pondered the tingling where he touched her. *Have I grown so used to people walking away from me that I think that every kindness is love?* She pulled the blanket to her chin, dreading and anticipating tomorrow.

****

Nora sat on the side of the bed after the nurse had helped her bathe and dress, her suitcase with all her worldly possessions placed beside her. She had never realized before how little of her own she possessed. Fingering the old scuffed leather case with the belts at the top, she still smelled the circus in its seams. The road had always been her life, except for the five months of every year spent in Peru, Indiana. Even then, every week was practice for new extravaganzas planned for the next season.

Dr. Mallory intruded on her thoughts. He stood in

front of her with a wheelchair and crutches in hand. "I see you're ready to go." He handed her the crutches, and she pulled herself up. "I'll take you out of the building in the chair, and then you can use the crutches on our journey."

She sank onto the wheelchair and tucked the crutches beside her. Mallory gently set the case on her lap and wheeled her out of the room. The warm humid breeze washed over her when they were outside the building, and a carriage awaited on the circular drive. A pleasant-looking blonde sat in the rig, and a young man who resembled the doctor stood up from a passenger seat.

Mallory stopped the chair by the step-up and waved his hand toward the man. "This is my brother, Robert, and the young lady is Miss Thea Lindstrom." He turned to Nora. "This is Miss Lenora La Rue." Pleasantries were exchanged. "I needed Robert to help lift you into the carriage."

Nora frowned. "Why can't I do that myself?" She pulled herself up with the crutches.

Mallory half-smiled. "I'll show you."

Nora stood in front of the step-up and tried to hoist her foot while balanced on the crutches. She immediately fell back into the waiting arms of the doctor, with an "Oh!"

Mallory righted her. "You have to wait for an artificial leg to be able to do that. Ready, Miss La Rue?" He lifted her into his arms and gave her to Robert, who set her on the seat across from Thea. Mallory set her case and crutches beside her. Robert sat next to Thea, and Mallory climbed into the driver's seat.

The city streets rolled past, and Nora was amazed to see people walking casually from building to building. Most of the time, when she was in any town, the streets were lined with cheering crowds. She felt a slight pang. Despite her family's treatment of her, she had loved working in the circus.

"What do you think of Milwaukee, Miss La Rue?" came a feminine voice intruding on her thoughts.

Nora glanced at Thea. "You may call me Nora, if you'd like."

"Thank you. You may call me Thea. Do you like Milwaukee?"

"I don't know enough about it to say. All I've seen was the hospital." She shaded her eyes. "It is interesting how the schooners appear to come into the city streets."

Thea nodded. "That's because they come up the river for a ways." Thea continued to point out buildings and sights on their way. They entered the shopping area of the city, and before them loomed a building with a clock tower. "That's the passenger depot."

Nora put her handkerchief to her nose. There were all kinds of smells coming from the river, and the burning coal from the factories and train engines overpowered her senses. And people complained about the odors from the circus!

Mallory pulled up the horses near the loading platform. He jumped down and stood by the step of the carriage. Robert helped Nora up and lifted her over the step to the waiting arms of the doctor, who set her on her foot. The crutches were handed down to her. She settled into what was now a normal stance for her and walked with Thea to wait on one of the benches while Mallory went to purchase the tickets. Robert brought her suitcase and their overnight bags, and when Mallory returned, Robert said his goodbyes.

Nora glanced at Mallory with surprise. "Isn't Robert coming with us?"

He shook his head. "No. Thea and I can handle this."

She watched as Robert turned the team back to the street. A wave of uncertainty flowed over her. "Are you sure?"

"The train is a lot more stable to get in and out of."

In a few minutes, with a snort and a loud wheeze, the engine pulled up to the passenger depot. Mallory handed their bags to the porter, and then the three went to the end car. Mallory called over the conductor and spoke to him. The man nodded and reached for a small step stool, which he set by the iron steps to the back of the car.

Mallory had Thea stand at the top of the steps and he stood behind Nora. "Now, Miss La Rue, put the crutches on either side of the stool."

Nora did so. "What do I do?"

"Push up with your foot like you're going to hop, then swing it forward."

Nora willed her muscles to do what she asked of them. The toe of her shoe brushed the stool, but she was up, feeling triumphant. She turned her head. "How should I take the steps?"

"Thea will help you grasp the top of the railing, and I'll steady you around your waist. Push hard with your foot and pull with your arms."

Nora gave a couple of practice bounces and hopped as hard as she could. She felt his hands on either side of her waist. Her athletic muscles still responded to her commands as she drew herself toward Thea, who had her by the arms. Two times got her up the iron steps. Mallory handed her the crutches. "You're doing wonderfully well, Miss La Rue," he exclaimed.

She smiled as she settled onto the crutches. "Thank you, Doctor, but I think I must sit down now."

Thea opened the door to the car, and the three of them found seats. Nora was by one of the windows. This was certainly different from having her own room on the circus train. The doctor was beside her, and Thea took the seat across. Soon she heard the conductor call, "All aboard!" and the cars began to move.

The conductor walked the center aisle, punching tickets. Mallory gave him the three of theirs, and Nora watched the city go by. Mallory and Thea pointed out things to her as they passed, but Nora barely heard them. This had been a very exhausting morning, and the clack-clack of the wheels lulled her to sleep. A patting of her hand pulled her out of the Land of Nod.

Thea had leaned forward. "Nora? We're almost in Waukesha."

Nora paused until she had her wits about her. "Oh, I must have dozed off."

Mallory smiled. "That's all right. You're still weak. Time with my aunt will help you."

Nora glanced out the window and watched a quarry going by. Then a river came into view, with trees and small farms nearby. They headed into a surprisingly busy town, with a few factories belting out smoke. "It's larger than I thought it would be. I expected just a few resorts." The large depot loomed ahead, and the train entered into a sheltered station and stopped with a mild jerk. Some people were gathering their things, and

Mallory helped Nora rise.

The conductor entered the car and announced, "Waukesha stop. We'll be here for fifteen minutes."

The three waited until the other disembarking passengers had exited the car, and then Mallory led them to the back steps again, where the conductor had the step stool on the ground. Mallory went down first. "Miss La Rue, this will be a little easier if you follow my instructions." He held out his hand. "First give me the crutches." When she did, he motioned to the railing. "Hold on to either side, raise yourself, and push forward like you do on the crutches."

Nora landed on the step down. "Now what?"

Mallory handed the crutches back to her. "You're low enough to push and balance with the crutches. I'll catch you if you fall."

Nora called on all her muscles to maneuver and found a way down masterfully. "This is getting easier!" she exclaimed with pride.

The three turned when a "John! You, John!" came echoing down the station. A large, ruddy-faced woman wearing a hat with a billowing ostrich feather moved surprisingly fast to the group. She grasped Mallory by his shoulders. "John, Thea, how nice to see you again!" She turned her gaze on Nora. "This must be Miss La Rue. I'm Elinore Weeks, and you will be staying in my home."

Nora eyed her hand for a ring. "How do you do, Miss Weeks?"

She gave a hearty laugh. "I do very well, Miss La Rue. Come with me, all of you." She led them out of the building to a strange-looking wagon. There was a step up in the back with hand rails on either side and four rows of two seats facing front. "This is what I use for outings with my patients."

With her and Mallory's help, Nora was soon seated in the open-air conveyance. When all were settled, the old man with the reins turned. "Home, Miss Weeks?"

"Yes. We're ready, Auggie."

The man slapped the reins of the two roan horses, and they went off at a fast walk, hooves making a *plop-plop* on the dusty street. With a rumble of wheels, they went over the bridge across the river and into a tree-lined road downtown. The stone business buildings rose in a canyon on either side of them, and shingles of various shapes dangled over the flagstone sidewalk. The streets turned from dirt to brick and the dust went away. At the end of the street was a tall church steeple where they went to the right and past a park entrance with the words "Silurian Spring Park" emblazoned over the drive. Auggie turned the horses to the right and into a drive by a large gabled house. The sign by the road proclaimed Sunny Meadows Sanitarium. They were obviously on the outskirts of town, because few buildings graced the landscape.

There had been conversation going on all this time between the other three, but Nora had been deep in study of her new surroundings. She heard a voice. "Now, Miss La Rue, let's get you down." Miss Weeks stood by her.

Mallory and Thea were already off the wagon, and Miss Weeks stood behind her. Nora turned, "Do I do the same thing as I did off the train?" Miss Weeks nodded. Out of the corner of her eye, she saw Auggie come around with a wheelchair. "No! No wheelchair. I can use my crutches."

Mallory stood in front of her. "Miss La Rue, you've only been using them on even surfaces. You have to learn to walk on the dirt and grass gradually."

She paused, wanting to give an angry retort, but she only huffed, "All right." She came down copying her moves off the train and landed between Mallory and Thea. Before they could grab her arms, she headed toward the wheelchair on her own, but when she hit a patch of wet grass and went tumbling over, a scream of fury escaped her lips, and she beat the ground with her fist. "You should have let me die!"

Mallory went to his haunches beside her. "Miss La Rue, this is your challenge. You can either roll over and be a burden to everyone, or you can live independently. It's your choice. But to do that, you have to learn new ways." He rose and extended his hand. "Now, may I help you up?"

She paused, wanting to boil him in oil. Then she braced her foot, and he pulled her to a standing position. Auggie pushed the wheelchair behind her, and she sat. "All right, you win this one, Doctor."

Miss Weeks took the chair in hand. "We will set you up in the cottage in back with your two roommates."

They went to the back of the large house, and there was a cheery white clapboard building with a picket fence that enclosed a small garden where a woman was hoeing. Another was on the porch shelling peas into a wooden bowl. It wasn't until the woman in the garden straightened up that Nora saw she had but one arm. The other woman came off the porch with an obvious limp.

Miss Weeks waved them over. "Ann Foster, Livy Shane, this is your new roommate, Lenora La Rue.

Could you help set her up in the third bed and show her where to put her things?"

Nora felt a little pang of disgust. Cripples always bothered her. In the back of her mind, she realized she was now one of them. She managed what she hoped was a pleasant smile. "Pleased to meet you." At the two women's nods, Mallory handed Nora the crutches, and he and Auggie unloaded her suitcase from the wagon, taking it inside. Miss Weeks helped her on the step to the porch and over the threshold.

The little cottage was charming, and it reminded her of storybook doll houses she had seen as a child. The living area had a small kitchen in the corner, a table, and a couch and chairs. A bedroom was closed off by a curtain which now was tied back. Miss Weeks pointed to a door at the far end of the bedroom area. "That's the door to the water closet." She laid a hand on Nora's arm. "Why don't you get settled in with your two companions, and the rest of us will return in a few minutes."

Nora managed her crutches to what she assumed was her bed, since Auggie had deposited the suitcase on it. She had begun unbuckling the case when she heard, "Lenora, may we help you with that?"

She turned as one-armed Ann unsnapped the strap on her sunbonnet. "Can you?"

Ann gave her a faint smile. "Of course we can."

Livy opened the door of a large wardrobe. "We keep our clothes in here." There was a pole across the upper middle, with wooden hangers, and a shelf above that.

Nora unpinned her hat and put it on the top shelf. "All right, let's get busy." Nora opened the case and shook out her first dress.

****

Elinore Weeks tapped on her teacup as she frowned at John. "Is Miss La Rue always this disagreeable?"

John studied his hands. "She does tend to be headstrong at times." He sighed. "I'll be in once a week to check on her. We can see when we'll be able to get her an artificial leg."

"Do any of her relatives plan to help in any way?"

John snorted. "All her father is going to trouble himself to do is wire money. They don't seem to care anything about her."

"That's probably why she's so angry."

They went on for a while, chatting about family and such, until John pulled his watch out of his vest pocket. "Thea and I should be getting to the station to catch the train east."

Elinore nodded. "I'll have Auggie ready the wagon."

John went to the cottage and rapped on the door. "Miss La Rue?"

He heard the *thump-thump* of crutches on the wooden floor. The door opened. She stood there with a less than pleasant expression. "Yes, Doctor?"

He paused. "I'm leaving you in the capable hands of Miss Weeks. She has all your medicines and tonics. I shall return this time next week to look in on you."

She pressed her lips together in a tight line. "Wonderful, Doctor." She closed the door in his face.

As he walked down the porch steps, he wondered why she would be so impolite to him. He had set everything up and brought her out himself. He could chalk it up to her being a prima donna, but there was something else he couldn't put his finger on. Another thought came to him: why did he care? He and Thea gave their goodbyes to Elinore and climbed into the wagon. Auggie gave the horses a slap with the reins, and they were off.

Thea studied him for a few minutes. "What's bothering you?"

John told her about his parting with Miss La Rue. "I don't know why she's so unhappy with me."

Thea thought for a moment. "Maybe it's because everyone in her life seems to be walking out on her."

He pondered that. "You may be right. Poor child."

The smell of coal smoke grew stronger as they neared the station. John helped Thea down and flipped Auggie a quarter.

Auggie smiled a snaggle-toothed grin. "Thank ya, sir!" Then he turned the wagon toward home.

John's mind was full of the prima donna all the way back to Milwaukee.

Chapter 4

Elinore Weeks proved to be an excellent nurse, and within a few days Nora was using her crutches to get to the main house for therapy after the noon meal. She was slowly getting back the balance that had been honed since she was a small child doing circus acts.

She sat on an examination table in one of the small rooms in the back while Miss Weeks changed the dressing on the stump. "Your stump is almost healed. John did an exceptional job on it." She straightened her back as she stood up. Gathering the clean dressing, she began to wrap the wound again. "You should be ready for the artificial leg in a week or two."

Somehow, that brought no comfort to Nora. It reminded her of what she had lost. "I'm still a useless person."

Miss Weeks raised herself up to her full height and scowled at Nora. "I never want to hear you say you are useless. You're just missing one leg. Everything else is intact." She waved her hand toward the door. "The men here have more problems than a missing limb. Most were in the war and have wounds in the mind that a doctor can't treat."

Nora felt her cheeks heat. "I have a habit of feeling sorry for myself. I can still hear my parents."

"Look forward, Miss La Rue. If you lock backward, you'll find remorse. That won't do any good." She finished with the dressings and handed Nora the crutches. "You need to get out and socialize. The patients who are able will be going to the concert at Silurian Springs this evening."

Nora glanced at her old clothes. "I don't have anything suitable to wear to a concert."

Miss Weeks smiled. "It's held on the grounds, with illuminations afterwards. What you're wearing will be fine."

Nora pondered this the rest of the day. She knew how people felt about circus workers. Ann and Livy had grown silent when she told them where she came from. They never warmed to her, though they were polite. Nora admitted to herself that she didn't know how to socialize with the general public. She didn't have to, before.

The sultry August breeze had cooled by the time Miss Weeks came to the porch with a wheelchair. Nora was sitting in a wicker rocker, and Ann and Livy were inside getting ready. Miss Weeks waved her hand toward the chair. "Take your crutches with you. It will be easier on you to go to the springs in the wheelchair then to use the crutches to get around." Nora opened her mouth to protest, but Miss Weeks shushed her. "I will hear none of that."

Ann and Livy joined them, and Nora was envious of Livy's artificial leg. She had a limp, but at least she wasn't stuck in a chair. Nora came off the porch and seated herself on the hated contraption. The group went to the front of the house, where two of the men and Auggie waited. One of the men had lost his arms and was fitted with one artificial limb. The other was being pushed in a wheelchair by Auggie. Miss Weeks made the introductions. Both of the men looked to be in their forties, so Nora suspected they had war wounds. Seth, the armless one, seemed to be quiet and shy. Frank, she found out, had been paralyzed from the waist down from a shot to the spine in the war.

· Frank regarded her with a sad expression. "It takes courage, Miss La Rue, to go out like this among people."

"I traveled by train here from Milwaukee and didn't have any trouble."

"Ah, then you were where people rushed and lived in their own thoughts. It's different when you are in a recreational place. I wanted to warn you."

Nora pondered this while they went across the street and west half a block. The entrance split into two roads sweeping by a small hill. As they rounded a corner, a beautiful pond came into view, with a band platform in the middle of it. A large colorful building with a tower graced the other side of the drive. Out of the corner of her eye, she noticed a group of older boys watching and pointing at them.

One of the boys stepped forward with a sneer. "Here come the cripples!" he cried, mocking Livy's limp. The others let out peals of laughter.

Nora glanced at Frank, and his cheeks were reddening. "I see," she said. *That's just like the freaks are treated in my father's side show.*

Miss Weeks took the boy by the scruff of his collar and shook him. "That's enough of that! Don't you boys realize that, but for the grace of God, here go you? Think about that!"

The boys, cowed, went off into the crowd. Miss Weeks could be intimidating when she wanted to be.

The boys were gone, but the stares from the crowd were bothering Nora. Of course, crowds used to stare at her during the circus performances, but it wasn't the pity and revulsion she saw in their eyes now.

She turned her attention to the band stage illuminated with colorful Chinese lanterns as the sun started to sink along the horizon, sending pink and violet streamers along the clouds. A young boy came with a tray of glasses filled with spring water. Nora drank of the cool liquid and admitted it was as good as she had heard.

The bandmaster came to the fore and announced, "Good evening, ladies and gentlemen! We shall proceed with the night of music. First will be 'Tales of the Vienna Woods' by Johann Strauss."

Nora felt a chill down her spine. That was one of the pieces they played for her act. She noticed a tree a few steps away and hoisted herself on her crutches. Working on the uneven grass, she made her way to the trunk and leaned against it. Closing her eyes, Nora was carried away to the circus. She was on King Charles again, and with every strain of the music her muscles followed the performance she had learned so precisely. When the piece ended, as she waved her right arm into a graceful bow, she felt something soft and wet smack her neck.

Boyish laughter echoed close by, and Nora opened her eyes to see a ripe tomato splattered on her shoulder. Moving fast, she leaned on her left crutch and tripped the hoodlum with her right, and he sprawled on the ground. "Hey, whatcha tryin' to do?" She put the tip of the crutch on his chest.

"To teach you some manners," she said, pushing

lightly to keep him down.

Miss Weeks and a red-faced man hurried over. The man grabbed Nora by the arm and turned to Miss Weeks. "Don't you know any better than to let your inmates harass innocent children?" Nora made note he didn't talk to her.

Miss Weeks gave him a glare that should have melted the skin off his face. "Miss La Rue was standing quietly by the tree and your *innocent child* pelted her with a ripe tomato. I think he owes her an apology."

He released his grip on Nora's arm, and she removed the crutch to let the boy get up. The man hauled the child up by the scruff of his collar. "I told you not to bother mental inferiors!" And he led him back into the crowd.

His words caused a blow to Nora's stomach, as if he had buried his fist there. For someone who was used to accolades and awe, she didn't know how to handle this.

Miss Weeks wiped the tomato juice and seeds off Nora's clothes. "I'm not going to apologize for the crude people in the world, but they are all over, and you have to understand that." She stopped and studied Nora. "We can go back if you want to."

Nora wanted to run away and never have to face crowds again, but something steeled her deep inside. "No. We came here to listen to the music, and I'm not going to go running because of some unruly child."

Miss Weeks gave a slight smile. "You're learning. Good."

Nora followed Miss Weeks back to the wheelchair and sat again. Frank patted her hand. "You did well, Miss La Rue."

Outside of a few stares and glares, the rest of the concert and fireworks went well.

****

John stared incredulously at his father. "What did he say?"

"I said Mr. La Rue has run into financial difficulty and had to cut his daughter loose. We have to cancel the artificial limb."

"No. If she has to earn money, she needs a way to get around. No one I know would hire someone in a wheelchair or on crutches."

Dr. Ben Mallory sat back in his desk chair and studied his son. "What do you suggest we do? The girl has worked in the circus all her life. What could she possibly do?"

John leaned in. "For the answer to the first question, I could cover it and she could pay me back when she starts earning money." He paused. "For the answer to the second, I don't know, yet."

"John, I warned you not to get involved."

"Father, someone has to help that girl. Everyone she has ever known has turned their backs on her."

Ben paused. "Are you sure she's worth doing all this for?"

"She can be an angry prima donna, yes. But I found out that when the storm came through, she kept the horse from trampling people. She could have easily gotten out of the tent when the wind first hit."

Ben sighed. "Well, it looks like you're going to make a pet of her no matter what I say. Just remember, I warned you."

John straightened up. "Yes, sir. I have to go on my rounds now." He closed the office door behind him.

All day he thought about Miss La Rue's problem. He had planned to go to Waukesha the next day to check up on her anyway. She was an intelligent girl; there must be something she could do.

The next morning, John watched the trees and farmland move by his train window. Armed with educational books, he hoped he could bring Miss La Rue up on her reading and arithmetic. When he arrived at the Waukesha station, he walked the two blocks to a livery stable and hired a horse. He buckled the books into the saddlebags and set off for his aunt's sanitarium.

It was a hot and sultry August day, and John, although wishing he had brought a canteen with him, knew there would be a cold drink available at the sanitarium. He rode into the drive of his aunt's home, and when he turned in at the back by the women's cottage, a sad tableau unfolded before him.

Miss La Rue was in the wicker rocker on the porch with Ann and Livy soothing her. She had her face buried in her hands, and bits of paper were scattered on a small table and in front of her. Ann glanced at John. "Good morning, Dr. Mallory."

John removed his hat as he stepped onto the porch. "Good morning. What seems to be the trouble?"

Miss La Rue raised her face and revealed her red-rimmed eyes. "I've been cut from my family."

John looked down. "I know. My father received a similar letter."

"The sanitarium was paid for three months. After that, I don't know where I'll be."

"Miss La Rue, I want to help you with that, if you'll let me."

Elinore had joined them. "John, you may use the

examining room. I've placed a pitcher of cold well water and glasses in there, too."

He nodded to her. "Thank you, Auntie." He turned to Miss La Rue. "Shall we go?"

She paused a moment, then pulled herself onto the crutches. Without a word, she followed him up the steps to the back porch of the big house and into the small examining room. Elinore pulled the door shut behind them and helped Miss La Rue onto the table while John washed his hands.

A battery-operated fan hummed by the open window, cooling the room somewhat. Elinore had the dressing off when John came over, wiping his hands on a towel. He studied the stump. "Looks like it's healed. Good. We can try the artificial leg next week. Recline on the table. Aunt Elinore, help me measure her left leg, so we can have it sized." Miss Weeks held a tape measure at the top of Miss La Rue's thigh, and the doctor read the number by the arch of her foot.

Miss La Rue pursed her lips. "I can't afford an artificial leg now. I haven't any money."

John glanced at her. "That is one of the things I want to discuss with you." He turned to Elinore. "Do you have any knitted leg caps to put over the stump?"

She went to a cabinet and pulled one out. It fitted over the stump like a stocking. Elinore poured two glasses of the cold water as she asked, "Would you like to talk in here or on the back porch?"

John made a nod toward the porch. "It's a lot less stuffy out there." When he had helped Miss La Rue off the table and handed her the crutches, she hobbled outside and sat on one of the wicker chairs on the wide shaded porch. John sat across from her, a small table between them.

Elinore set the glasses on the table. "I'll leave you alone to discuss things," she said, and stepped inside. The screen door squeaked behind her.

Miss La Rue took a sip of the water. "Well, Doctor?"

He paused. "First, I want to say how sorry I am for your circumstances. I want to make you an offer. I'll pay for your artificial limb and you can pay me back when you gain employment."

She frowned. "How do you know there is anything I can do? Who's going to hire a cripple?"

"The artificial limb will help with that. We have to find out what you're good at."

She snorted. "I'm good at jumping on the back of a horse and doing acrobatics. No, wait, I can't do that anymore, can I?"

John rose and hurried off the porch. "I'll be right back." He went to the horse and pulled the books out of the saddlebags. Bringing them to the porch, he set them in front of her. "You told me you didn't have much schooling, so I brought these four books to help you." He picked the first one up. "Since I know you can read some, I brought the fourth grade McGuffy Reader. It has spelling, grammar, and diction. This is intermediate arithmetic, this is geography, and this is business practices." He pointed to each in turn.

She studied him for a moment. "Why are you doing this for me? This isn't a medical concern. I don't want your pity."

"It's not pity, Miss La Rue. It's extending a hand to a person who needs it. I expect you to get a job and pay me back."

There was a dark cast to her eyes. "I guess, Dr. Mallory, I'm not used to people thinking about me and my needs. If I seem impolite at times, it's just my defenses." She took the reader from him and riffled the pages. "Thank you for the use of the books. I shall study them."

He picked up the books and took the reader. "Let me carry them to the cottage for you. I'll be back next week."

She was quiet on the way, then turned to him before he stepped off the cottage porch. "I am sorry for the way I've treated you. I shouldn't have prejudged."

"That's all in the past." He took her hand and lightly squeezed it, not ready for the slight jolt to his system. A look in her brown eyes told him she had felt it, too. The summer breeze played around her black hair, trying to loosen it from the tie binding it at the nape of her neck. Tendrils waved around her rosy cheeks. John hadn't been aware until that moment of how lovely she was. He shook off his feelings and masked his face. "Good day, Miss La Rue." He tipped his hat and went to the main house, where Aunt Elinore waited for him at the back door.

He stepped into the kitchen, and Elinore poured two glasses of lemonade. She glanced at him. "Let's go to the front porch. There's shade there now." They settled on two wicker rockers, and John stared across the green expanse toward the few buildings on the other side of the street.

Elinore took a sip and studied him. "John, I think you've ventured into dangerous territory."

"Why?"

"I noticed you clasping Miss La Rue's hand and

gazing at her for over a minute. Aren't you getting too involved?"

He pressed his lips. "It's just that someone has to help that girl. She doesn't seem to have a friend in the world."

"You have to be careful. You don't know what sort of a person she is. You may end up hurt or disappointed."

He watched a hawk soaring on heated air. "I think there is a good, smart woman deep down, a woman who has been ill-used. I'm going to try to draw her out." They went on to other topics of conversation until John had to leave to catch the train back to Milwaukee.

He went back to his horse and noticed it had been moved into the shade and provided with a bucket. Miss La Rue waved from the cottage porch. "I hope you don't mind. The trough is now in the sun, so I moved the horse and gave him some cool well water."

"Thank you, Miss La Rue." He climbed into the saddle and headed to the livery stable. *She seems very good with animals. Well, she was raised among them. I wonder.* He pondered the thought all the way home.

Chapter 5

In spite of herself, Nora was looking forward to Dr. Mallory's visit. She had worked hard all week on the books. In arithmetic, she had already known addition and subtraction. Now she was learning the multiplication tables. She had them memorized to seven. In geography, she knew all the states and capitals. The circus had traveled to most of them. And with the business practices, she was sure she'd be able to clerk in a store.

Livy had been a schoolteacher before she lost her leg, so she helped Nora with her drills. Nora felt confident she could find a job soon.

When Dr. Mallory showed up in a carriage with Thea, Nora couldn't help a pang of jealousy. She shoved the feeling as far down as she could and went out to greet them. After the doctor helped Thea down, he rummaged in the rear of the carriage and removed a long package. "Here we go, Miss La Rue. Your ticket to freedom."

Miss Weeks had joined them. "Why don't Thea and I help her into it?"

Nora followed Miss Weeks and Thea into the examining room. Miss Weeks opened the brown paper wrappings and extracted a wood, leather, and canvas contraption. She inspected the workmanship and pronounced it, "Good." She turned to Nora. "Lean on the examining table and give me your crutches. This all goes under your dress and petticoats, so we have to remove them." After that was done, Nora was directed to sit on the table.

Miss Weeks removed the knitted cap from the stump and smoothed on some ointment, then replaced the cap. She put a small cushion at the top of the artificial leg and slid it onto the stump. The knee of the leg was hinged, so it rested in a natural position. Nora gazed at it. "It doesn't look like the peg legs I've seen many wear."

Miss Weeks smiled. "There have been many advancements in the limbs lately. You have received one of the best."

Nora felt the blood run from her face. "I know I couldn't possibly afford this."

"The doctor figured if you get the best, the sooner you can get a job and pay him back. Come, come. Let us help you up and finish strapping you in."

There was a band of canvas that had two buckles securing the leg to the thigh. Then a lighter panel stretched over the side of her hip. A strap was put around the left side of her neck and hooked onto the hip panel from the other side. Nora studied the braces. "That will take some getting used to."

Miss Weeks and Thea stood on opposite sides of Nora and supported her arms. "Now, take a step," Miss Weeks ordered.

Nora noticed that the hinged knee had snapped lightly into the standing position, so it didn't give way. "How do I move the knee?"

"Just give it a snap forward. It's made to move like a natural limb."

Nora hadn't used her right leg for so long, she had to consciously think about how to walk. Slowly she moved her right thigh forward. The knee moved like it was supposed to. Then, before she could shift her weight, the knee buckled and the women saved her from a fall. "What happened?" Nora steamed.

Miss Weeks soothed, "You have to pull your weight forward when you step, and that will straighten out the knee. Now, let's try it again."

It took several tries and a few angry words from Nora to get the steps right. Miss Weeks handed her the crutches. "Do you want me to try it alone?" Nora asked, surprised.

Miss Weeks nodded. "When you get better, you can walk without crutches like Livy does."

Nora set her teeth and put her right leg forward. The artificial foot came to rest on the floor and she pushed her weight over it till it clicked, then held it there until she moved her left leg. It was painfully slow, but she managed without any mishap.

Miss Weeks waved her hand at the table. "Go back there and we'll help you dress. Then the doctor can check your stump for any rubbing."

Nora, fully clothed, was sitting on the table when the doctor came in. "I hear it went well," he exclaimed. He undid the buckles and moved the limb aside so he could examine the stump. His warm hands on her thigh heated her cheeks. "It looks like a capital fit. Do you think you can manage taking it off and putting it on by yourself?"

Nora didn't hesitate. "I'm sure I can." She replaced the limb and buckled it.

He grinned, and her heart skipped a beat. "Good.

Now, if you have any problems, be sure to tell me next week when I visit." He pulled out a jar from his doctor bag. "Here's the ointment to put on the stump before you put the leg on."

She slipped it into a pocket in her skirt. "Thank you, Dr. Mallory. I will find a job as soon as I can."

He patted her shoulder. "I trust you will. I have every faith in you."

Nora reached for the crutches and slid off the table onto her new limb. "I'm getting used to this."

Dr. Mallory held the door for her. "I'll help you with the porch steps."

Nora went to the end of the porch. "Now what do I do?"

The doctor stood at the bottom of the two steps. "Put your crutches on the next step and move your right leg down. Let the knee snap in place, then lean on the right crutch and raise up a bit to move your left leg down."

Now Nora understood why Livy had that peculiar gait. Slowly, she followed the doctor's instructions and made it down the steps. "I'm getting better at this!"

Mallory smiled, which enhanced his boyish good looks. "If you need help with anything, Miss Weeks is very knowledgeable."

"Thank you, Doctor!" Nora turned and walked back to the cottage. It felt so good to be almost human again.

****

The next day off John had, he took Thea to the state fair. His mother always entered one of her pies in the contest, so he wanted to show up to support her. They walked to the gate from the depot, taking in all the colorful flags and streamers waving in the breeze. Shouts, screams, and laughter came from the carny section with its rides and game booths. John paid the admission and picked up a map of the grounds.

Thea studied the map and pointed to the left. "The food judging is in exposition hall number two."

They wound their way through the crowds of milling people to the double doors of one of the permanent buildings. Row upon row of foods in glass cases filled the floor. They found the baked goods section, where the smell of the desserts hung on the warm summer air. His mother waved to him from a few rows down. His sister Franny was there as well, Franny was a fantastic cook in her own right.

His mother beamed at him. "They finished judging only minutes ago, and look!" Sitting in front of her was one of her rhubarb-and-cherry pies with a large wedge taken out of it and a blue ribbon pinned on the cloth in front.

He stuck his finger in the gooey fruit filling and tasted its sweet tartness. "Delicious! You outdid yourself this year." He turned to his sister. "How did your spiced quince preserves do?"

Franny shrugged and brushed back a roan-colored curl from her eyes. "I have third prize on those, but not bad for a first attempt."

John kissed her cheek. "You're just seventeen. Just think what you'll do with a few years of practice." He questioned Thea, "I'm going to the racetrack stables to see Will. Do you want to come with me?"

She shook her head. "John, you know all those animal smells bother me. I'll stay here."

John tipped his hat to them and picked his way

through the milling people. The racetrack was on the east side of the fair park. Upon entering the stable, he heard angry voices. A tough-looking balding man stormed out of the building and nearly knocked him over. "See here now, watch where you're going!" John called after him, but the man waved him off. John went into the stall area and found his friend, Will Canton, brushing down his copper-colored standard-bred horse, Chance. John pointed to the retreating figure. "What was that all about?"

Will greeted John and replied, "That was the man who owns Chance's brood mother. He claims that Chance was sold without his knowledge by his partner, and he wants the stallion back. Funny, he was the one who said Chance was a runt, until he started winning races."

John scratched the horse's white-blazed nose, and Chance nickered. "I would love to raise horses on the side. I may, someday."

Will studied him. "With Thea's breathing problems around animals? That may be tricky."

John sighed. "Yes, well, you might be right. I'm finding there are many things we don't agree on. That's why I've been putting off proposing." He paused. "Does your uncle still run that general store in Waukesha?"

"Yes. In fact, I keep Chance at the stable in back with his draft team. Why?"

"One of my patients at a sanitarium there is in dire need of a job. Would he consider hiring a woman clerk with an artificial leg?"

"I'll ask. Isn't that far and beyond what doctors usually do?"

"Her family disowned her. I'm just trying to help."

"A stray puppy dog, eh? I'll see what I can do." They went on to discuss former friends in the neighborhood they grew up in.

John turned to go. "I left Thea with Mother and Franny, and they must be missing me by now. Thank you in advance for your help, Will."

Will waved him off. "Think nothing of it."

John looked forward to seeing Miss La Rue and telling her of the prospect. He hurried back to the exposition building.

****

Nora was learning to garden from Livy, since Ann had returned home to her family. Miss Weeks came to the fence and shaded her eyes. "Miss La Rue, can I see you for a moment?"

Nora leaned the hoe against the porch and removed her gardening gloves. Walking to the fence, she said, "Yes, Miss Weeks?"

"I received a wire from Dr. Mallory, and on his visit next week, he has arranged for you to see Bart Canton, a general store owner downtown. I noticed your clothes could use mending. Do you need some needles and thread?"

Nora wavered and felt her cheeks heat. "I don't know how to sew."

Miss Weeks pursed her lips. "How have you managed before? Didn't your mother teach you?"

"My mother didn't sew, either. Everything was done by the seamstress." That was the first time Nora had ever seen Miss Weeks speechless.

Finally she said, "Well. I see your education is lacking in domestic skills, as well. Bring your best shirtwaist and skirt, and I will show you."

That afternoon was spent poking thread through the eye of the needle, or trying to, It kept splaying until Miss Weeks showed Nora how to wet the thread with spit. After a couple of attempts, Nora got the thread to knot at the bottom, and small stitches were made through worn seams and hems and then the thread was knotted again. Nora's fingers were wounded several times, but at the end, she proudly held up the mended clothing.

Miss Weeks gave it a critical eye. "Not too bad for the first time. Tomorrow, I'll show you how to do laundry."

During the next few days, Nora received intense training in the housekeeping arts. She experienced no real mishaps in laundry, except she learned it was advisable to pick the iron off the stove with a rag. Besides two broken plates, dishwashing went well. Carpet sweeping, dusting, and wet mopping came off without a hitch. Feather dusting lost one of Miss Weeks knickknacks when a hapless little black-and-white ceramic puppy broke his neck on the floor. Nora was devastated until Miss Weeks assured her it wasn't a priceless item, although they might be able to mend it with a bit of sticking plaster.

The morning of Dr. Mallory's visit, Nora was busy in the kitchen of the big house, fixing mid-day supper for the residents with Miss Weeks' help. Chicken soup with small dumplings and vegetables simmered on the stove. Nora's raspberry pies, that she had learned to bake the night before, were in the warming oven. Fruit compote was also on the stove, and they were assembling ham-and-cheese sandwiches for the men.

Miss Weeks answered a knock at the back door, and Dr. Mallory stepped in and took a deep breath. "My, it smells wonderful in here."

Nora looked up and moved her hand over her sweaty brow. "Thank you, Doctor. I made most of this myself."

Miss Weeks followed the doctor in. "Yes, I've been teaching her housekeeping and cooking. A very satisfactory student."

Dr. Mallory nodded. "Well done. Miss La Rue, I'm here to escort you to the general store to meet Mr. Canton. I suppose we could leave—after the meal?" He quirked his eyebrow.

Miss Weeks laughed. "Seeking an invitation, John? Yes, stay!"

Miss Weeks, Dr. Mallory, and Nora took their meal to the back porch's table to take advantage of the cool breeze on the summer day. The doctor savored the last bite of his raspberry pie slice and took a sip of coffee. "That was very good for a first attempt. Miss La Rue, are you sure you're up to walking two blocks to the store? You've been off your crutches only a couple of days."

Nora nodded. "Miss Weeks said I could borrow one of the walking canes. That should be enough."

Miss Weeks put a hand on the doctor's arm. "Years of acrobatics seem to have helped in her recovery."

He smiled. "Yes, she is quite fit." Nora's cheeks heated.

Miss Weeks rose and gathered the dishes. Nora went to help but was waved off. Miss Weeks carried in the dishes and brought out a cane. "You'd better get started. Katrine and I can take care of the cleanup."

Dr. Mallory helped Nora down the steps, and they walked to the road. Nora took care to travel on the evenest part of the ground, and her well-versed muscles automatically kept her upright. Then she stumbled when her artificial foot hit a half-buried rock. With the help of the cane, she managed to keep herself from falling. Dr. Mallory took her arm and looped it through the crook of his elbow. "You're still a little new at this. It takes practice."

Nora remembered the irritation she used to feel when she was learning a new trick and not quite good enough yet. She swallowed down an angry retort and stared straight ahead, setting to memory the route to the store.

Past the Congregational Church, they crossed the street to a stone building with double doors. "Canton's General Store" was emblazoned in black paint on the side of the second-story and on a shingle hanging in front. Dr. Mallory turned to her. "Here we are. Now, answer truthfully any question he asks of you, and do any task put to you."

Nora took a deep breath. "I'm ready." Her stomach churned like a butter-maker.

A balding man with spectacles turned from arranging soap cakes on a shelf when the bell pealed on a brass spring. "Is that you, John Mallory? I haven't seen you in ages." He glanced at Nora. "Is this the young lady Will told me about?"

"Yes, this is Miss Lenora La Rue." He introduced her to Bart Canton.

Mr. Canton shook her hand. "May I call you Lenora?"

She smiled. "I go by the name Nora."

"Now, Nora, what jobs have you done in the past?"

She hesitated a moment then swallowed. "I used to work with a circus."

"In what capacity?" Nora didn't understand the word and paused. "What did you do?" he urged.

"Oh, I was a bareback performer."

"Did you ever handle money?"

"No, sir, but I've been learning. I'm a fast learner."

He stroked his chin. "I see. I need someone to work the material and notions section. Show me how you would measure twelve yards of material and seven feet of trim. I have that on the counter over there." He indicated a showcase across the room with a bolt of cloth and a twist of trim on a cardboard.

Nora went to the counter and noticed a yardstick fixed to the edge. She started unfolding the bolt and put the edge to the end of the yardstick and covered it across. When she worked to the other end, she held it with her finger and returned that portion to the beginning, and repeated the measure eleven more times. Scissors were handy and she carefully cut the edge of the material. She took the trim and measured two yards and one foot, then cut.

Mr, Canton nodded. "Now, take the brown paper and package it."

Nora studied the paper roll on the back counter with the holder of string next to it. She carefully folded the material and wound the trim loosely around her fingers. Pulling the paper until it looked enough to wrap the merchandise, she tore it along the blade that was set across it. She put the paper on the counter and laid the items neatly on it. Nora had some trouble folding the paper, and when she reached for a length of string to tie it, it came apart. She was not going to let these things get the better of her, so she wrestled with it and managed a closed package.

Mr. Canton glanced at his pocket watch. "Twenty minutes, Nora?"

She felt her cheeks heat and was convinced she had failed. "I'm sorry, Mr. Canton. I'm sure I can do well with practice."

"Would you be able to stand for long periods of time?"

She hesitated slightly. "Yes, I'm sure I can."

He studied her for a moment. "I'm willing to give you a try. You will be expected here by eight in the morning and until six in the evening, Monday through Saturday, for twenty-five cents a day. You can start Monday next."

She grinned triumphantly. "Thank you, Mr. Canton. I'll be here as you say." They shook hands.

Dr. Mallory, who had been leaning against the opposite counter during all this time, then came and offered Nora his arm. "Shall we go, Miss La Rue?"

She picked up her cane from where she had stood it by the counter. "Yes, Doctor." As she took his arm, her nerves gone, she was fully aware of his nearness, thanks to the tightening of her chest and the tingling like she had touched an electric current machine.

When they were back on the street, the doctor pointed across the way. "Let's stop at the ice cream parlor for a few minutes. I want to talk to you."

In that establishment, which smelled like sweet chocolate, she sat at a small table while the doctor bought two phosphates from the fountain counter. He set a tall glass with the bubbly liquid in front of her and offered her a straw, then sat across from her and took a sip of his own glass. She smiled. "Thank you, Doctor."

"Miss La Rue, this is my last visit as your doctor. You are completely healed and seem to be able to get around quite well on your own. I attribute that to your youth and fit health."

Nora felt a small panic in the pit of her stomach. "I hope that doesn't mean I won't see you again. Who is going to be my doctor, if I need one?"

"There are some fine doctors in Waukesha who will take care of you. You will be seeing me again because of the matter of your artificial limb. Since you have a job now, you can lay aside some of your money each week to pay me back."

"How much was it?"

"One hundred and thirty-six dollars." He took a pencil and paper out of his pocket and started writing figures. "Let's see, you'll be making around twelve dollars a month. You can rent a room in Waukesha for about six, so you can live on three with three set aside for me."

Nora was stricken. "That's quite a bare existence."

"Not if you learn to budget. You still have two months at the sanitarium paid for, so you can save what money you make in that time. In the business book I gave you, it will tell you how to do that. I suggest you open a savings account at a bank, so you can also acquire interest."

Her brain was close to bursting. She had never thought about what it would be like to live on her own. Everything up to this point had been taken care of by others, and no one had ever bothered to teach her. "How do I keep track?"

"We'll pick up a ledger on the way back, and I'll show you how to bookkeep."

They finished their phosphates and stopped by the general store again to purchase a ledger. At the cottage, he showed her how to enter her income and purchases. Nora promised to enter any transaction immediately. He then showed her how to balance at the end of the month.

Finally, he stood and removed his hat from a peg. "I must be going, to catch my train to Milwaukee. Goodbye, Miss La Rue, and the best of luck to you."

Nora couldn't help it. She felt that sense of someone coming into her life and leaving again. Was she fated to always be abandoned? Holding her hand out, she rasped, "Goodbye, Dr. Mallory, and thank you."

He grasped her hand a beat longer than he should have. A mixture of emotions crossed his face and some sadness lingered there, and he turned quickly and left.

She went to the door and watched him go. Tears tracked hot paths down her cheeks, and she dashed them away.

An ache in her heart was here to stay.

Chapter 6

Three weeks after leaving Miss La Rue, John was constantly thinking of her. Thoughts of her would crop up at the funniest times.

"John—John? Are you listening to me?"

He focused on Thea, who was tapping the spoon in her teacup. "I'm sorry. I was thinking of something else. What did you say?"

"Oh, John. You seem very distracted these days. You have been working too much. It's been ages since we've done anything on your days off."

He paused. "We went to the state fair."

She sighed. "That was over a month ago. Honestly, since you've been at the hospital, we don't do half the things we did before. And the two of us don't seem to be moving forward."

"What do you mean by that?"

"I mean, you have been courting me for over a year and nothing has happened. Mother was asking me about that a couple of days ago."

"Do you mean marriage? I'm not ready for that, yet. I'd rather wait until I get regular hours at the hospital."

She frowned. "First it was until you graduated, then it was when you got a practice, and now it's when you get regular hours. Really, John, how long do I have to wait for you?"

He rubbed his temples. "I'm sorry, Thea. I'm very tired. Please excuse me for the evening."

She sat silently as he gathered his things to go. Glancing up, she said, "Good evening, John."

He leaned in and kissed her cheek. "Good evening, Thea." He cursed himself as he walked away from her house. He and Thea had grown up together in the same neighborhood, and their families assumed they would eventually marry. He enjoyed her company as a friend, but there were too many things they disagreed on. Looking into their future, he could see strife. *I don't know how to resolve this.* He walked into his apartment and fell asleep in the armchair.

****

Nora busied herself during slow periods by replacing the material bolts on the shelves. She had been doing well, with few mishaps, on her new job. At least, Mr. Canton seemed pleased with her. The door's bell made her turn around. A young blond-haired man with a mustache strode in.

"Excuse me, miss, is Uncle—er, Mr. Canton here?"

She stepped over to him. "He's out back loading supplies on a wagon for a customer. May I help you?"

He studied her for a moment. "You must be the young lady John told me about." He put his hand out. "I'm Will Canton, Bart's nephew. And you are?"

She shook his hand. "I'm Lenora La Rue, but you can call me Nora."

Mr. Canton came in, wiping his hands. "Will! Good to see you. Are you off the racing circuit already?"

Will shook his head. "No. I've got a race at Fountain Spring House this Saturday, so I thought I'd bring Chance here to stay until then."

Nora's ears perked up. "Oh, you've got a race horse? How splendid!"

"Would you like to see him?"

Nora glanced at Mr. Canton. "May I?"

He waved his hand toward the back door. "Go ahead, since there's no one here, but be right back."

She followed Will into the yard, and gasped at the copper-colored horse. "He's beautiful! Is he a sulky or a jockey racer?" She let Chance sniff her hands and scratched his nose. The horse nickered.

Will grinned. "He seems to like you. He's a sulky racer." He paused. "Have you been around horses much?"

"I've been riding since I was a small child. Did Dr. Mallory tell you anything about me?"

"Only that you had lost a leg and were looking for work."

She sighed. "I wish I could see the race, but I have to work on Saturdays."

He motioned to the stable hand. "Dan, take Chance to his stall and bed him down."

Dan took the reins. "Yes, Mr. Canton." Nora reluctantly watched him lead the horse away.

Will frowned. "Come, Nora, let me talk to my uncle." They went back inside the store where Bart Canton was setting up the flour barrels. "Uncle, do you think you'll need Nora here all day Saturday?"

He straightened up. "I certainly do. Saturday is our busiest day. That's why Jean and Caleb come in to help."

Will thought a moment. "Nora, there's an exposition race on Sunday. The only difference is you can't wager on the Sabbath. Would you like to go to that?"

She chewed on her lower lip. "I'm sure the ladies will be in their Sunday finery. I don't have anything suitable to wear to something like that."

"You can watch from the entrance gate. Nobody there will look down their noses at you."

She smiled. "I'd love to."

"Good. I'll pick you up Sunday morning after church. You're at Miss Weeks' sanitarium, aren't you?"

"Yes, I am, but I don't attend church. My family never has. We were always working or traveling on Sunday."

"I see." He tipped his hat. "Getting to know you sounds very interesting. Good day, Nora." And he left with a wave to Mr. Canton.

Nora went back to the material bolts. *Will seems nice. I do miss Dr. Mallory a lot, but he's spoken for. I have nothing to lose to venture down another path, for now.*

A lady came in for lace trimmings, and Nora ceased her musings.

****

Sunday morning, Nora studied herself in the full-length mirror. She had taken her one good dress and fixed lace trim over the worn spots on the sleeves and neckline. She turned to Livy, who was packing her case. "What do you think?"

Livy glanced at her critically. "I think it will do. The lace covers nicely."

Nora gazed at Livy's case. "I'm sure you're looking forward to going home today. It will be lonesome in this cottage without you."

"Well, at least I'm not going home as an invalid. My parents were worried about that. Teaching school shouldn't be a problem, so I can still help support the family."

Nora hugged her. "I'll miss you."

Livy smiled shyly. "I'll miss you, too. I'm sure you'll succeed at anything you put your mind to."

Nora heard a carriage in the yard. "That must be Will. Goodbye, Livy, and take care of yourself."

Livy walked with her to the porch. "I will. You, too."

Will hopped off the driver's seat and met Nora at the gate. He removed his hat. "You look fine in that dress. Let me help you up."

Nora settled in the seat and shaded her eyes as Will climbed on beside her. "Are you sure I won't be in the way?"

"No. Once everyone's in, the entrance gate is clear of people." He touched the whip to the horse's rump and the carriage headed for the road. "John didn't tell me about you. Do you have family around here?"

She paused. "My family is in Peru, Indiana."

A puzzled shadow crossed his face. "Then what are you doing here?"

She hesitated. *Will he still like me, if I tell him I'm from a circus family?* "I had the accident here over two months ago. My family travels most of the year, so it was easier if I stayed." She prayed that would be enough of an explanation for now. He remained silent. Nora thought it was because he was waiting for her to tell him more, but she asked, "How long have you known Dr. Mallory?"

"John? We grew up in the same neighborhood. Our

families were friends."

"I see." She carefully channeled him to tell her more about the east side of Milwaukee, so she wouldn't have to answer any more of his questions.

Soon, they were on a drive with a magnificent building in front of them. Will waved his hand toward it. "That's the Fountain Spring Hotel."

Nora appreciated the four-story building with it's line of gables and chimneys graced with a long three-story porch clinging to the walls. "It looks like a new hotel."

Will half-smiled. "Actually, rebuilt. The original burned down." He turned toward the racing stables. "Here we are." He helped Nora off the carriage. "Chance should be over here."

They found their way to one of the enclosed stalls, and Chance put his head over the door to greet them. The horse nickered and bumped Nora with his nose. She laughed. "And a hello to you, my handsome lad. That's the way he's been greeting me every evening when I stop to see him after work."

It was Will's turn to laugh. "It's too bad you can't race. He'd probably do anything for you."

"Lucky for me," came a voice from behind them. They turned, and there stood a small man in racing silks of green and yellow.

Will grinned. "You're job is safe, Trenton. Come meet Miss Nora La Rue. This is my driver, Trenton Casper, one of the best on the circuit."

Nora nodded acknowledgment. "Pleased to meet—oh!" She felt herself being bumped from behind. Her artificial knee buckled slightly, and Will caught her by the arm. Chance swished his tail and looked innocent.

Will studied her. "Do you know how to braid a tail?"

She smiled. "I've done that many times."

Trenton handed her the bands. "You're welcome to it. He won't stand still for me."

Will opened the stall door, and Nora went in. She patted Chance's neck and whispered in his ear, "Quiet and calm." In moments, the horse stood still, and Nora completed the work.

As Nora came out, Will and Trenton looked at each other. Trenton shook his head. "She has a way with horses, all right. I wish she could come with us."

Will turned to Nora. "I'll show you where you can stand. Everyone will be hitching up the sulkies in a few moments." As if on cue, a number of men were gathering in the stable drive, and Nora followed Will out to the gate. He waved his hand to a bench attached to the outside wall. "You can sit there until all the drivers are through. You have a capital view of the track from here."

While Will went back, Nora busied herself watching the fine ladies and gents heading to the covered bleachers on the other side of the track. She had a sad flashback to when she used to watch a similar parade while standing by the main tent at the circus. Her family may have been indifferent to her, but she had loved being in the circus, and missed all the respect and awe she'd received when she did her act. She could almost imagine being astride King again in her sequin-covered satin costume. Nora jumped when she felt someone touch her shoulder. She turned to find Will grinning at her.

"You were lost in quite a reverie. It must have been a happy one. You were smiling."

She glanced down, her cheeks heating. "I'm sorry. I was just thinking of times gone by."

The horses were lined at the gate, waiting for the signal to parade in. Some were calm, others stomped impatiently, and a few were lathered with nerves. Will pointed to the fourth in line. "There's Trenton and Chance." Chance was one of the ones stomping.

The trumpets announced the call, and one of the men opened the gate. The horses and drivers flashed by with a blur of shiny coats and bright-colored silks like a circus parade. She couldn't stop the tear down her cheek that she hastily brushed away.

Will put a hand on her arm. "I'm going to the owners' seats. You'll have a perfect view from here. I'll be back after the race."

Nora leaned against the wooden fence and watched the horses line up in front of gates. A gun went off, and the gates were opened by men on top of each gate. The horses set off with a smart trot, and she found herself cheering on Chance and Trenton. The bend to the finish line was right in front of her, and she felt dust kicked up off the track, but she was caught up in the excitement. Unfortunately, Chance came in a close second.

She brushed her clothes off and stepped back from the fence to sit on the bench again. The parade of dusty drivers and sweaty horses came back a lot more slowly than they went out. Will came up when the horses were in their stalls. Nora followed him to Chance's stall, where he turned to her. "Would you like to brush Chance down?"

She brightened. "I would love to. Where are the

brushes and curry comb?"

He pointed to the back of the stall. "Hanging over there."

Trenton had returned with two buckets of water he dumped in the stall's trough. "Anything else, boss?"

Will shook his head. "No. You can go change."

Nora had removed the bands and was brushing out Chance's tail while the stallion drank deeply. She handed the bands to Will. "I don't know where you want these."

He tucked them in a small case hanging in the stall. When Nora combed and brushed the horse until he shone like a new penny, Will put a light blanket over Chance's back. "I'll hitch him on the back of the carriage when we go into town." He handed her a towel. "You can wash up, and we'll get some refreshments."

Nora stared at him for a moment. "I'm not dressed to associate with the fine people."

Will shook his head. "They've gathered into groups, and I doubt they'll even notice you."

They walked to the green, where booths of refreshments were set up. People milled in little groups, and the rumble of conversation was all around. Nora found a small table near the rail fence, and Will purchased some sparkling water, cucumber sandwiches, and finger cakes.

While they were eating, a heavyset man with a sweaty bald head came striding over. "Mr. Canton! I see you're still entering that colt that is rightfully mine."

Will's mouth drew into a tight line. "Mr. Leaver, I have the bill of sale on Chance. Any argument you may have on ownership should be taken up with the one who sold him."

Leaver raised his top hat and swiped his head with a handkerchief. "I'll take this to court, if I have to. Be warned." He turned on his heel and disappeared into the crowd.

Nora leaned forward. "What was that all about?"

Will paused. "The man who sold me Chance was being goaded by Mr. Leaver to sell him the colt. Leaver and his bunch have a reputation of mistreating their animals, so he wanted to avoid selling Chance to Leaver. He made a quick sale to me before any bidding could take place."

Nora had visions of Chance being mistreated, and it made her sad. "As long as you have the bill of sale, I don't think he can do anything about that."

Will sighed. "You don't know these types. They won't stop at anything." He rose. "Come. We should be going."

Nora stood and brushed a few crumbs off her dress. "I'm ready." They started walking off the green, and she noticed a few disapproving glances her way, followed by whispers behind fans. Would she ever fit in anywhere?

When Will took his leave of her, back at the sanitarium, she thanked him for the outing. The small cottage seemed so quiet without anyone else there, but Nora wanted to be alone for a while.

Chapter 7

John was finding he couldn't shake Lenora La Rue. He thought when he released her from his care, that would be the end of it, yet he couldn't stop her from wandering into his thoughts and dreams. That lovely summer day when her raven hair was carried in wisps around her reddened cheeks, and those deep brown eyes... His body hardened at the thought.

One of the orderlies brought the mail into John's office and set it on his desk. "Morning, Dr. Mallory. A bit quiet today, isn't it?"

John nodded. "It's nice to have a breather once in a while."

"Good day to you, sir." The orderly left to continue his rounds.

John shuffled through the envelopes and found one from his Aunt Elinore. He opened it and unfolded the stationery. Two tickets fluttered to his desk.

Dear John,

Since you need to pick up the payment from Miss La Rue soon, I've enclosed two tickets to the Harvest Ball at the Fountain Spring Hotel in two weeks. You can see it's the evening of Saturday, October twelfth at seven o'clock. I will not take no for an answer. Miss La Rue and Will Canton will be there, as well.

Love to you,
Aunt Elinore

God help him. He pounded his fist on his forehead. He was pulled so strongly to the lovely yet scandalous Lenora La Rue. A surgeon who worked in a prestigious city hospital, the son of the head of surgery, *can't* fall in love with a circus performer. John sat back with a peculiar sense of relief. This was the first time he'd admitted this fact to himself. But what to tell Thea? *God help me. And has Will been seeing Lenora?* A shot of jealousy went through his heart like an arrow.

John removed some stationery from his desk and wrote a response to his aunt, telling her they would accept the invitation and thanked her. It was time to face up to his feelings for Lenora rather than live with a lifetime of regrets.

****

Nora stared at Miss Weeks like she had lost her senses. "Me? Go to a fancy hotel for a ball with all those society types? Absolutely not! I got a full dose of snobbery at the race with Will."

A patient smile graced Miss Weeks' features. "My dear, you will be completely on your own in a little over a month. Your social skills are sadly lacking. You need to know what it takes to get along with people in leisure time pursuits."

"But one thing I don't have and can't afford is a ball gown. I certainly can't wear my old worn dress."

Miss Weeks stood back and studied her for a moment. "Wait here. I'll be back in a few minutes." She disappeared out the cottage door.

Nora marveled at how much she hadn't been taught by her parents. They seemed to have trained her to ride horses and nothing else. She guessed that was all they had needed her for.

Miss Weeks came back with a rolled tissue paper package. On one of the beds, she carefully unrolled it. "This was the dress for my first ball when I was eighteen." She held up a war-era gown of ivory silk with ecru lace and a purple silk flower trim.

Nora felt a disappointed stab run through her. "That's over twenty years old. I'd really be a laughingstock in that."

Miss Weeks tsked softly. "Miss La Rue, this is where sewing comes in handy. You can take this old dress and alter it into today's fashions."

"But I just learned to sew. I don't know how to alter at all."

"Don't worry. I will teach and help you." She pulled some magazines out of the bottom of the tissue. "I even brought some recent fashion plates to help us. You can look at those while I go get my dress form and pins."

Miss Weeks took Nora's measurements and adjusted the dress form accordingly. They found a style that satisfied Nora and set to work. Cutting and coaxing the full skirt into a draped bustle in back and redoing the bodice took several days. Miss Weeks taught Nora how to use the sewing machine. She managed to get the seams fairly straight, and she put on the trim by hand.

Finally, the gown came off the dress form, and Nora tried it on. Miss Weeks made sure all the pins were out of it and helped Nora put it over her head. In front of the full-length mirror, Nora watched as Miss Weeks buttoned the back together. The silk material settled into its new form. Nora hadn't felt this elegant since the fine costumes she had worn at the circus. "It's beautiful, Miss Weeks. Thank you."

Miss Weeks took a step back. "It looks wonderful on you, my dear. It sets off your dark hair perfectly. I'll help with your hair the evening of the ball."

In the remaining days before that special evening, Miss Weeks taught Nora the finer points of social etiquette—what to say, what to eat, even how to hold a fan had its rules of order. Nora was ready for her head to explode.

The afternoon of the ball, Miss Weeks helped Nora get dressed while heating up the curling iron on the stove in the cottage. Nora had purchased a lace fan, a reticule, elbow-length gloves, and a tiered necklace from Bart Canton's merchandise. They lay ready on the table in front of her.

Miss Weeks picked some white roses from her bush and worked them into Nora's hair, which she had pinned up except for some she arranged over Nora's shoulder. She brought the heated curling iron over and made those locks into two long curls with a sizzle of hair against the hot metal. Nora rose and looked at herself in the mirror. She blinked a few tears. "I haven't looked like this for some time."

Miss Weeks folded her hands and smiled. "You look beautiful, dear. People shouldn't look down on you tonight." She retrieved a small jar from the table. "Here's some rouge, if you like."

Nora put some on her lips and cheekbones. "Please help me with the necklace?" When Miss Weeks clasped the jewelry behind Nora's neck, the gold chains fell into scallops held together by the links of garnets.

A clatter of horse's hoofs and carriage wheels announced that her escort had arrived. Miss Weeks opened the door of the cottage and waved. "Nora will be out in a few moments."

She heard Will call, "No hurry."

Nora finished getting her things together and reached for her old cape. Miss Weeks put a hand on her arm. "Nora, that old thing will never do." She went to the satchel that had transported all her instruments from the house and drew out an ivory cape that matched the material on the dress. "Wear this."

Nora laughed. "I really feel like Cinderella. Thank you, Miss Weeks!" She stepped out onto the porch as Miss Weeks hung the lantern on the iron hook fixed to one of the posts. In the dim light, she could see the carriage with the forward coach lanterns lit.

Will hopped out of the driver's seat. "You look lovely! John and Thea are coming with us."

She glanced at the seats to the rear. "Dr. Mallory?"

A shadowy form rose and removed his hat. "You may call me John, if I can call you Nora."

She hesitated. "Yes, of course." She then greeted Thea. Will helped her into the seat, and they headed to the hotel.

Fountain Spring Hotel was awash in electric lights strung around the huge porch. It looked like a magical fairyland, and Nora sadly compared it to the circus tents at night. Will let the three of them off at the entrance and went to find a space for the carriage.

Seeing how handsome Dr. Mallory was in his formal clothes made her fidget a bit. "I'm sorry, Dr.—um, John. If I'd known you were going to be here, I would have brought the payment with me."

He grinned and shook his head. "Don't worry about that. Thea and I have rooms here tonight. I'll stop by to see you in the morning."

Will came bounding onto the porch. "Come on. Let's go in."

They stopped at the hat check, and Will took Nora's cape. She noticed John sucked in a quick breath and stared at her for a moment, then flushed, offering his arm to Thea as he said, "Shall we find a table?"

Will offered his arm to Nora, and they went into the ballroom. Nora noticed people looking at her, then turning away when they noticed her peculiar gait. *No matter how you dress it up, a cripple is always a cripple.*

John found a table not far from the dance floor, which was fine with her. She slipped into the seat feeling like a duck out of water. Will and John left to get refreshments, and Thea chatted about things that meant nothing to Nora. She hoped she nodded in the right spots.

The men came back when the orchestra started to play. As people around them got up to dance, Will put out his hand to her. "Would you like to dance?"

She shuddered. "Please don't ask me. I never learned to dance, and I couldn't possibly now."

He turned to John. "Are you going to dance? If not, may I ask Thea?"

John waved his hand. "Go ahead."

When they left the table, John studied Nora. "Working in a circus, you never learned to dance?"

Nora shook her head. "Not socially. We did theatrical dance steps, but that's all I ever did. I've never attended a ball before."

"There are dances you could do on your limb. Would you like to try?"

She took a deep breath. "Not in front of all these

people."

He glanced around. "The hallway over there is deserted. Let me show you." He rose and held his hand out.

She clasped it and wasn't ready for the tingle that ran up her arm and tightened her chest. She stood, and he led her out of the ballroom. "What do I do?"

"Put your left hand on my shoulder like this. Then I put my hand on your waist, and we hold the other hands."

Nora did what she was told. "Now what?"

"Now I'll step forward and you step back, like this." They took one step. "Then a step to your left. Then I'll step back and you forward. Then a step to your right." They completed the square. "That's how you do a waltz." They did it a few more times. Her artificial knee buckled, but John held her up. "Now let's try it to the music."

They started well enough, but after a few rounds, toes were stepped on and legs were tripped. Nora went down on the floor with John. She started laughing. "Graceful I'm not."

John was laughing, as well. "I didn't say it was going to be perfect." He hopped up and helped her to rise. "It was fun, though."

The music had stopped, and they held hands longer than was polite, gazing at each other. Nora got lost in those beautiful eyes of his for a moment, but she quickly pulled herself out of the trance and stepped back. "Thank you for the dance."

He quirked his eyebrow at her. "My pleasure." He offered his arm. "Shall we return?"

They turned to the doorway, and there stood Will

and Thea. Will looked amused, and Thea had an unreadable expression.

Nora felt her cheeks heat. "Did you see that?"

Will chuckled. "I see why you didn't want to dance."

"I'll be content just listening to the music." They returned to their table, and John took Thea to the dance floor while Nora slid into her chair.

Will regarded her for a few moments. "You sure have John Mallory smitten."

She paused. "Why do you say that? Isn't he engaged to Thea?"

"First, he's more involved with you than with any other patient. Second, he's been with Thea for several years and never asked for her hand. Third, I saw the look he gave you, and he doesn't look at Thea like that."

"How about you? You're the one who invited me to the ball."

Will half-smiled. "I like you. You're interesting and mysterious. I have a feeling John knows more about you than I do."

"There is some information about me I don't share with anyone. He knows because he was my surgeon and was there when my world fell apart." A shaft went through her heart again.

"I have a feeling something terrible happened to you. John is kindhearted like that. He used to rescue small animals that were hurt or mistreated and nurse them back to health. I'm surprised he didn't become a veterinarian."

"Do you think he feels sorry for me?"

Will gave her a straightforward look. "No. He

would have treated all his patients kindly, but you are the first he has done anything for beyond medical treatment."

Nora pondered that as John and Thea returned to the table. Times during the evening, Nora would stand up and walk around. She noticed men giving her admiring glances but quickly studying the floor when she stepped out with her peculiar gait. *A cripple is to be pitied, not admired.*

John paid more attention to Thea the rest of the evening. Will and Nora said their goodbyes when it was over, since John and Thea had rooms in the hotel for the night. John wore his businesslike mask when he said good night to Nora. She remembered the playful side of him she had found in the hallway and was sad Dr. Mallory had returned. Thea wished them good night also, but there was a cold chill in her eyes.

Will snapped the reins, and the carriage headed down the drive. Nora sighed and glanced at Will, who patted her hand. "You were absolutely beautiful tonight."

She snorted. "For a cripple?"

Will shook his head. "No," was all he said.

****

John and Thea watched the departing carriage until Thea turned an icy stare on him. "Is there anything going on between you and Lenora La Rue?"

He tried to look innocent. "She was my patient."

"When did that include dance lessons?"

"We *were* seeing Will and Nora socially tonight."

"John, it's one thing to try to help a poor unfortunate, but to socialize with a scandalous circus person is quite another! I don't think Will knows what she is or he wouldn't be seen with her."

John had never seen this side of Thea before. "You should be ashamed of yourself! Nora has been loosed from her family and is bravely trying to find her way alone in the world. I don't know if she told Will where she came from, but he doesn't spurn her."

She sneered. "Well, maybe someone should."

John glared. "Keep your nose out of it. If Will gets told, let it be by Nora."

Thea turned on her heel and marched inside. "Good night, John!"

John leaned against one of the posts, holding his tongue. He wanted to throw something. He closed his eyes for a moment to gain control. During his years as a doctor, he'd noticed how people treated cripples not just with pity but with the belief they were mental inferiors, like losing a limb made them suddenly stupid. Nora had another strike against her by coming from a circus family. Most other folks believed circus people to be tramps and thieves. Oh, they'd come see the show, but in no way associate with the riffraff who worked there.

He pulled the hotel key out of his vest pocket and tossed and caught it a couple of times. Then, blowing a breath that frosted in the crisp fall air, he turned and headed to his room.

Chapter 8

Nora rocked in the wicker chair on the porch of the cottage. She had a shawl on against the fall morning chill, but she loved this time of year. The smell of burning leaves made a sharp but lovely perfume.

A clip-clop and rattling noise announced a carriage arriving in the drive, and Miss Weeks appeared at the back door. John came around the side of the house and met her. Nora watched them come toward the cottage and to the porch.

John removed his hat. "Good morning, Nora."

Nora picked up a brown envelope she had on the table beside her. "Here's your payment, Doctor." She paused. "You may count it, if you like."

He blew a slow breath. "No, I trust you. I'm guessing you are keeping records."

"Yes," came out tersely. "I am going to rent an apartment and open an account at one of the banks. I'll send a bank note to you, so you don't have to trouble yourself to come out here every month."

Miss Weeks glanced at both strangely. "John, would you and Thea like to stay for some tea?"

"No, thank you, Auntie. We have to be getting back."

Miss Weeks nodded and started back to the house. "Good day, John. Take care of yourself."

John hesitated and gazed at Nora. "I feel like I

should be apologizing to you for something." His fingers tapped a beat on the rim of the hat in his hand.

Her emotions were fighting to overwhelm her. "No need." An unbidden tear rolled down her cheek, and she brushed it away.

Suddenly, he had her in an embrace. "Oh, Nora, I'm sorry."

She wanted to push him away, but it felt so good to have someone who seemed to care about her feelings that she couldn't get her arms to obey her. A lifetime of hurt came flooding out as she cried into his rough coat.

A sharp bark of "John!" came from the corner of the house. Thea stood there with an unpleasant frown. "Are you coming? We'll be late for the train."

John pulled back and squeezed Nora's shoulders with his hands. "I'll be back next month."

Nora nodded, and she watched him hurry off the porch as she steadied herself with her hand on the table. After they disappeared around the corner of the house, she sank back into the chair. *I'm falling in love with him, and I can't stop myself. Am I doomed to be hurt by people all my life?* She watched a swallowtail butterfly doing its curious dance from flower to flower. She stood and went inside the cottage.

****

John stared out the window of the train,, not seeing the countryside go by. *Lord, I 've made a mess of things. I seem to have complicated the lives of two women in one fell swoop. And my own. Thea doesn't deserve this and neither does Nora. But I'm practically engaged to one woman and in love with another…*

Thea had been quiet most of the morning. He glanced at her, and she was watching him with a veiled expression. "John, I'm sorry about last night. I guess I'm jealous of Nora. Seeing you with her in the hallway, you seemed like a different person. Happier. More alive."

The clacking of the train and the murmur of voices in the car was all that was heard for a few moments. "Thea, I have an obligation to you. There's been an understanding between us—"

"For too long a time," she finished. "I always wondered why you kept putting off going any further than that. You love me, but you're not in love with me."

"Our families expect us to marry."

Thea shook her head. "You'll always have that regret hanging over us. That wouldn't be a happy marriage. I couldn't live with a man who was pining over someone else." She looked down. "Don't you understand? I'm releasing you."

Part of John wanted to cheer, but he hated hurting Thea. They'd known each other so long. That was probably the reason she knew what he was going through. He reached over and put his hand on hers. "Thank you, Thea, and I'm deeply sorry."

She managed a smile. "Don't be. You couldn't help it."

He settled back, watching the farms give way to the clutter of factory houses on the outskirts of the city. The smell of coal smoke told him they were close to the depot. Robert was there to meet them and placed their cases in the carriage.

He turned to glance at John. "How was the ball at Fountain Spring?"

John paused. "Interesting. I'll talk to you later." He wondered how in hell he was going to tell his family he and Thea had split. Hopefully, they'd understand and accept Nora. The problem was his father knew what she was.

When they arrived at her house, Thea kissed John on the cheek. "Don't worry about me. I'll be all right. I wish you well."

As John helped her down and carried her case to the porch, Robert gave him a puzzled look. John returned and hopped up beside Robert, who wiped his hand over his mouth. "What was that all about?"

John sighed. "You may as well know. Thea and I decided to part ways."

"You stepped on her toes too many times?"

"Mostly her heart." He paused. "I can't ask her to marry me because I'm in love with someone else." He went on to tell his brother about what had taken place that weekend.

Long after he finished his story, all that was heard was the clip-clop of the horse's hoofs on the brick street. Robert turned to him. "You really left Thea for a one-legged circus performer?"

"Nora isn't a performer anymore. And I give her credit for being able to hold a job and pay her own way. There's a lot of grit in that girl."

Robert stopped the horse in front of John's apartment. "Good luck in telling Mother and Father. They won't be pleased."

John climbed down and pulled his case off the back. He frowned. "I know that. Thank you for the lift, brother."

Robert tipped his hat. "Good day to you, and you're welcome." John watched the carriage go down the street. Good day, indeed.

****

During a break at the store the next morning, Nora approached Mr. Bart Canton as he poured nails into a bin. "Mr. Canton, do you know of any rooms for lease close by? My time is running out at the sanitarium, and I need to find a place of my own."

He straightened and looked thoughtful. "I think Mr. Lawrence has a room over his china shop across the street. Since it's slow right now, why don't you go see him?"

Nora picked up her cape off the back of her chair. "Thank you. I'll be back directly." She carefully avoided the horse waste in the roadway and walked inside the cheery china shop with all its delicate treasures. The brass bell tinkled as she opened the door. Mrs. Lawrence was dusting the display shelves and glanced at Nora. "May I help you, dear?"

"Yes. Is your husband in? Mr. Canton told me he might have a room to rent."

Mrs. Lawrence hesitated. "He does. But we usually don't rent to single ladies. Our reputation, you know."

"I'm coming out of the sanitarium in a couple of weeks and need a place. I have no family or friends here. This is right across the street from my work. Please let me talk to him?"

Mr. Lawrence appeared from the back of the shop. "Miss La Rue, I heard what you said. I think it would be all right, but we absolutely forbid any gentlemen visitors." He paused. "I know of your—difficulties. Would you be able to get up and down the steps?"

"Yes. Slowly, but yes." Nora stared steadily at him.

He turned to his wife. "My dear, would you step into the back room with me?"

Nora studied the lovely china sets and figurines that dotted the shelves. *It would be wonderful to be able to buy some of those treasures, but I'm poor now. I used to live in a mansion with servants, and now...* She quickly dashed a tear from her eye when she heard the Lawrences enter the room.

His eyes pierced her. "We will rent the room out to you, but let's be clear. If there's any scandalous behavior, out you'll go."

Nora gave an inward sigh. "Yes, sir. Is the room furnished?"

"Yes, it is. We can let you have it for twelve dollars a month, due on the first. Is that agreeable?"

"Agreed. Thank you, Mr. Lawrence. I can move in on the first of November?"

He nodded. "Your first rent will be due then."

"You shall have it." And with that she happily went back across the street to the general store.

****

John halted the carriage horse in the drive of his father's substantial home. He had requested a dinner invitation, telling his father he had something to discuss with them. He sat there a few minutes gathering his thoughts, trying to figure out what to say to questions he could only imagine.

The street gaslight cast a yellow glow on the cream brick walkway to the porch as he approached, and the maid, Bess, opened the door to his rap with the brass knocker. "Dr. John, come in. Your family is waiting for you."

John gave his coat and hat to the maid. "Are they in the parlor?" At her acknowledgment, he went through the door.

His father rose and slapped him on the back. "Welcome, son. Why isn't Thea with you?"

"That's what I wanted to see all of you about."

His mother studied him. "I can tell by your face something has happened."

John blew out a slow breath. "There's no easy way of telling you this. Thea and I have parted."

Franny jumped to her feet. "What? Why?" she said at the same time his mother said, "Oh, John, no!"

His father's lips drew into a straight taut line. "Explain yourself."

John paused. "Thea told me she didn't want to marry a man who is in love with someone else." His family stared dumbfounded at him.

"Who is this other woman?" his father demanded.

"Lenora La Rue."

"Your patient?" his father exploded. "Boy, have you taken leave of your senses?"

"She isn't my patient anymore. She's a respectable clerk in a general store and is paying her own way."

Just then, Bess came to announce that dinner was on the table. When she left, Ben Mallory turned to his son. "John, we shall take this up after supper."

The usual mealtime chatter was almost nonexistent. Everyone seemed in shock with the news. Afterwards, his mother and Franny excused themselves to the women's parlor, and John went with his father to the library.

Ben Mallory pointed to one of the leather chairs. "Sit! Now tell me what is going on here."

John related his history with Nora, culminating with the discussion with Thea on the train back from Waukesha.

His father leaned against the mantel and lit his pipe. He puffed silently for a few minutes while the grandfather clock ticked in the background. "John, I seem to remember telling you not to get involved with your patients."

John passed his hand over his mouth. "I know, sir. I usually don't, but there was something about her that drew me in."

"You felt pity for her?"

"I was sorry how her family treated her, but I didn't want her to give up on herself. She had no one else."

"You weren't in love with Thea?"

John sighed. "I thought I was. We grew up together, but I have never felt ready to go further. Every time she questioned me about it, I kept giving excuses."

Ben puffed on his pipe a few more times. "You realize that Miss La Rue will never fit in socially, with her background."

John rapped on the arm of the chair with his fingers. "Father, in a way, I'm getting weary of all these rules of society. Becoming a rural surgeon in a small town is looking better to me."

"If you're talking about Waukesha, there is much high society there, being a resort town."

John put his head in his hands. "I don't know, Father. I've got to think this through. I don't even know how Nora feels about all this."

Ben tapped out the ashes into the fireplace. "Then you have some work to do. I'll explain things to your mother."

John had never felt so unsure of things in his life. He looked forward and dreaded his next trip to Waukesha.

Chapter 9

Nora received a letter from John that he would be in Waukesha that Saturday. Miss Weeks had helped Nora move her things to the new apartment a few days before. It was furnished by the Lawrences simply, but its one room was clean and neat, with a large arched window looking out over the street and a small one on the other side over the alley. Tucked away on one side was an iron-framed bed with a green braided rug next to it. A washstand and chest of drawers were along one wall. A pantry, gas stove, and a small table with two chairs were on the other side, and a large overstuffed armchair and reading table with an electric lamp was by the big window. This was her world now.

She sat at the table with her stationery and dashed off a note to John to meet her after the general store closed for the day. The postman came twice a day to the store, so she could give the letter to him to take back to the post office.

Nora shrugged on her cape against the frosty November morning and pinned the hat to her hair. Taking one more check in the mirror on the washstand, she picked up the letter and headed out to the street.

She met Mr. Canton unlocking the front door of the store. "Good morning, sir. I have a letter going out today. May I put it with your outgoing mail?"

He nodded. "Of course. You can place it in the

postal basket on my desk."

When she returned, she found several crates of new stock to put away at her station. About an hour later, Will strode in and right to her.

He had a concerned look on his face. "Nora, have you heard from John Mallory lately?"

"He sent a letter saying he was going to be in town this Saturday. Why?"

"He didn't tell you anything else?" Nora shook her head. "His sister spoke to me and told me John and Thea had parted ways. The family is quite upset."

Nora paused. "I'm sorry to hear that."

"Are you really? She said they split because of you."

Nora leaned on the counter. "Me? John didn't say a word to me."

He backed off. "I'm sorry. I thought you knew. Maybe he was going to tell you Saturday." He turned. "Excuse me, I have to check on Chance." He hurried out.

Nora was stunned. *What did I miss?* She went through everything that had been said and all that had happened when she last saw John. He had apologized and held her when she began to cry. She knew how she felt about him, but did he feel the same? Strange stirrings went on inside her. Part of her was hopeful she had finally found someone who cared about her, but there was that darkness, the fear she would be hurt and abandoned once again. She pondered that the rest of the day.

****

John's stomach churned as he drove the carriage to Canton's General Store. Will had told him about breaking the news about Thea and John to Nora accidentally. He wondered what kind of reception he was going to get. He had told Nora in the letter that he was going to take her to one of the downtown hotels for supper that evening.

He walked into the store, and Bart Canton looked up. "Evening, John."

"Evening, Bart."

Nora was straightening up her work station and wiping the shelves. "I'll be ready in a few minutes." She had worn her best dress to work. She finished up and put on her cape and gloves and pinned on her hat. "Good night, Mr. Canton."

He nodded to her. "Good night, Nora. Here's your pay for the week." He handed her a sealed brown envelope she slipped into her reticule.

John held the door for her and helped her into the carriage. "You look very nice tonight, Nora."

She eyed him carefully as he climbed up and took the reins. "Thank you." The steady clip-clop of the horse's hoofs on the bricks was the only sound heard for a few blocks, until they stopped in front of the hotel that was lit up for the evening. John helped Nora down and took the carriage to the side of the building. He returned in a few minutes to find her talking to the doorman.

He offered his arm. "Ready?"

She took it. "Yes, I am."

The doorman tipped his hat. "Have a very good evening." They nodded to him.

John found the host at the door of the dining room. "Dr. Mallory, party of two."

He checked his reservations ledger. "Yes, sir. Follow me." He took a menu board and led them to a table near one of the windows. After John pulled out the chair for Nora and took a seat across from her, the host handed him the menu. "The special tonight is braised pheasant," he said, inclined his head, and left.

John studied the menu. "How about the pheasant?"

Nora seemed distracted. "Yes. Anything you want."

He gave the waiter their order, then turned his attention to Nora. "Something is bothering you."

She paused. "The doorman recognized me from the circus. I'm trying to be as inconspicuous as I possibly can, because of what people think of circus performers, let alone the lame. I can't help my face was pictured all over this summer."

"As time goes on, that will fade. Cheer up. We're here to enjoy ourselves tonight." The waiter brought over raw vegetables and oysters on a half-shell.

Nora ate one of the oysters and nibbled on a carrot. "Will came over for Chance the other day. He told me that you and Thea had parted ways."

John dabbed his lips with the napkin. "What else did he tell you?"

"That it was because of me. John, are you sure you aren't being hasty?"

"For whatever reason, I have deep feelings for you. Thea noticed it. That's why she said what she did."

She seemed to be going through some sort of internal dialog. "How do you know it isn't infatuation?"

John was fighting the impatience gnawing at him. He knew everyone in her life had hurt her. "I know why you're asking these questions, and believe me I understand. I know the concern I've had for you from the beginning has been turning into caring and wanting to protect you. Last time I was here, I experienced a deep feeling I'd never had before. I wanted to stay with you and be with you."

"And is that love? I've never had anyone who cared that way. I thought I had it with Rico, but—you know what happened."

John was angry at the thought of Rico. "Excuse my language, but Rico was an ass."

Nora wasn't shaken. She smiled. "I've heard ten times worse language from the roustabouts. It's a wonder I haven't spouted off some choice words already, with the frustrations of this leg, or the lack of it."

The waiter came with their main course, and they ate their way through the tender, herb-braised meat with root vegetables, rolls and butter, and small stemmed glasses of white wine. Dessert was a cherry tart and coffee.

She sat back at the end of the meal. "Thank you, John. I don't think I've ever had a meal this elegant."

He rose and helped her up. "Good food and good company. Come, let's go. I'll escort you back to your apartment." He paid the tab, and while she put on her cape, he got the carriage. The drive back was chilly, and he heard tinny music coming from several saloons they passed by. The smell of coal smoke lingered in the air from the blacksmith's shop on the corner. He stopped the horse in front of the china shop. Impulsively, he took off his glove, putting his fingers on her cheek, and cupped her chin. The cold skin suddenly radiated warmth. "Understand, Nora, I am falling in love with you."

In the warm amber of the streetlight, her eyes glistened. "Are you sure about that? How do I know you're not telling me this just to leave when you tire of me?"

"Please give me a chance to prove myself. I don't give my heart lightly. My feelings for you go back to when I first saw you that night at the circus. Infatuation at that time, yes. Since I've known you, that has turned into respect and love." She shuddered under his touch. He placed a chaste kiss on her cheek, then put his glove back on. "Let me help you down." He went around to her side of the carriage and took her down into an embrace. "I'll give you time. I won't push you until you're ready."

Nora buried her face in his shoulder. "I want to believe you," she murmured. "Good night, John. Thank you for the evening. Here's your payment for this month." She pulled back and drew an envelope out of her reticule. After she handed it to him, she started up the stairs to her apartment. He lingered there to see that she got in safely, then turned and climbed onto the carriage again. He gave the reins a snap, and the horse made it's way to the livery.

****

Sunday morning was sunny and crisp. Nora woke chilled, and waited until she heard the popping of the furnace in the cellar. She arose and slipped on her artificial leg. Walking a few steps, she waved her hand over the radiator under the small window. Heat was coming out finally. The men had probably come to stoke the coal.

She shrugged on her robe and, not wishing to start hot water on the rickety stove, opened the pantry and took out a bottle of Silurian water she'd purchased at the spring, and poured it into a glass. Unwrapping the brown paper around a new loaf of bread, she cut a couple of slices and spread some honey on them. Then she sat and nibbled on the bread with a wry thought. *I'm down to bread and water now.* She thought about storing some perishable food on the enclosed part of the walk-up outside, where it would stay cold, at least during the winter. There was a funny sort of freedom in deciding things for yourself, she found.

A church bell pealed in the distance. Her desire to meet people burned within her. She had never felt this alone before. Hoofbeats in the street brought her to her feet, and she pulled the curtains back on the large front window. Will was bringing Chance back from a race yesterday. Nora shed her robe and got dressed in her shirtwaist and skirt, fastening her cape as she hurried out the door.

Will glanced up from brushing Chance when she stepped into the stable. "Will, I hope you're not angry with me. I don't want to lose your friendship."

He paused, then smiled. "I'm sorry I acted as I did last time I saw you. I've been friends with John and Thea since childhood, and I was upset about their parting. I don't blame you."

Nora scratched Chance's nose, and he gave a deep-throated nicker. "I'm glad you don't."

Will finished his job and led Chance into his stall. "Would you like to go to St. Matthias with me for Sunday service? It's Episcopalian."

"I never belonged to a church, although I know my father's family were Catholic. To my knowledge, I was never baptized. But, yes, I'll go with you." She looked down at her clothes. "Is this suitable to wear?"

He nodded. "You'll do fine. It's just a few blocks;

we can walk." He waved at Dan, who was in the tack room repairing harnesses. Dan waved back to them and wished them good morning.

The last of the brown leaves on the oak trees were stubbornly clinging for dear life to the sparse limbs. Nora was drawing frosty air into her nostrils, and some rime ice outlined the leaves on the ground. The lofty spire of the stone church came into view. Many people were already making their way up the steps.

The warmth of the building and the people amazed her. The compact sanctuary held wooden pews, and Will led her to one in the back. Nora was sure it was because of her clothes, because most of the congregation were fairly well-dressed. Will glanced at Nora and gave her hand a squeeze. She was grateful for his friendship.

At the end of the service, Will and Nora were almost the first ones out. The reverend was greeting everyone as they left. He shook Will's hand. "Bart Canton's nephew, Will, isn't it? We don't usually see you after the season."

Will nodded. "Racing is closing down now, and I'll be in Milwaukee most of the winter."

He turned his attention to Nora. "You're new here. You are…?"

She paused. "Lenora La Rue, but I go by the name Nora." She shook his hand.

He looked back at Will. "A special lady of yours?"

Will smiled. "A friend. She works at my uncle's store."

They moved to go as the reverend called. "Hope to see you again, Nora." He went back to greeting the parishioners.

They were a couple of blocks away when they noticed a column of smoke towering over the buildings, and the fire bell started pealing. Will stopped in his tracks. "That looks like it's coming from the direction of the store. Nora, do you think you can make it the rest of the way by yourself? I'm going to run and see."

"Of course. Go!" Will took off in a sprint, and Nora carefully navigated the flagstone sidewalk. She heard pounding of horses' hooves and assumed it was the fire department. Crossing the street, she happened to glance a block down and noticed a man on a horse leading a riderless steed, going away from the fire. She shaded her eyes. *That looks an awful lot like Chance. But no, that can't be.*

She made it to the street in front of the store and gasped as she turned the corner. Fire equipment was in front of the store, and the column of smoke was coming from the back loading yard. *The stable? Oh, no!*

Will appeared in the street leading the two draft horses, and Bart Canton arrived on horseback and gave the reins of his horse to Will to hold while he ran to the back. People were coming out of their houses and apartments to watch. The constables held them back at a safe distance. Nora was still across the street and leaned against one of the shuttered business' storefronts.

Will noticed her and came over, leading the horses. "Nora! The stable is on fire, and I can't find Chance. He wasn't in his stall. Could you hold the horses for me while I search for him?"

She took the reins and the two halter leads. "I'll take them around the corner to the vacant lot. There's some grass and a trough that might keep them calm."

Will paused. "On second thought, I'll borrow my

uncle's horse." He took the reins back and climbed on.

In the excitement, Nora forgot to tell Will what she had observed in the other street. She chastised herself as she tied the two draft horses to the post by the water. The steeds seemed to be calmed a bit by being away from the noise and flames, but she stayed with them.

Nora filled her time by talking to the horses and scratching their noses until she saw Mr. Canton round the corner. "Nora, Will told me you had the horses. Good thinking to get them away from the crowd. I'm surprised you're strong enough to handle them."

Nora stood from a bench by the trough. "I've been around horses all my life. I guess I naturally know how to calm them."

Mr. Canton glanced at the ground with a sad expression. "I may have to transfer you to the stable for a while."

"Why?"

"Dan was killed in the fire," he said with a rasp in his voice.

Nora put her hand to her mouth in shock. "Oh, no! Oh, poor Dan."

"The thing is, he was found at the door of the tack room with a rifle in his hands. The constable fears foul play."

"You mean someone deliberately set it?"

"He thinks so. Chance's stall was open, and he's missing."

"Mr. Canton, I think Chance was stolen." She told him what she had observed one street over as she came from the church.

He untied the halter leads on the horses. "I'm going to take them to the livery stable for now, until we get my stable rebuilt. Why don't you go back to your apartment now? I'll tell Will what you told me." They parted, and she went gratefully home.

****

Dr. Ben Mallory tapped his pencil on the desk as he glared at John. "This is the second patient in a row that has developed an infection in the incision. You're usually more careful than that. I can't keep sending other doctors to take care of your mishaps on your days off. What do you have to say for yourself?"

"I'm sorry, sir. It won't happen again."

Ben rose and came around the desk to face his son. "Your life has become a distraction for you. I want you to put the needs of your patients ahead of your problems. Otherwise, I'll have to rethink about your working here."

"Yes, sir. May I go?" At his father's nod, he opened the door and walked out. Closing it again, he leaned against the wall and wiped his brow with his hand. *Thea released me, and Nora is unsure about me. What am I supposed to do? Until I can get this resolved, I'd better keep my mind on my work, or that's going to be decided for me.*

Since John had finished his rounds that morning, he made his way to the hospital lounge and poured himself a cup of coffee. Sitting down at one of the tables, he gazed outside at the drab and damp November weather.

Henry came over and sat down. "The old man really raked you over the coals this morning."

John paused. "Seems like everyone in this hospital knows what happened."

"Not everyone. I was the one who had to take care

of your patients while you played."

John felt like someone had hit him in the chest. "Everyone gets days off. But thank you for your help." He stopped. "What do you mean 'played'?"

Henry sneered. "You were with the little gimpy hussy, weren't you?"

John jumped up and grabbed Henry by the arm and slammed him against the wall. "Don't you ever call her that!"

Henry snorted. "You let go a lady for a tramp."

John pulled a roundhouse punch to Henry's jaw, sending him into the table, which went over with a crash. Several people ran out, while the janitor came in to deal with the splattered coffee and broken cups.

Dr. Ben Mallory appeared at the door, looking like a thundercloud. "Dr. Mallory, Dr. Chase. My office. Now."

Henry glared at John as he rose off the floor. John went ahead but was wary of where Henry was. The senior Dr. Mallory held the door open and closed it purposefully behind them, then strode to his desk and sat studying the two combatants. "Can someone please tell me what *that* was all about?"

John and Henry glanced at each other like two naughty schoolboys. John took a breath. "A disagreement, sir."

"Oh? What about?"

Henry's jaw muscles tensed. "I'd rather not say, sir."

Ben Mallory made a sound deep in his throat. "It must have been some disagreement." He rose and strolled around to face the two doctors. "I don't know who started this, but I'm going to end it." He turned to

Henry. "Dr. Chase, forget about the two days off you requested. Get back to your job."

"But sir—"

"Now, Dr. Chase." Henry slunk out of the office.

Ben turned his ire on John. "My God, boy. I just chastised you for neglect of your duties, and now you're fighting like a rowdy in a bar? What did he say that got you so angry?"

"He insulted Nora." John stared at the toe of his shoe.

Ben put his hands behind his back and rocked a couple of times on his feet. "You realize that, because of what she was, that's going to happen. Especially with people who know her past. If you choose her for your wife, both of you have to live with that."

John was quiet for a moment, gathering his thoughts. "Father, do you know any of the surgeons at the small hospital in Waukesha? Maybe I could go to work there."

"The facilities there aren't as modern as what you're used to. The pay won't be as much, either, because there aren't as many people there."

"It's time for me to make a decision. Waukesha is where my heart is. I can't work in a place where I'm becoming unhappy and garnering insults. Nora isn't sure about my feelings for her yet, and being there will make it easier to win her over."

Ben put a hand on his son's shoulder. "Sleep on it tonight, and if you still want to make the move tomorrow, I'll get in touch with Elinore. She knows all the doctors there and can maybe put in a good word."

John paused. "Thank you, sir. And I'm sorry for losing my temper."

Ben went back and sat at his desk. "Just do the best for your patients."

"I will, sir." John strode out of the office and back to do his rounds again.

Chapter 10

Canton's General Store had some fire damage, but they were able to open Monday morning. The windows in the rear of the store were boarded, but the merchandise inside was unscathed. The equipment in the yard was damaged beyond repair, and Bart Canton had to replace that, along with everything in the stable.

Nora set up boxes of notions in the display case while hearing the wrecking team tearing down the rest of the burnt walls of the stable. Mr. Canton set up a battery-powered fan by the front window to blow the odor of charred matter out of the store, and Nora pinned on a wool shawl against the November chill.

What looked like an official in uniform came into the store and went to Mr. Canton. "Bart, anything damaged in here?"

Mr. Canton straightened from pouring nails into a barrel. "Some equipment in the back by the windows took some water, but no harm came to them. I'm just blowing the smell of smoke out." He gestured toward the fan.

The stranger turned to Nora. "You must be Miss La Rue. I'm Fire Chief Cork. I want to thank you for taking care of the horses yesterday. Many times they want to run back into their stalls even though the stable is on fire."

She nodded her head. "I know that very well. I was

raised around horses."

"Excellent. Good day to you both." They acknowledged him as he left the store.

An hour later, Mr. Canton turned off the fan and closed the front windows, then stoked up the potbellied stove in the middle of the aisle. The worst of the smell was gone, but a trace lingered in the air.

When Will came in with a dejected expression, Mr. Canton greeted him with, "Any sign of Chance?"

Will shook his head. "No. Whoever it was got away." He turned to Nora. "Did you see who it was?"

"I just had a glance at the rider. I was studying the horse he was leading. The man had a dark Western hat and a long tan coat. His horse was black. I'm sorry, but that's all I remember."

"You couldn't see his face?"

"No. His hat was pulled down."

Will paused. "Well, at least that's something. I have a suspicion of who did it."

Nora pulled back in horror. "You mean Mr. Leaver? That terrible man we saw on race day?" She thought a moment. "This man wasn't as heavyset as Mr. Leaver."

"He has many people working for him. He could have sent a wrangler." Will patted her hand. "Thanks for your help. I think I'll pay Mr. Leaver a little visit."

"Be careful." He gave her a half-smile, and then he was gone. Nora tried the rest of the day to draw a face out of her memory.

****

John waved at Aunt Elinore as he stepped off the train with his suitcase. "Thank you for meeting me here, Auntie."

She gave him an embrace. "I'm glad you decided to come. We need more surgeons here. You can stay in the cottage until you find a place of your own. We haven't had any female patients there since Nora left."

Auggie was waiting with the carriage and took John's case, storing it behind the seat. He tipped his hat to Elinore. "Home, ma'am?"

She shook her head. "Up the hill to the hospital."

John helped his aunt into the carriage and climbed in himself. In the sharp November breeze, he smelled snow in the air. A few of the oaks held stubbornly to their brown papery leaves that waved from the twisted limbs. They went past the lookout tower where people had a view of the whole town. Auggie stopped the horse in the drive of the large clapboard farmhouse that served as the hospital.

John and Elinore went inside, and John was hit with the familiar antiseptic odors. Strangely, it made him feel right at home. Elinore nodded at a young man at a reception desk. "I'm Miss Weeks, and this is Dr. John Mallory. We're here to see Dr. Gables."

The young man rose from his chair. "Yes, ma'am, I'll see if he's in." He went down the hall and rounded a corner. After a couple of minutes, he was back. "He's in his office."

"I can find the way," Elinore said. She led John to a door that read Head of Surgery and rapped on it.

A jovial, middle-aged gentleman with graying hair at his temples opened it to them. "Elinore! It's so good to see you again. This must be your nephew, Dr. John Mallory." He held out his hand.

John shook it. "You must be Dr. Gables."

"Yes, yes. Now come inside and sit down, both of

you. We miss Elinore here sorely, but her sanitarium has done wonderful work in rehabilitating many of our patients. She told us you were looking for a practice in Waukesha."

"Yes, I am."

"Why on earth would you want to leave your situation in Milwaukee? They have modernized equipment that we couldn't begin to afford."

John paused, gathering his thoughts. How would he answer that? "I long for a slower pace. The city life is taking up so much of my time," he said carefully. "There aren't as many people here, and I could take more time with each patient. I believe that the care of each person is as important as the care of the body."

Dr. Gables sat silent behind his desk, studying John. "I can only offer you ten dollars a week for your services." He consulted a ledger on his desk. "Right now, I'll put you on Monday, Tuesday, and Friday. The two other surgeons we have on the staff also each have a private practice that keeps them busy when they aren't on call here. You may look into that. Also, make sure you have a telephone installed. We call any of you for Saturday or Sunday emergencies."

"That sounds all right. I can do that."

He rose, and so did John. Dr. Gables held out his hand. "Then it's settled. I'll give you the rest of the week to let you establish yourself, and I expect you bright and early on Monday next."

John shook it. "I will be here. Thank you, sir."

John and Elinore took leave of Dr. Gables and climbed onto the carriage for the trip to the sanitarium. Elinore patted his hand on the way back. "I'll give you some help tomorrow. I know of a few places that are vacant downtown, only fifteen minutes' travel to the hospital."

John set up his clothes and toiletries in the cottage. He was determined to see Nora and tell her he was here. A half hour before the general store was slated to close, he set off down the street.

The bell rang merrily as he stepped into the store. Nora turned, and a stunned look settled on her face. "John, what are you doing here?"

He swept off his hat in a grand gesture. "Say hello to Waukesha's newest surgeon!"

Bart Canton came in just then. "Did I hear you right, boy? You left the busy practice in Milwaukee to work in a resort town?"

"I like the slower pace."

Bart snorted. "A snail's pace, you mean. After the tourists leave, most of the business goes, as well."

John stole a sidelong glance at Nora. "I'll survive."

Bart shook his head and went back to closing up. Nora spread her hands out with the palms up. "Why?"

"Because, my dear Nora, I want to be where you are and prove to you I mean what I say." He put his hat back on. "I'm staying at the cottage at the sanitarium until I can find a place of my own." He held her right hand and kissed it. "I'll be in touch." He left Nora staring wordlessly after him.

****

Nora wasn't sure if she was happy or not about John moving to Waukesha. She had deep feelings for him, yes, but she had been hurt before. The wound that Rico left still festered, and she was filled with self-doubt. She gazed out on the dark street with the lamp post casting a yellow glow on the sidewalk. Every once in a while a drunk reeled out of the saloon next to the store and weaved his way home. When white flakes started to drift to the ground, she stared at them with some concern. How was snow going to affect her artificial limb? Well, she'd dealt with challenges before.

Sighing, she closed the curtains and made ready for bed. *I'll worry about all of this tomorrow.* She fell into a deep sleep.

Nora woke to the sound of brushing outside on her staircase. She put on her limb and a robe, and went straight to the door. The noise was getting closer to the entrance. She opened it and found John out there with a broom that was full of snow. "John?"

He grinned with a twinkle in his eye and held it up. "I thought I'd give you a hand this morning." His words made white clouds that drifted in the air.

She looked down the steps and saw they all had been brushed clear. She shivered as an icy breeze hit her. "Thank you. You know I can't invite you in."

"I'm warm enough. I'll help you for the first time walking in snow." He sat on the top step.

Nora went back into the apartment and set a coffeepot on the stove to heat while she got dressed. The aroma of coffee wafted about when she finished. Taking two ceramic mugs from the cabinet, she poured the hot liquid. She took one of the mugs and gave it to John, who warmed his hands around it gratefully. When she had put on her boots, coat, gloves, scarf, and hat, she stood by him and sipped on her own mug. "Would you like some bread? I'm sorry, that's all I can afford for breakfast lately. I have some apple butter Mrs. Lawrence gave to me."

He nodded. "Thank you."

Nora went in and cut a couple of slices from her day-old loaf and spread the apple butter on it. She handed one to John. "Payment for clearing my steps."

He took a grateful bite. When he finished, he asked, "Is money very tight right now?"

"I had to purchase these winter things. All of my old winter clothes are at the house in Indiana."

"Your parents didn't send the rest of your things to you?"

She snorted. "They probably sold them." She took a swig of coffee to wash the bitter gall down her throat. "Anyway, they don't know where I am. I haven't heard from them since that letter cutting me off."

"You didn't contact them?"

She frowned. "I don't need any more aggravation than I already have." She brushed the crumbs off her cape and took the empty cups back into the apartment. "I should be getting across the street."

When she came back, John pointed to the top step. "Sit there for a moment." As she did, he pulled out of his pocket two lengths of rubber with small stud points and elastic bands. "You have treads on your snow boots, but the studs will give you extra protection from slipping." He attached it to the boots. "Now, stand up."

She pulled herself up with the handrail and stood until she got used to the unaccustomed height. "I'm ready."

John went ahead of her and backed down the stairs. "Take them one at a time. Don't worry. If you fall, I'll catch you."

Nora stepped on the first tread with her limb, and it felt like she was on something hard and springy. She gave a little bounce to bring her left foot beside it, and it held on the wet stair. "I did it!" Each step she took gave her more confidence, and when she came to the ground, she gave a squeal of victory.

John shouldered the broom he had placed at the base of the stairs against the building. "Now, I'll walk you across the street." They waited for a couple of carriages to go by, and then he helped her off the curb and into the slushy street. She put her arm through his.

Mr. Canton was brushing off the sidewalk in front of his store. He glanced up and waved. "Take your time. I should have the entrance cleared in a moment."

Nora had tiny slips, but was able to stay on her legs. "Challenge won!" She grinned.

John nodded. "This was only an inch or so of snow. It's going to get harder with more."

Mr. Canton laughed. "As long as we don't get snow like '81, she should be all right."

John helped her to the front door. "We'll hope we won't see that much snow again." He turned to Nora. "I'm going to find a place to live that has room to open a practice." He kissed her on the cheek. "I'll be back when the store closes."

Nora couldn't help it. Her heart swelled with love for this man. He really seemed to want her. Maybe she should let down her guard this time. Maybe.

****

John whistled in the frosty air. The November sun had turned most of the snow to puddles during the day, and some of the small puddles were starting to freeze. He arrived at the store just as Nora was coming out with Mr. Canton. John stopped the horse by the curb. "Come on, I want to show you something."

Mr. Canton helped Nora into the carriage. She

gazed at John. "Did you find a place today?"

"I did. I want to know what you think." He snapped the reins, and they went through downtown and turned on Maple Avenue, a lovely residential street. Stopping in front of a white picket fence, he hopped down and helped Nora out. A formidable two-story white clapboard home with a wraparound porch was at the end of a brick pathway. A yellow glow came from large front windows with leaded trim.

"That is a beautiful house." She glanced at him. "Can you afford something like this?"

He smiled. "I have some money saved, and Father is going to loan the rest to me." He put her arm through his, and they strolled up to the front door. John turned the bell key below the frosted glass oval set into the door panels, and an older man with graying hair opened the door.

"Good evening, Dr. Mallory, do come in." He waved them in.

John acknowledged him. "Mr. Edgers, I'd like you to meet Miss Lenora La Rue."

He inclined his head. "Welcome, Miss La Rue."

She nodded. "Thank you." She glanced around. John watched her as she surveyed the large hallway with a parlor on one side and a dining area on the other. A fire was crackling merrily in the parlor fireplace. The electric lamps were on in all the front rooms, showing their rich carpets, drapes, and furnishings. "What a lovely home! My compliments to your wife."

Mr. Edgers lowered his eyes. "My wife passed a few weeks ago. That's the reason I want to sell."

"Oh, I'm so sorry."

John made a sweeping gesture with his hand.

"There's plenty of room for a practice here, don't you think. Nora?"

"I'm sure there will be."

John turned to Mr. Edgers. "Then it's settled. I'll take it. I'll have the money next week."

Mr. Edgers shook John's hand. "Give me a couple of weeks and I'll be out. I'm moving in with my daughter and her family."

"Thank you, sir. Let's be going, Nora." They said their goodbyes, and John helped Nora back into the carriage. He climbed up on the seat, and the horse took off at his command. Turning to Nora, he asked, "What do you think?"

"I don't feel it's my place to say, but it will make a fine practice for you."

He paused. "I'm going to need a nurse and an office clerk. Would you like to be the clerk for me?"

"What are my duties, if I agree?"

"There is a telephone installed. You would take calls, set appointments, do bookkeeping, and greet patients."

Nora mulled this over. "That sounds like something I could handle. What would be my pay?"

"I'll offer you fifty cents a day." That was met by a sharp intake of breath.

Nora stared at him. "That's double what I make at the store. Can you afford that?"

He grinned. "With my father's help, yes, I can. There's a small cottage in back of the house on Maple. You can move into that so you wouldn't have far to travel."

"You've got this all figured out, don't you?"

He laughed. "It's not sordid. I'm going to hire a

live-in nurse, too. She will share the cottage with you."

She studied him. The light from the lamp posts sailed over her as they went down the street. "You make a very tempting offer. How can I say no?"

He stopped the horse in front of her apartment. "Don't. Say yes."

Her eyes twinkled in the dim yellow light. "Yes."

"Wonderful! I'll let you know when I'm ready for you. You can tell Mr. Canton." He hopped down and helped her up the steps to her door. He flipped the toggle switch for the light in the shelter and gazed at her. "Nora, I want to say—" He was stopped as she threw her arms around his neck and kissed him. She smelled so sweet from the frosty air. His groin tightened and he held her close.

She stepped back and took a breath. "That was too forward, wasn't it?"

He rested his gloved hand on her cheek. "No. Goodnight, Nora." He turned and left with enough warmth to carry him home.

Chapter 11

John paused before he went into his father's office. He had brought the figures that he needed for his practice. Would his father agree to them? Rapping on the door, he heard a voice from the inside say, "Come in."

He opened the door and leaned in, taking off his hat. "It's me, John."

Ben glanced up from behind his desk. "Well, boy, what happened in Waukesha?"

John told him what had transpired. "Did you speak to the head of the hospital about me pulling out?"

Ben nodded. "We have backup to take care of the patients you have left. However, there is trouble on another front. Your mother and sister are sorely distressed about you and Thea. She has become like family to them."

John frowned. "This was a mutual parting between me and Thea."

"Your mother doesn't see it that way."

"What should I do?"

Ben studied his son. "Bring Miss La Rue to dinner with us on Saturday next. Maybe if your mother and Franny meet her, they won't be so upset. Robert and his fiancée, Julia, could come, as well. Robert seems to like Miss La Rue."

John was silent for a moment. "I'll talk to Mr.

Canton. He will probably give her the day off if I explain it to him." He put the papers he'd brought in front of his father. "Here's what I'll need to start off my practice."

Ben glanced at the sheet. "I can let you have the things from my old practice, that I have in storage. They're old, but you can replace them as you can. I'll hire a wagon to move them to your address in Waukesha." He rose and came around the desk and slapped John on the back. "I'll miss seeing you, son."

John grinned. "I won't be that far. Just an hour's ride from here on the train."

"I'll also have the hospital supply put a package up. I'll send that along on the wagon. I'm sure there's a place where you can supplement your supplies as you need them."

"I'm setting up an account with one of the drugstores." John put his hat on and picked up the papers. "Thank you, Father. I'll make good, you'll see." They said their goodbyes, and he went to catch the train back to Waukesha.

****

Nora was finishing up with a customer when John came into the store. She handed the woman her change as John called to Mr. Canton. He greeted John with, "What can I do for you?"

"I bought a house on Maple, and I'm going to need a few furnishings for it." He handed Mr. Canton a list. "Can you order these for me?"

Mr. Canton ran his finger down the paper. "Yes. Some of them could take a while."

John nodded. "I can wait. Also, I have to ask a favor."

"What is it?"

"Could you spare Nora on Saturday? I want to take her to dinner at my parents' home."

Mr. Canton peered at her over his glasses. "We have help on Saturday, and she has been a reliable clerk. Yes, she can have the day off."

Nora jumped in. "But that means I won't get paid for Saturday."

John shook his head. "I'll make up for it."

She glanced from one to the other. "All right, but I wish you had asked me first." Mr. Canton went back to work, and John steered Nora to the other side of the store. She pursed her lips. "I hope you understand I only have that one dress to wear. I don't think that ball gown would be appropriate for a dinner, and I can't afford another for a while."

John paused. "It will be only the family. My father knows your situation." He tipped his hat. "I'll pick you up Saturday morning, and we can catch the train into Milwaukee. Pack an overnight bag. It will be easier for you to stay overnight at my parents' house. We can come back in the morning."

"I don't want to impose."

He kissed her cheek. "You won't be." He left her dreading the whole thing. She went back to stocking the shelves to keep herself busy.

****

Saturday morning was cold but sunny. John helped Nora into the carriage and set her bag and crutches in the back with his case. Tendrils of black curls swirled in the frosty breeze around the hood of her cape. Her eyes were those of an alert doe who had just heard a noise. "Nora, relax. You'll be fine."

She snuggled her hands into her rabbit fur muff and sighed deeply. "I guess I'm wary of new people. I haven't met many who won't prejudge me."

He dropped her off at the depot and seated her on a station bench with their bags next to her before he took the carriage to the livery nearby. When he returned, he purchased their tickets for the train and sat beside her. They waited together for the train to come into view.

The engine finally came, puffing and snorting like an angry bull, and stopped in front of them with a squeal of brakes and a loud hiss of steam. The bell on the engine pealed its arrival, along with the steam whistle's notification. The coal odor cloaked the air around them.

John gave their things to the conductor to hold while he helped Nora into the coach. She settled into a seat by the window, and he put their bags on the seats facing them, then stood her crutches by the window. In a few minutes, the train gave a jerk and slowly pulled out of the depot. Soon the clickity-clack of the wheels reached a steady rhythm.

They talked about mundane things as the frozen scenery flew by. John sensed that she was starting to relax around him, and that made him glad. He'd prove she was worthy of being loved, and he would be the one to not walk away.

Robert was waiting for them with the carriage at the Milwaukee depot. The brothers slapped each other on the back, and Robert took Nora's hand, giving a nod. "Welcome back to Milwaukee, Nora."

She smiled. "Thank you." John helped her into the carriage while Robert put their things in the back and climbed into the driver's seat. Robert gave a whistle and a snap of the reins, and they were off.

Nora snuggled against John, and through all her winter clothes, he felt her shudder. He didn't know if it was the cold or her nervousness. Probably both.

In a little while, the carriage turned into the drive by the Mallory house. Robert let them off by the front door while he took the carriage to the stable. John had his case and her crutches, and she had her bag. At his knock, Bess was at the door. "Come in, Dr. John. We've been expecting you." Bess had their things taken up to their rooms, and John led Nora into the parlor.

Ben Mallory rose and greeted her warmly. "Welcome, Nora. Let me introduce the rest of the family." John's mother, Lillian, and his sister exchanged pleasantries with impassive faces. Julia smiled and nodded. Ben directed at Bess, "Could you take them up to their rooms?"

She turned. "Yes, sir. Follow me." John and Nora took the flight of stairs after her.

John put a hand on Bess' arm. "I know the way to my room."

"Yes, sir."

John watched as Bess led Nora to one of the guest rooms down the hall. He turned and entered his childhood room. His mother had redone it since he'd lived there, but the window still looked out over the oaks in the backyard and the lovely flower garden, which had taken on the late fall browns and grays.

He poured some water from the pitcher into the basin to freshen up. After he was finished, he opened the door to go downstairs and found Nora waiting for him in the hall.

She put her arm through his. "I didn't want to go

down by myself."

He patted her hand. "You'll be fine. You look lovely." He watched her cheeks redden into a charming blush, and a faint trace of a smile played on her lips.

Robert was in the hallway taking off his coat and hat for Bess to put away as they came off the staircase. He hurried past them up the stairs. "I'll be right down," he said as he flew by.

John and Nora stepped into the parlor, and Ben rose. "As soon as Robert joins us, we can go into the dining room for supper." In a few minutes, Robert reappeared, and they all went to the table.

John noticed that his mother had set out the china service, unusual for the midday meal. He pulled out the chair for Nora. She hadn't said a word since she came down.

Dalia, their cook, brought out the food and set it on the table. Ben led the grace and started sending the food around. Nora took small portions of the ham, potatoes, and suet pudding with fruit.

After a few minutes of silence, John's mother dabbed her lips with the napkin and glanced at Nora. "Well, Nora, who's your family?"

Nora took on her frightened look. "Jacques La Rue. We're from Peru, Indiana."

"Really? What are you doing here?"

Nora paused. "My family travels much of the time on business."

John made a face at his father, and Ben shook his head.

Lillian sat back. "All of you? What kind of business is he in?"

Nora looked at John for help. He thought fast. "Her

family has a troop of entertainers that travel from town to town."

Nora chewed on her lower lip. "I might as well tell her." She turned to Lillian. "My family owns a circus."

All except John and Ben were struck dumb.

The blood had drained from Lillian's face. "John! This is the type of person you bring into your father's home?"

Nora jumped up and went out the front door. John slapped his napkin on the table. "Mother! What's the matter with you?" He took off after Nora. He found her in a heap at the bottom of the porch steps. He gathered her up, and she buried her face on his chest.

"I knew this was a mistake!" she sobbed.

John held on and rocked her. "I'm sorry. I didn't know Mother would react like that."

Ben came out with a contrite Lillian behind him. "John, is she all right?"

John nodded. "She seems to have fallen down the steps." He looked at Nora. "Can you stand?" He helped her up. "Any pain?"

She shook her head. "No. I'm all right."

Ben turned to his wife. "Well, Lillian?"

She took a deep breath. "Ben explained things to me. Nora, I'm truly sorry for what I said. You have to understand that the news startled me. Most circus people are unsavor—"

"Lillian!" Ben barked.

John put his arm around Nora's waist. "Father, may I speak privately to Nora in the library?"

His father nodded. "I'll speak to the rest of the family."

John helped Nora up the steps and found Franny

glaring at them from the door. She opened her mouth to speak, and John cut her off with, "Don't you dare say a word!" They moved past her and went into the library. John closed the door. "Sit on the couch." He joined her and put his arm around her shoulders. "Talk to me, Nora."

Her eyes were sad. "I truly don't know where I fit in anymore. I knew there was bad feeling about circuses in the public's mind, but I guess I was isolated from it. I was thinking the other day that if I had stayed in, I probably would have married Rico and raised a family of circus performers, never feeling what the public thought. Seeing things from that side of the fence, it was quite bearable. People hated us, but they paid their money to see the show." She paused. "We were rich. I was a star. The cyclone took that, as well as my leg."

John was moved more than he realized. What courage it took to admit that to herself as well as to him! He tenderly embraced her, and her body slumped against his. "Nora, I'm really sorry for my family's reaction. You have to understand, though, that they treated Thea like a relation, and when we parted, they took it hard. There's probably some resentment to you, even though it wasn't your fault."

Nora pulled back. "I'd like to lie down for a while."

He rose. "I'll walk you up to your room." After he closed her door, he hurried downstairs. His mother and Franny were doing needlework in the ladies' parlor.

He sat in a chair next to them. "Mother, I have never seen you so ungracious to anyone before."

She peered at him over her glasses. "Don't start with me, John. Your father gave Franny and me the same lecture." She took a deep breath and removed her glasses. "I don't see that Nora is worthy of your attention. You're so much better than she is. Thea was more of a lady."

"Thea was a dear childhood friend, but I didn't love her in a way that leads to marriage. I didn't break it with her. She was the one who noticed how I feel about Nora. And Nora, well, she could have dug a hole and crawled into it after she lost her leg, but she fought her way back. I admire and love her the way she is. She is indeed worthy of my attention."

Franny glanced at him. "I'm sorry, John. I'll give Nora a chance."

Lillian put her fingers on her son's cheek. "As will I, for your sake."

He kissed her hand. "Thank you, Mother, Franny." He left to go into the library to do some reading, but Bess found him.

"Excuse me, sir. There's a Mr. Canton here to see you."

"Will?"

"Yes, sir."

He made his way to the hall after thanking Bess. Will was standing by the reception table with a concerned look. "John. I saw you come in with Robert. I have to talk to you."

"I was just going to the library. We can talk there." John closed the door behind him and waved his hand toward one of the armchairs in front of the fireplace. "Sit."

They were seated facing each other, and Will leaned forward. "I need your help. I think I know where Chance is, but I need someone to check and see. Leaver wouldn't let me in, so I have to find someone he doesn't know. Someone who has seen my horse."

"Where is this place?"

"Kenosha."

"That's quite a trip. I'm embroiled in setting up a practice in Waukesha. It would be hard to justify a two- or three-day jaunt."

Will paused. "If you leave on the evening train to Milwaukee when you get off work, you can get to Kenosha and back in one day."

"That's an awful lot of travel, but if I just check out Leaver's stable, it should work."

"Take Nora with you."

"Why Nora?"

"She knows Chance as well as I do. You can pose as a couple looking to buy a horse." He took a folded newspaper clipping out of his jacket pocket. "Here's an advert for his stables."

John paused. "You helped me find a job for Nora, and I'll help you with this."

Will blew out a breath. "I'll be forever grateful to you if I can get Chance back."

A knock came on the door. John glanced up. "Yes?"

The door opened a crack, and Nora's voice came through. "Bess said you were in here. May I come in?"

John and Will rose. John drew her in. "Yes, of course. As you see, Will is here, and we have something to discuss with you." They told her the plan to find the horse.

Will asked, "Can you help me?"

Nora chewed on her lower lip. "Mr. Leaver saw me at the race that day. Do you think he'd remember me?"

Will shook his head. "He gave you hardly a glance. He was more concerned with me."

"What about my job at your uncle's store? He won't be very pleased having me take time off again."

"I'll talk to my uncle and let him know what you're doing."

Nora gave Will a nod. "I'll be glad to see if I can find Chance." She turned to John. "I think you should take me back to Waukesha now. Your family doesn't want me around."

John gripped her gently by the shoulders. "Nora, I talked to my mother and sister. They're willing to give you the benefit of the doubt. Please, for my sake?"

Many emotions passed shadows on her face "For you, I will try."

John glanced at Will. "Why don't you stay for dinner? I'm sure there's enough food."

Will put his hat back on. "No, thank you. I have things to take care of at home. I'll be in touch." He got his coat from Bess, and they said their goodbyes.

Things went more smoothly at dinner between his family and Nora. His mother and sister gave her their sincere apologies, and Nora visibly relaxed.

The next morning, after breakfast, while John was readying to go back to Waukesha, his father knocked on the bedroom door. "Yes, Father?"

"I want you to know, son, that Nora has made a favorable impression on your mother. She told me she was contrite since dinner last night. She and Franny now approve of your choice. She was a little hesitant, because of Nora's injury, but Nora seems to get around in great fashion."

A weight lifted from John's heart. "I'm glad to hear

that. It will make Nora happy, too." His father slapped him on the back and disappeared out the door again.

****

Nora welcomed the company of Franny, who helped her pack. She was curious about Nora's life in the circus. Nora informed her about the good and the bad.

Franny folded Nora's dinner dress. "For being so rich, you have some out-of-season clothes."

Nora sighed at her worn dress. "We took very few clothes with us when we traveled. We were wearing mostly the costumes for the show or our practice clothes." She paused. "Be grateful for the family you have. Love wasn't known in our family. I doubt if I'll ever hear from them again."

Franny's eyes misted, and she held Nora's hand. "We'll be your family, Nora."

Nora smiled and embraced her. "Thank you. You don't know what that means to me."

Franny picked up Nora's bag. "I'll carry it down for you." Franny went down the stairs at Nora's side, even though Nora took the steps slowly.

John and Robert were waiting in the hallway, where John took the bag from Franny. "We have the carriage in the drive."

Lillian came from the parlor and put her arm around Nora. "Come see us again, Nora."

Ben joined them. "Yes. You're always welcome here."

Bess brought Nora's winter wraps, and then John helped her into the carriage. As they moved down the drive, Nora turned and waved to the smiling assemblage watching from the porch.

Robert turned and glanced back from the driver's seat. "Julia said how much she liked you, when I drove her home last night."

Nora nodded. "Tell her I enjoyed her company, too."

John hugged her with one arm. "For things starting off so badly, I think you made a good impression on the family."

Nora snuggled. "I hope so. I'm still new to social graces, and there's a part of me that has self-doubts."

"You did wonderfully well. And we can work on those doubts in the future."

The train was already at the depot when they hurried in after bidding Robert thanks and goodbye. John quickly purchased their tickets, and they entered the cozy steam-heated car for their trip. Nora sat by the window and watched the villages and farms on an endless march. She turned to John. "Do you think this could be dangerous, what Will is asking us to do?"

He shook his head. "I think if we just look at the horses, all we have to do is report to Will if we find Chance. Like detective work."

"When should we do it?"

"I have Thursdays off. I'll let Will know, and he can talk to his uncle about letting you go."

"Maybe I should quit at the store and help you set up your practice. The thing is, I still owe on the leg."

John laughed and kissed her forehead. "Since things are the way they are, I'll forgive the rest of the debt. You've worked very hard, and I'm proud of you."

Tears welled in her eyes. "Nobody close to me has ever praised me before."

John pulled her into a discreet hug. "It's about

time. You deserve it." He hesitated. "Nora, I do love you."

Oh, she wanted to believe him, truly she did. "John, I want to trust your feelings for me. I have been hurt so much in the past, but I want you to know I'm trying."

He rocked her gently. "That's all I ask for now."

"I'll tell Mr. Canton I'll stay on until he can find someone else. By then, you should have the house."

He pulled back and smiled. "You're doing it again."

"What?"

"Changing the subject when we talk about us." There was a bit of a sparkle in his brown eyes.

She opened her mouth to say something, then closed it again. He returned his arm around her shoulders, and she leaned against him. The southern-slanted sun cut in through the windows of the car, and the passing trees and buildings threw shadows over them.

Back in Waukesha, John rented a carriage from the livery and took Nora to her apartment. He helped her up the steps and set her bag by the door. The reflection of the late afternoon sun from the building windows bounced into the shelter.

Nora gazed at the strikingly boyish but handsome face and her breath caught. Deep down, her love for him was overwhelming. Still, she couldn't quite say the words yet.

John gathered her into his arms. "I'll be in touch with you about the trip to Kenosha. Good evening, sweetheart."

She placed her hands on either side of his face and

kissed him. "Good evening, John." She felt like melting into his warm embrace and remaining there forever.

Chapter 12

Nora was more nervous than she had ever been in her life. She'd never dreamed she would be called to do detective work like she had read in crime novels, but here she was, dressed to the nines in a rich new outfit and a large plumed hat. Watching out the window, she saw John stop in front of the building with a carriage.

She donned her heavy woolen cape and her gloves, and grabbed her muff as John knocked on the door.

"Are you ready?" He looked as nervous as she felt. At her nod, he continued, "Will is going to meet us at the depot in Milwaukee."

"Is it wise for him to go with us?"

"He'll stay at the station, and if we find Chance, he's going to the police."

She blew out a slow breath. "And so starts our detective work."

When they got to the Milwaukee station, Nora saved their train seats while John went to get Will. The two men hustled into the railroad car only a few minutes before the conductor's "All aboard!" rang out.

John slid into the seat beside Nora, and Will took one of the seats facing them. He pulled a couple of calling cards out of his pocket and leaned forward so only they could hear. "You have a one o' clock appointment at the stables. I've arranged for your transportation from the station. Here are cards for you.

You are Leonard and Martha Jacobs of West Allis, looking to buy a standard bred horse for racing. Nora, I think you know horses enough that he can't flim-flam you. He's been known to talk unsuspecting people into substandard horses for a big price."

Nora nodded. "I should be able to tell."

"If he asks you for a sale, tell him you want to think about it overnight and check your finances. That should give you a way to get out of his stable. Don't let him corner you."

John took the cards and put them in his waistcoat pocket. "We'll do our best, won't we, Martha?"

Nora grinned. "Yes, Leonard."

At the Kenosha station, they exited the railroad car and found a carriage waiting for them. Will went into the passenger room, and John approached the driver. "Hire for Leonard Jacobs?"

The driver tipped his hat. "Yes, sir. To the Leaver Stables, am I right?"

"Yes." John helped Nora into the carriage and climbed in beside her. In moments they were at a good clip to Leaver's business. John checked the time on his pocket watch. "Good. We're right on time."

The driver stopped in front of a huge stable building with many gables and turrets. Leaver came out to greet them as John helped Nora from the carriage. Leaver held out his hand. "Mr. Jacobs, I presume?"

John shook it. "You must be Mr. Leaver. May I present my wife, Martha?"

Leaver gave a nod of his head. "Charmed."

John turned to the driver. "Wait for us." The driver agreed. John pulled a card out of his waistcoat. "Here's my card. Could you show us your horses?"

Leaver waved his hand. "Come with me."

He took them into the dimly lit stable. It had few windows for its size, only two small ones in the back; the rest of the light was from one bulb hanging from the center rafter. What horses Nora could see on either side looked healthy. Several of them hung their heads over the door to see what was going on. John engaged Leaver and the stable hand in a conversation, and knowing a woman wouldn't be expected to take an interest in business, she could walk around.

There seemed to be an aisle of stalls on either side of the central one. Moving slowly, she tried to appear as though she was browsing casually back to the door. No one was watching her, so she walked to the aisle on the right. The light was even dimmer down this row, but it was enough to see the horses in these stalls weren't like the ones that were being shown. Most were very thin, and some had scars across their hindquarters. She knew they were whip scars, because she had seen the same thing in the circus. As she came to the end of the row, a dark horse put its head over the door and nickered at her. She went over, and the horse nudged her with its nose and nickered again.

She studied the horse carefully. No, that couldn't be Chance, it was the wrong color. Then she remembered a trick her father used to do to get all the show horses the same. She took a handkerchief out of her reticule and spit on it, then rubbed it on the horse's nose. Brown dye came off on the cloth. She hurriedly put it back in her reticule. "Chance, that has to be you," she said quietly. She scratched his ears. "We'll get you out of this horrible place." She checked the brass plate fixed to the door: *Maximus 26*.

"Lady! What are you doing?" she heard from the head of the aisle. The stable hand was glaring.

She turned. "Just looking at some of the horses."

"These aren't for sale."

She innocently walked to the stable hand. "I'm sorry." She followed him back to the center aisle.

John glanced at her, and she gave a slight tilt of her head. John turned back to Leaver. "I can't decide between those two horses. Let us sleep on it, and I'll check my finances. We'll be back in the morning."

When they arrived at the station, Will had a policeman standing with him. "This is Sergeant O'Brien. I went ahead and talked to the police. What did you find out?"

John and Nora told them what had happened at the stables. Nora showed O'Brien her handkerchief with the brown dye.

O'Brien nodded. "I always thought they were horse thieves. We never had any proof before." He turned to Will. "I think they should come along with us, since Miss La Rue actually saw the horse."

Nora felt a pain in her stomach and glanced at John. "Do you think we should?"

John nodded. "We have to stop Leaver."

O'Brien pointed at a police wagon. "You three get inside. I'll stop by the station to pick up a warrant. Then we can go to the stable."

At the station, O'Brien added to their group a patrolman to help him. Soon they were back at Leaver's stable. Nora gripped John's arm; her one good leg was like rubber. O'Brien and the patrolman went to the door, and O'Brien rapped it with his nightstick. "Police! Open up!"

One of the stable hands peeked out. "What do you want?"

"We have a search warrant for the premises. Find Mr. Leaver."

The stable hand darted back, and they could hear him calling. In a few minutes, Mr. Leaver appeared at the door. "Why do you have a search warrant?"

"We believe a stolen horse is being housed here."

"Nonsense."

O'Brien pushed his way past. He waved his hand at the patrolman. "She said the horse was down the aisle to the right."

The group went to the end of the row of stalls until they found the plate, *Maximus 26,* and Nora gasped. Standing in the stall was a dapple-gray horse. She pointed to the animal. "That's not the horse that was here."

Leaver had a smug look. "You must be mistaken. He's been here for days."

She pulled her handkerchief from her reticule. "The horse in here had brown dye." She showed him.

"No, my dear, this is a gray horse."

"You must have moved him."

Will took Leaver by the coat lapels. "Where is my horse?"

O'Brien broke between them, saying "Calm down." He turned to the patrolman. "Henry, make a search outside, and we'll look in here."

They went through the large stable, and Chance was not to be found. They went outside just as Henry was coming back from his search. O'Brien queried him, "Did you find anything?"

Henry shook his head. "There wasn't any horses

out in the pasture or around the outbuildings."

Will was in Leaver's face. "What did you do with him? You can't just make a horse disappear!"

Leaver smiled serenely. "The horses in the stable are all I have."

Will raised his fist to strike him, but O'Brien put his hand on Will's arm. "Mr. Canton, that won't help get your horse back."

Will snorted. "It would make me feel better."

Leaver nodded slightly, then turned back to the stable. "Good day, gentlemen, lady."

Back in the patrol wagon, Will pounded on his forehead with his fist. "Nora, he must have recognized you after all."

O'Brien nodded. "He must have moved the horse someplace else after the both of you left."

Will sat back. "Damn! Excuse me, Nora. I have to come up with another plan."

O'Brien studied him. "Is the horse a racer?" Will nodded. "Maybe you could wait until the racing season starts and find out where Leaver is registered for an entry. It would be my guess he would race the horse out of state to avoid running into you."

Will thought for a minute. "There's the spring race in Chicago in late April. I'm sure he'll enter Chance in that. If he's going by the name Maximus, I'll look for that."

"He may change the name, since you know about it."

"If he registered the name, he can't change it without going through all the paperwork again." He glanced up at O'Brien. "Do you know anyone on the Chicago police force?"

O'Brien nodded. "I have a cousin who works in Chicago. I'll get in touch with him and tell him about your situation. He can get an extradition to Milwaukee for you. His name is Seamus Finney, Station Twelve."

Will took out a note pad and jotted the information down with a pencil. "Thank you for your help."

"It's worth it to get another horse thief off the streets."

On the trip back, Nora was bothered. "I should have exposed him when I found Chance. I'm sorry, Will."

Will shook his head. "Don't be. There's no telling what he would have done to both of you. At least now I know he has him."

John put in. "And we can tie him to the fire at your uncle's store and the murder of the stable hand."

Will chuckled. "That should put him away for a long time."

Nora relaxed somewhat, and they talked about ordinary things the rest of the trip. Will got off in Milwaukee, and the stars were coming out in Waukesha when John and Nora arrived at the station. John got the carriage from the livery and helped Nora up.

"The hotel dining room should be open. Would you like supper?" he asked.

Nora felt her stomach growl. "Oh, yes."

At a table later, John's eyes sparkled in the dim lights. "It was fun being a married couple, if only for a short time."

Nora's cheeks heated. "We do work well together, don't we?"

"I'm trying to prove that to you. How am I doing?"

She smiled wickedly. "Better than you think."

Their order came and the conversation turned to fixing up the house and cottage for the practice.

Back at her apartment, he went up the steps with her. The stars shone brightly in the inky black, cloudless sky. The air was frosty. John said not a word but ran his hands down from her shoulders to her fingers, which he raised to his lips.

She freed one of her hands and rested it on his cheek. "I love you, John."

She heard an intake of breath. "Say that again."

"I love you, John."

He embraced her. "That sounds so sweet. The words I've been waiting to hear." They kissed, and Nora took no notice of the tears running down her face.

Chapter 13

The next few weeks were busy with setting up John's practice. Ben, Robert, and Will helped put the furnishings on a freight, and the crates were delivered to Waukesha station, where they and John picked them up with a contracted wagon.

With Elinore and Nora's help, the house on Maple had been transformed. The hallway was now the reception area where Nora's desk would be. Drapes in the parlor doorway were removed and the room became a waiting room. The dining area was appropriated for examinations, and the library became John's office. John would sleep in the master bedroom upstairs, and the rest of the bedrooms would be for patients he wanted to observe overnight.

Nora and Elinore fixed up the little cottage behind the house for Nora and a live-in nurse. It was like an apartment with two bedrooms and a water closet.

Finally, everything was ready and the group admired the new doctor's office. John's heart swelled with pride.

Ben put an arm around John's shoulders. "I'm proud of you, son, but it needs one more thing. Come with me outside."

They all put their winter things on and crunched through the December snowfall to the end of the walkway by the flagstone sidewalk. There, on a gatepost, Ben had nailed a pole with a wooden arm. From that he hung a shingle with the words, *Dr. John Mallory, Surgeon.*

John's eyes misted. "Thank you, Father." His father slapped him on the back.

Elinore announced, "I made some coffee and sandwiches. Let's go inside."

At the table in the kitchen, Ben turned to John. "You know we want you for Christmas festivities next week, and you must bring Nora. You can stay overnight."

Nora looked panicked. "Oh, no! I forgot! I haven't any gifts to give."

John put a hand on her arm. "We can go shopping this week."

She relaxed a little and said politely, "Thank you, Dr. Ben, for inviting me."

Ben took a sip of his coffee. "No one should be alone at Christmas."

Their conversation lasted an hour, and then Ben, Robert, and Will had to catch the train to Milwaukee. They said their goodbyes and took the wagon back to the livery.

Nora and Elinore cleaned up while John put the finishing touches on his office. The bell rang at the front door, and the postman handed them the afternoon delivery. John took the mail into the office and settled behind his desk to open the envelopes. One, postmarked Peru, Indiana, caught his eye. He eagerly pulled the contents out.

Dear Dr. John Mallory,

I received your letter of Wednesday last and had to write a reply. I see you are asking for the hand of my daughter. I hope you don't expect any monetary help from me. Between the loss of the trained horse and her medical expenses, she has drained any inheritance she would have received from us. I have already washed my hands of her, and if you want to take on a cripple for the rest of your life, you are welcome to her.

Yours,

Jacques La Rue

Poor Nora, to have been raised by such beastly parents. With a little polish, a true gem was emerging. She didn't deserve this kind of attitude from her family, not after working so hard to make her own way. John resolved to talk to his father about this reply at Christmas. He was not going to tell Nora about it—yet.

At the end of a light supper that Elinore and Nora had fixed, Elinore set down her napkin. "John, I think I've found a perfect nurse for you. She has been helping me at the sanitarium and is very vigilant with the patients. Twenty years experience."

He paused. "Would she be interested in working at a largely outpatient practice?"

"She told me she had worked in a hospital for many years and was looking to slow down a bit."

"Tell her to stop by tomorrow, and we'll see if she's interested. What's her name?"

"Nellie Gatling. She's originally from Louisville, Kentucky." She glanced at her watch pin. "I'd better be getting back to the sanitarium."

John rose. "Thank you for your help, Auntie."

She laughed. "Think nothing of it. It's good to have you here in Waukesha."

At last, John walked Nora to her new home. He paused by the door of the cottage and was taken by a wave of lust. Gritting his teeth and washing it back down, he reasoned with himself that it wasn't proper now.

Nora glanced at him with a puzzled expression. "Did I do something wrong?"

He half-smiled. "No. I'm thinking of how beautiful you are."

She put her arms around his neck. "Then let me know."

He made a low noise in his throat and kissed her thoroughly. The blood raced through his body and stiffened his groin. Slowly, he pulled back and took a deep breath. "Nora, I can't do this now."

With a teasing smirk, she said, "Manners and propriety, I assume. All right, I'll keep your good-boy reputation intact—for now." She opened the door to the cottage and flipped on the light switch. She laid her gloved hand on his cheek. "Good night, Dr. John." Then she went inside and closed the door.

John sat on the step of the porch, gathering himself. He wanted with all his heart to go in there and deflower her, but he hadn't been raised like that. Finally, he headed to the house. Sleep would do him good.

****

The next morning, Nora was organizing her desk and file cabinet when the telephone gave two short rings, which was their signal of an incoming call. She put the receiver to her ear and spoke into the bell-shaped speaker on the wall, "Dr. Mallory's office."

A woman's voice replied in a soft southern accent, "This is Miss Nellie Gatling. I would like to come over and speak to the doctor about the nursing job."

"Oh, yes, Miss Gatling. Dr. Mallory is expecting

you. Come over anytime."

"Thank you." And the call was cut off. Nora replaced the receiver on the horseshoe-shaped spring holder on the side of the wall box.

John appeared at the door. "Who was that?"

"Miss Gatling. She'll be over today about the job." Nora entered a note in the appointment book.

"Nora, it might be better during business hours that we refer to each other by our last names."

She smiled. "As you wish, Doctor." He came over and put his arms around her, leaning down for a kiss. Nora put her fingers on his lips. "No kissing during business hours, then."

He had a wicked grin. "Nobody's here." He planted a kiss and went back to his office.

Nora went to work entering the business receipts in the ledger. Later, the front door opened and a solidly built woman entered. She took off her coat and gloves, laying them over one of the chairs in front of Nora's desk. "I'm Miss Gatling, come to see Dr. Mallory about the job."

Nora closed the ledger and rose. "Just a moment. I'll tell him." She went to John's office. "Miss Gatling is here."

John glanced up. "Show her back."

Nora nodded. "Yes, Doctor." There was a slight teasing lilt to her voice. She led the woman to the office, then went back to her post.

Some time passed, and John came out followed by Miss Gatling. "Miss Gatling this is Miss La Rue. She will be your cottage mate." After nods from both women, he continued, "You may move in any time you are ready."

She gathered up her coat. "I don't have much. I can move in this evening, if that is all right."

"Yes. Let me know, and I'll help you."

She waved him off. "No need. I'm perfectly capable of doing it myself. Thank you, Dr. Mallory." She put on her things and left.

Nora turned to John. "My goodness, she is a take-charge kind of person, isn't she?"

He smiled. "That's why she got the job. I need a nurse with a lot of experience."

A knock came on the front door, and John went to answer it. A tall man in a frock coat stood there, hat in hand. "I assume you are Dr. Mallory." At John's acknowledgment, he went on, "My name is Wirt Jones, my father, Long Jones, runs Bethesda Park and the Terrace Hotel. I want to invite you to the New Year's Eve Ball at Putney Hall downtown. It's put on by the Knights of Pythias Lodge, of which I am a member. I was sent to see if you would like to join our brotherhood, as you are new in town."

"I thank you for your kind offer. I would be pleased to accept your lodge's invitation."

"Are you married, Doctor?"

"No."

"Then please bring a guest with you. I'll have an invitation sent straightaway." The men shook hands, and Mr. Jones left.

John turned to Nora and gave her an elaborate bow. "Will fair lady honor me as my guest?"

Nora picked up the appointment book. "I'll have to see if I'm free that night," she teased.

He grabbed her and embraced her. "You will be."

At once the phone gave off its ring. Nora pushed

back. "It looks like your adverts in all the papers are working. I must get to my job, Doctor."

He kissed her. "Later, then." He went back to his office.

That evening, Nellie Gatling moved into the cottage, with the help of Miss Weeks. Auggie drove the horses with the wagon of Nellie's things. She was soon settled, and Miss Weeks and Auggie went home.

Nora helped Nellie hang clothes in Nellie's wardrobe and then went to brew some tea. "Would you like some tea and sugar cookies?" Nora called to her.

"Yes, I'd love some," came the reply. Nellie came out in a dressing robe and slippers, her long gray-brown hair in a braid over her shoulder. She took the seat across from Nora at the small, leafed table.

Nora poured the tea and pushed the plate of cookies toward her. "I learned you came from Kentucky."

Nellie nodded. "I've been in Wisconsin for ten years. I worked at the surgical hospital in Racine. That's where I met Elinore." She paused. "Is it too personal to ask what happened to your leg?"

"It was crushed under a horse in an accident."

"It's unusual to see a cripple employed. Was Dr. Mallory your surgeon?"

"Yes, he was."

Nellie sat back and studied her. She waved her finger. "I can tell there's something going on between you two."

Nora felt her cheeks heat.

"Ha! As I thought."

"Since you're finding out about me, I have a question to ask: why aren't you married?"

Nellie paused. "I guess that's fair. I never found anyone who would want to be put second in line. My work has always been most important to me, and not many men would put up with that. Where are you from, Nora?"

"I'm from Indiana."

"What brought you to Wisconsin?"

Nora didn't know what to tell Nellie. She had felt the sting of rejection too many times. "I was traveling with my family when the accident happened. They had to travel on, so I stayed."

Nellie looked startled. "They abandoned you?"

"Yes."

"You poor dear. I admire how brave you are."

Nora changed the subject, and they went on to other topics of conversation. She was grateful Nellie didn't ask anything else about her family.

The next day, Nora walked the two blocks to the downtown shops to purchase some Christmas presents with the savings she had stored in the bank. They weren't elaborate things, but she hoped they would please.

Chapter 14

John packed their overnight bags and the box of presents on the carriage. He called back to Nellie, who stood on the porch. "Are you sure you won't come with us? My mother cooks more than we could possibly eat."

Nellie waved her hand. "No, no. Elinore invited me to dinner at the sanitarium. Thank you for the invitation, but I'll stay here."

John helped Nora into the carriage, and they were off to the train station. They joined the happy throngs of people on their way to merrymaking with families in Milwaukee. Even the station had a cheery tree in the passenger area. The aroma of gingerbread wafted from the bakery down the street. John was full of the Christmas spirit, and Nora seemed contented, too, so different from the last time they had gone to his family home.

Robert picked them up in the carriage, and they were greeted with warmth by the rest of the family when they arrived at the house. Nora went upstairs with Bess and Franny, while John took the opportunity to talk with his father.

Ben closed the library door. "What is it, son?"

John took an envelope out of his pocket. "I wrote to Mr. La Rue, asking for the hand of his daughter. This is the reply I received." He handed the paper over, and Ben opened it.

Ben's eyebrows furrowed. "This is a very callous letter. That poor girl. I would take it that he gives his permission, in a off-handed way."

John scowled. "He thinks the only reason I would want his daughter is for his money. He doesn't realize what a gem she is. Nora was a big help to me in opening my practice."

Ben nodded. "I must say, she has changed from the hellion that came to us last summer. Have you asked her yet?"

"No, but I will now."

Ben slapped his son on the back. "Perfect time to announce an engagement. Congratulations, John."

"Thank you, sir." They went to join the family in the parlor.

The women of the household had done a splendid job of setting up the tabletop tree and the garlands across the windows and hearth. The warm evergreen smell brought memories of many beloved Christmases while John was growing up, even those before there was electricity in the house. There were no young children in the home now, but in a few years…? John smiled as he looked at Robert and Julia whose wedding would be in March.

Nora and Franny came down to join them. Nora had changed out of her traveling clothes into her simple but presentable skirt and shirtwaist. Her beautiful raven hair had been gathered into a bun perched on the top of her head. All the men rose as the two young women came in.

John held his hand out to Nora. "How lovely you look. Come with me to the library. I have something to say to you in private." He turned to his father. "May we be excused?"

A small smile played around Ben's lips. "You may."

She turned to him as he closed the library door. "What is it? Have I done something wrong?"

He gripped her shoulders. "Oh, no, my dear. I have something important to ask. Sit down."

She sat on the armchair by the hearth. A quizzical expression crossed her face. "You seem dead serious."

He pulled a caned chair beside her. "I am. Nora, I wrote your father for his permission for your hand in marriage. Will you marry me?"

She lowered her eyes, then looked back at him. "You do realize, don't you, I won't bring anything to this marriage? I'm sure my father let you know that."

He took her hand gently. "Money was the last thing on my mind, believe me. I love you and am so proud of your strength. I need a partner in life, not just a dutiful wife. You do understand that my patients will come first, don't you?"

The corners of her lips curled up. "I've been on the receiving end of that. That's your job and passion. I don't think I would have come to love you as much if you were anything else." She paused. "You have my love and devotion. That's all I have to bring."

He raised her fingers and kissed them. "If that means yes, then that's more than enough." He rose and drew her up with him. Taking her into his arms, he held her close, loving the feel of her body next to his. He had never felt this protective yet lustful in his whole life. She raised her face to him and they kissed for a long moment.

When he pulled back, she had tears running down

her cheeks. "I dared not dream that anyone was going to love a cripple."

He cupped her chin. "Your leg is just a fraction of your physical body. Your soul is intact."

"I thought that was fractured, too."

"At first. You fought so gallantly to fit in. You found what your parents almost destroyed." He kissed the tears off her face. "Come. We have an announcement to make."

Back with the family, there were hugs and smiles all around at the news. John was grateful his family had finally accepted Nora. She was learning what love of kin was about.

Will came over after dinner to wish everyone a Merry Christmas, and John gave him the happy news.

Will paused a moment before saying, "Congratulations," as he shook John's hand. He embraced Nora and murmured, "Best wishes," then lingered a minute before he let her go. He gave them a half-hearted smile, but John sensed something was bothering him. From the look on Nora's face, he knew she noticed it, too.

After Will left, Nora turned to John. "What was wrong with Will, I wonder?"

John shook his head. "I don't know. Well, maybe he'll tell us another time." They went back to the warmth of his family.

****

When Nora and John arrived in Waukesha the next day, Nora's head was still whirling from how fast everything was happening. She stashed her things in the cottage, while John bedded down the horse in the stable behind the house. She found a note from Nellie saying she would be back that evening.

Joining John in the house, she put away the food Mrs. Mallory had given them of the leftovers from the feast, and as she closed the icebox door she heard music coming from the parlor/waiting room.

John had put a wax cylinder on the gramophone, and waltz music came from the horn. He stood in the middle of the room with his hand outstretched. "We are going to try the waltz again. I want to dance with you at the ball on New Year's Eve."

Nora's feet were glued to the floor. "That turned out very badly last time."

He pursed his lips. "That was the first time you tried. That's why I think we should practice."

He went to her and laid his hand on her waist, and she laid hers on his shoulder. They clasped their other hands together, and then he took a step forward. When she stepped back, the knee joint gave, but he caught her before she went down. She gritted her teeth. "I'll never be able to do this."

He crossed the room and stopped the music. "Let's try this slowly and see if we can manage it." He came back, and they started with the first step again, with the same results. John stood and studied the situation for a few moments. "Instead of stepping backward, why don't you stay in place for the first step?"

It took some practice, but Nora's circus training kicked in. She concentrated on the repetitive movement until she didn't think about it anymore. In about an hour or so, they were dancing to the music. When the gramophone stopped, they flopped on the couch, holding each other and laughing until they were breathless. Then Nora's body became very aware of the nearness of John's, and her throat tightened. What felt like electric sparks were flying along her skin, and from the look in John's eyes, he was feeling it, too.

John planted a kiss on her lips, then worked his way along her jawline to her ear. Nora quivered in her stomach, and her breath caught. *This is just like the night Rico—no, I won't think about that. But John will know if my barrier is missing.* A panic shot through her, and she stiffened.

John pulled back. "Something is wrong, isn't it? You're not ready for this yet."

Her heart was racing. He will find out either now or later. She took a few deep breaths. "I need to tell you before you find out for yourself. I'm not a virgin."

He looked like a runner frozen in mid-stride. "Who?"

"Rico. I was a stupid child." She covered her face with her hands and wept.

He gently pulled her hands down and wiped her face with his handkerchief. "I don't care. That was in the past. I love and forgive anything you've done."

"Most men would run."

"I'm not most men. Nora. When you truly love someone, you can forgive them anything."

She gently stroked his face with her fingers, in awe of this man who was so loving and forgiving. She wondered if she really deserved him. He made a small noise in his throat and planted his lips on hers once again. She couldn't help herself. Her body rose to meet his. Sensations rocked her. Before she was fully aware, their clothing was shed, and she felt the luscious warmth of his skin on hers. This was nothing like with Rico. Her soul seemed to mesh with John's.

Slowly, gently, he sheathed himself inside of her. Everywhere he touched caused a sensual vibration. She gripped his shoulders as he begin to move, panting, sweating. Finally she released, and ended up sobbing in his arms. Then she pulled back. "I'm—I'm sorry." She gulped. "I never knew intimacy could be so wonderful."

"I love you, Nora. God help me, I do. I never knew it could be this way, either." He kissed her damp forehead and they both stood, rearranging their clothes.

Nora went to the mirror in the hallway and tsked at her appearance. Her hair was impossibly mussed. As she was taking the combs and pins out, she heard hoof beats on the drive. Peeping through the curtains, she gasped. "Nellie is back. Oh, heavens, my hair is down."

John was putting on his coat. "Don't worry. I'll escort her back to the cottage."

She had managed to get the ebony tresses back up and pinned by the time she heard Nellie enter the kitchen. She hurried there and found Nellie putting away more food.

Nellie glanced up. "This is from Elinore. I thought we could have some for supper tonight."

John entered then and hung his hat and coat. "I'll get the dining room, if you girls will ready the food." He gave Nora a secret wink as he passed her. Her cheeks heated, and she concentrated on the potatoes she was dishing up. They warmed the food on the gas range and brought it to the table that John had set.

They told Nellie of their engagement, and she paused. "Wait right here." She was back in a few moments with a wine bottle and stemmed glasses. Opening the bottle, she poured the wine and handed the glasses around. "Congratulations! Here's to a happy

New Year for you both!" They raised their glasses and celebrated the engagement.

Nora settled into her bed at the cottage that night happier than she had ever been.

****

John watched out the window for the enclosed carriage he had hired for the evening. Nellie was helping Nora upstairs with her ball gown. They had a man with a broken leg in one of the rooms, and Nellie was going to be up there in case she was needed.

Finally, he saw the carriage turn into the drive. "Nora, the carriage is here," he called.

"Coming!" She came down the steps and pulled on her gloves while John took her hooded cape off the coat rack and put it around her shoulders. He already had his cape and gloves on.

He turned to Nellie. "Mr. Graves shouldn't be any trouble tonight. I gave him a little laudanum to help him sleep."

She nodded. "Yes, Doctor." Pausing, she leaned against the stair post. "My. The both of you make a very handsome couple. Enjoy yourselves."

John opened the door for Nora. "We will. Goodnight, and happy New Year."

She waved and mounted the stairs again.

The night was crisp and clear. Countless stars glittered overhead as John helped Nora into the carriage while the driver held the door. Moments later, they heard a whip crack, and the horse started its journey to Putney Hall. Nora gripped his arm. "You're nervous, aren't you?" he observed.

"Yes," came her voice from under the hood. "I remember what it was like at the last ball I went to."

He patted her hand. "You'll be fine."

Soon they were at the entrance, and John tipped the driver as he again held the door of the carriage. "When should I pick you up?" the driver asked.

"Half past midnight will be fine." The driver touched the brim of his hat and left.

John pulled the envelope with the invitation out of his pocket, and Nora silently slipped her hand through his offered arm. Inside, the lobby was a flurry of activity. People were checking winter coats and capes into the rack area. John took Nora's cape and went to check both his and hers.

Mr. Wirt Jones, who had been the one who stopped by to invite him, came over as John was turning around. "Dr. Mallory! I'm so happy you accepted the invitation. Please come in with me, and I'll introduce you around."

John spotted Nora. "Just a moment, I have to get my guest." John brought her over and introduced them.

Wirt gave her a brief nod, then led them into the hall. Colorful balloons and streamers swayed from the light fixtures, and the aroma of warm food filled the air. A woman decked out in gaudy jewels and ostrich feathers hurried over with a young woman in tow.

She leaned in and spoke to Wirt. "Is this the young surgeon, Dr. John Mallory?" At Wirt's nod, she went on, "I'm Mrs. Robert Porter, and this is my daughter, Agatha."

Soon a swarm of young women gadflies were buzzing around John, and he couldn't get a word in that they heard. One of the "ladies" elbowed Nora back. John stuck his hand in the air and said loudly, "Please stop a moment, ladies!" They looked startled, but settled behind their fans. John drew Nora to his side. "I want you to meet my intended, Miss Lenora La Rue." A groan was heard from behind the fans.

Mrs. Porter gasped. "But Mr. Jones said you were unmarried."

"I am. I became engaged over Christmas."

Mrs. Porter turned to Nora. "I've never heard of the La Rues. Is your family new in town?"

Nora paused. "My family is in Indiana. They're not here."

One of the girls spoke up. "She's a clerk at Canton's store. I've seen her." Nora's cheeks flushed.

Another giggled. "She's the one with the wooden leg."

John almost broke society protocol by chastising every silly one of them, but he took Nora's arm and said, "Excuse us," leaving the gaggle of geese behind. He gripped her shoulders. "I'm sorry, Nora. That didn't start very well."

There was a sad but angry fire in her eye. "It was just like the children lobbing tomatoes at me."

"We can leave if you want to."

"No. I'm not going to run every time this happens. I can't let them win." The musicians started to play a waltz. "Let's try our new way of dancing."

He led her onto the dance floor and noticed a firm set to her jaw. They glided into the steps they had rehearsed, and John saw eyebrows raised by the people watching. *I'll bet they never saw a cripple dance before. Thanks to Nora's years of acrobatic training that help her do this!*

At the end of the music, Nora's cheeks were flushed, and she looked radiant. John felt a presence and turned around. Mr. Wirt Jones nodded to both of them. "Would you and Miss La Rue like to join my friends at our table?"

John smiled. "Thank you, we will." He offered his arm to Nora, and they followed Jones to a table near the front of the hall. He introduced them to his wife Ella and several others who were with them.

When they were seated, the woman next to Nora patted her hand. "You dance very well in spite of your—um…" She seemed flustered.

"Wooden leg?" Nora finished.

"I'm sorry. I meant it as a compliment. It didn't come out that way."

Nora relaxed. "That's all right. I'll take it as such."

"May I ask what happened to your leg?"

Nora paused. "It was crushed under a horse. John was my surgeon."

John hoped they didn't inquire further. Nora didn't need any more stigma attached to her. He spoke up. "She has made a wonderful recovery, thanks to her youth."

Wirt sat back in his chair. "You seem to be a fine doctor, John Mallory, I'll ask at the next meeting if you could be nominated for membership in the lodge, if you are interested."

John nodded. "I would be honored, sir."

Things went better for the rest of the evening. Eventually, they got into the carriage and made their way home. John walked her to the cottage door and gave her a long kiss. "Happy New Year's, darling. I wish we didn't have to part."

She put her hand on his cheek. "Thank you for protecting me. I did notice. At least, you'll be able to get into society here. That should help your practice."

"I love you. Sweet dreams." They kissed again, and his body warmed with the memory of the intimate bond shared. He reluctantly entered the house to see how his patient was doing.

****

Nora and John attended his brother's wedding at St. John's Cathedral in downtown Milwaukee in March. The reception at the Pfister Hotel was an elegant affair. Nora was taken aback with the grandeur of the cathedral and hotel. For someone who lived in a large house but traveled on trains and slept in tents, this was eye-opening. Somehow she had trouble getting over her fish-out-of-water feeling.

John was best man, so Nora was with the Mallorys most of the day. Again, the people who didn't know her avoided contact once her disability was discovered, but blessedly the Mallorys had embraced her as one of their own and kept her from feeling alone.

Sitting at the groom's family table at the reception, she practiced the social manners she had been taught. Miss Weeks, who was sitting across from her, gave her a smile and a nod when she looked inquiringly at her before she made a move. Miss Weeks was Lillian's sister, and Nora could tell the resemblance between them as they sat next to each other.

Nora was concentrating on her plate of roast beef when she heard Lillian address her. "Nora, you've been very quiet this evening. Have you and John discussed a date?"

Nora glanced up. "Date?"

"To get married, child."

She shook her head. "Not yet. I don't think any of my family will come, so it wouldn't be a proper

155

wedding." She wished this line of questions would go away.

Miss Weeks and Lillian glanced at each other, and Lillian frowned. "We can't let that happen. Nora, talk to John about having a garden wedding at our home. Maybe in May?"

Nora paused, and her eyes misted. "I wouldn't have anyone to give me away."

Miss Weeks waved her hand. "Tsk! If your family is that callous, give yourself away. You don't need them."

"We'll talk about it and let you know." The waiter removed the dinner plates and attention was turned to the bride and groom cutting the cake. The musicians assembled on the raised stage at the far end of the hall and started to play "The Bride's Waltz." Robert and Julia took to the floor for the couple's first dance. John and Julia's sister Kate, who was the bride's maid, took to the floor after them. The other groom's men and bride's maids followed suit. The next dance was the parents and bride and groom.

Nora and Franny were standing on the side watching them all whirl by. Franny tapped her toe. "I can't wait until it's everyone's turn." She gave a little hop to the music.

Nora smiled. "I enjoy the whole thing."

John and Will appeared from the crowd. John gave an elaborate bow in front of Nora. "I have been released from my obligations. May I have the pleasure of the next dance?"

Nora winked. "You may."

Will made the same request of Franny, who eagerly accepted. John and Nora eased into their practiced steps and surprised many people. At the musician's break, Ben came over and slapped John on the back. "I never would have believed anyone could dance on a wooden leg."

John grinned. "Nora is a special girl."

"Come to the family table for refreshments. Your mother and Elinore have been after me to talk to both of you."

Lillian and Miss Weeks recounted the discussion at dinner. John turned to Nora. "Do you have any objections?"

"No."

"The date is set for May tenth, then," John confirmed.

Lillian clapped her hands. "Splendid! I'll start the plans."

Nora turned to Elinore. "Miss Weeks, I'd like you to help with my wedding dress, if that's agreeable?"

Elinore nodded. "Certainly, my dear, and in light of you becoming family, you can call me Aunt Elinore."

"Thank you, Aunt Elinore, I'd like that." Nora paused. "Could you be my bridesmaid?"

The family appeared stunned. Elinore ventured, "Why me?"

"Outside of John, you have been my mentor since I've been here. I feel very close to you."

Elinore softened. "I'd be honored to be your bridesmaid."

Nora squeezed the woman's hand. "Thank you."

The musicians had returned, and Will came to Nora. "I saw how well you danced with John. Can you show me how to do it?" He turned to John. "If you don't mind." John waved him ahead and Nora showed him the steps on the dance floor. He soon picked it up, and they weaved around the room.

At the end of the waltz, Nora laughed with joy. "That was perfect."

Will smiled, but it faded slowly. "Thank you for the dance."

"Is there something wrong?"

The smile came back. "No. I'm just—I, um… It's not important. I want to wish you the best on your engagement." He gave her a peck on the cheek, then wandered into the crowd.

Nora made her way back to the table and sat next to John. "Is there something wrong with Will?"

John shook his head. "Not that I know of. Why?"

Nora bit her lower lip. "He seems so sad. Maybe it's about Chance."

"Perhaps. You look tired. Should I walk you to your room?"

"No. I'll stay a while yet. Since Franny and I are sharing a room, I'll go up with her. No need to get the gossips' tongues wagging." She didn't tell him she would love nothing better than to melt into his arms like liquid honey, but there would be another time.

He stood and held his hand out to her. "Then I want another dance with you." She happily whirled away with him onto the dance floor.

Chapter 15

April in Waukesha brought with it sloppy, dirty snow and mud quagmires. Nora's skirt wicked up the water and mud from the wet street as she crossed it. *There are times I wish skirts weren't so long.* She made it back to the practice with her shopping basket on her arm and her hems sloshing around her legs. At the back door, she stepped inside and removed her boots and winter wraps to hang by the radiator. Taking the basket into the kitchen, she put away food in the pantry and icebox. Nellie came in to help her with the last items.

As she sat by the stove to dry out her skirt, Nora asked, "Anyone call while I was out?"

Nellie shook her head. "It isn't quite as busy on the days the doctor is at the hospital. Most of what comes in, I can handle." The telephone rang, and Nellie waved her hand. "Stay there. I'll answer it." A minute later, she was back. "Will Canton is calling. He wants to talk to you."

She went to the telephone and picked up the receiver. "Will?"

"Nora, I need to talk to you and John."

"John is at the hospital today and won't be home until late."

"I'm staying at my uncle's home tonight. May I see you tomorrow?"

Nora paused. "Why don't you come to dinner

tomorrow night? Six o'clock?"

"I will be there. Thank you, Nora." The line went dead.

Nora left a note for John before she retired to the cottage that evening.

The next day, Elinore came over for a fitting on Nora's wedding dress. Nora had been sewing the lace and trim by hand, and Elinore was using her sewing machine to do the seams. At midday, Elinore went back to the sanitarium and Nora slipped through the back door and into the kitchen, where Nellie was fixing a light lunch for all of them and soup for two patients upstairs.

Nora began to set the table. "How are our ague patients?"

Nellie wiped her hands on a kitchen towel. "Both are going to be collected by their families this afternoon."

John appeared. "I heard you come in. How is the sewing coming along?"

Nora gave him a peck on the cheek. "Fine. We only have a few more things to do."

"I left receipts for some of my purchases just inside the ledger."

Nora nodded. "I'll post them after we eat."

"Did Will say what he wanted to speak to us about?"

She paused. "No. But it sounded important."

The afternoon was quiet, so Nora had no trouble fixing a nice dinner for that evening. Will was at the front door at the promised time, and John let him in. Nora asked Nellie if she wanted to have dinner with them, but she declined and went out to the cottage.

Nora had finished putting the food on the table when John and Will came in.

She waved her hand toward the table. "Everything is ready. Please sit down." She took some bowls and dished up a savory beef stew that Elinore had taught her. A side of biscuits and butter was placed in front of the men.

"Smells heavenly, Nora," Will exclaimed as he dug in.

John beamed at her. "She's turning into quite a cook."

She dabbed the napkin on her lips. "Thank you both." After the meal was consumed, Nora poured the coffee. "Now what was it you wanted, Will."

He took a breath. "I wrote to O'Brien's cousin at Precinct Number Twelve in Chicago. That covers the race track. He said he'd heard from his cousin in Kenosha about my horse. They know about Leaver's dealings, and they want to catch him once and for all. He wants me to bring the bill of sale and a photograph of Chance, plus the handkerchief with the dye on it."

John studied Will with a puzzled expression. "What does that have to do with us?"

"I want Nora to come with me."

Nora pursed her lips. "Why me?"

"You can calm a horse better than anyone I know."

John furrowed his brows. "How dangerous will this be? I don't want Nora hurt."

"She can stay outside until Leaver is dispatched."

John looked at her questioningly. "I'll let you decide."

She blew out a slow breath. "If you think I'll be of some help, I'll go. When are you going to do this?"

Will checked a notepad. "Saturday next. The race is in the afternoon, so if we catch the early train to Chicago, we should be there in time. O'Brien's cousin, Seamus Finney, will be waiting at the station for us with a search warrant. We'll go with him in the patrol wagon." He glanced at John. "Would you like to go too?"

John shook his head. "I have to be at the hospital that day."

Nora chewed her lower lip. "You won't need me?"

"No. Nellie can take care of things while you are gone."

She turned to Will. "I guess I'm yours for the day."

Will grinned. "Wonderful! I'll be over at seven in the morning on Saturday. We can stay at one of the hotels in Chicago and come back the next day."

Nora hoped this would work. It would be one more person who wouldn't be abusing horses in the world.

Saturday morning, Nora had a quick breakfast and saw John off to the hospital. John kissed her before he left. "Be careful, darling. You never know what thugs like that are going to do."

She patted his cheek. "I'll stay out of the way."

Nora had finished packing at the cottage when Nellie called from the house, "Mr. Canton is here."

"Tell him to bring the carriage in the back." Nellie waved from the back door and disappeared. Nora set her bag on the step of the cottage when Will had the carriage next to it, and Will hopped down and stored her bag, then helped her into the rig.

"Ready?" he asked as he resumed his seat.

Nora sighed. "As I'll ever be. I hope everything turns out without any problems."

He slapped the horse on the back with the reins. "I hope so too. That's why I wanted you to come. If Chance gets frightened, I think you can help calm him."

Nora just answered, "All right." *But who's going to calm me?*

She and Will tried to engage in small talk on the train trip to Chicago, but she found she couldn't fully relax, and Will seemed on edge, too. In between conversations, she gazed out the windows and saw plants trying on their green spring outfits among the patches of stubborn gray snow. The animals on the farms were out and cavorting across the fields as if they were prisoners on a lark. She remembered spring in Indiana when she was a child and helping ready things for the circus, breathing in the clean, crisp air and hearing the birds twittering out their territories, taking in the aroma of the earth waking up from its winter sleep.

"You have a smile on your face," came Will's voice into her reverie.

Nora blinked. "Hundreds of miles away in land and time. Thinking about when my family was readying the circus for the season."

"Circus?"

"John didn't tell you?"

Will furrowed his brows. "You must be the girl who lost her leg when the cyclone hit last summer. Of course. John must have had you for a patient."

Nora watched his expression, waiting for the disapproval to set in. "I am the girl. Yes."

Half in thought, he continued, "That makes sense. You said you traveled with your family." He glanced at her. "Why didn't you tell me this before?"

She paused. "Because most people have prejudged ideas about those who work in a circus. I'm very selective about who I tell."

"I see. Actually, I'd be interested in your life at the circus."

They spent the rest of the trip discussing what she and her family did, until finally the call rang out for the Chicago station. Will helped her down and carried their bags. When he saw a burly red-haired policeman waiting by the passenger door, he waved at him. "Are you Sgt. Seamus Finney?"

The officer studied him. "You must be Mr. Will Canton." He turned to Nora. "And Miss Nora La Rue?" Both Will and Nora nodded. "Good. I have rooms for you at the Michigan Street Hotel. Bring your bags to the patrol wagon."

Outside the station was a wagon with a patrolman holding the horses. "This is Officer Raczkowski," Finney informed them. "We'll drop the bags at the hotel, then head to the track. Everything is set for the trap."

Nora hoped all would go well, but she couldn't get over the dread that was like a pickax in her stomach.

The track grounds were decked out like a grand party, with all the flags and streamers flying in the Lake Michigan breeze. People in their finery were being seen at the first race of the season. Finney called to the driver, "Raczkowski! Stop the horses." He turned to Nora and Will. "We can walk to the stable area from here. Raczkowski and I will put on our long coats. May as well not alert them in advance."

Will glanced at Nora. "Can you walk that far?"

Nora nodded. "I'm fine." Nora pulled the hood of

her cape up, and she noticed Will put his hat low on his face.

Many people were at the stables examining the horses for the race, so Nora prayed they wouldn't be noticed. Finney and his patrolman were ahead of them. They came to a corner and looked down the row of stalls. Finney held up his hand. "Leaver's horses are on this aisle. Miss La Rue, stay out of the way."

Nora glanced at Will, and he nodded. "You'll be safe."

She put a hand on his arm. "Be careful."

With a half-smile, he disappeared around the corner with the policemen. She leaned against the wooden wall by the open stable door and heard the commotion on the far end of the aisle. Angry voices were raised as the policemen showed the warrant. Then there was silence. She ventured a look and gave an inward gasp. Leaver stood in front of a stall, pointing a pistol inside. Nora heard him say, "If you try to arrest me, I'm shooting the horse."

A quick study of the aisle revealed a long bullwhip coiled on a peg by the side of the stalls. *If I've learned anything from living outside the circus, it's that women can move invisibly. Men don't pay attention to them.* She moved silently down the way, grabbing the whip as she came to the tense tableaux. Then she lashed out, and with a crack, the thin end of the whip wrapped around Leaver's wrist. With a shout from Leaver, the pistol was knocked from his hand, and Finney scooped it up from the floor. The men looked at her with stunned shock all over their faces, while Leaver took advantage of their surprise and grabbed Finney's arm. The gun fired wildly, and Nora watched in horror as Will crumpled to the ground. "No! Will!" She forgot her wooden leg and fell to the ground next to him.

Finney wrestled Leaver down. "Raczkowski! Get your handcuffs on him and take him to the patrol wagon. I'll call for the track doctor."

Meanwhile, Nora had unbuttoned Will's shirt and found where the bullet had entered. She made a compress from the handkerchief in his jacket pocket. "Hold on. The doctor is coming." Will just groaned.

The doctor came in a few minutes later and checked the wound. "Looks like the bullet broke the collarbone. I'll have to get him to the hospital. I have the ambulance outside." The drivers brought out a stretcher and lifted Will into the wagon. "Do you want to go with us, miss?"

Nora looked at Finney. "Should I?"

He patted her arm. "Go ahead. We'll take the horse and put him in a stall at the station stable." He helped her off the floor, and waved at the drivers. "She has a wooden leg." They nodded and got her into the wagon.

Nora sat beside the doctor next to the stretcher. The doctor laid a hand on her arm. "Are you his intended?"

She shook her head. "No. I'm a friend."

"Where is his family?"

"In Milwaukee."

"I'll need to get a wire to them."

The wagon stopped, and the doctor got out. Will glanced at her. "Nora? Sorry I got you into this."

She grasped his hand. "Don't worry about me. Stay quiet."

The doctor came back with two orderlies. "Come, miss, I'll help you out."

Nora gave Will's hand a squeeze before she left.

The orderlies removed the stretcher from the wagon, and she followed them into the hospital. They transferred Will onto a gurney, and Nora patted his hand. "I'll be waiting for you."

He looked at her with drug-drowsy eyes. "I love you, Nora," he said faintly. He was wheeled away.

Nora had been struck by a lightning bolt. Had she heard him correctly? Or was it just a drug-induced stupor?

"Excuse me, miss?"

Nora turned to a young man standing behind her. "Yes?"

"I'm the dispatcher. Could I have the address of Mr. Will Canton's family?"

She paused. "I don't know their address, but I could give you the address of Dr. Ben Mallory. He's a neighbor of theirs." She gave the address to him.

"Thank you, miss." He tipped his hat and went on his way.

Nora looked around and seated herself on a padded wicker chair in the lobby. The doctor found her a few minutes later. "I'm sorry, I didn't introduce myself to you. I'm Dr. Reynolds. You are…?"

"Nora La Rue."

"Miss La Rue, thank you for helping our dispatcher. I'm going to take Mr. Canton into surgery to remove the bullet and set the bone. I'll seek you out when I've finished."

"Thank you, Doctor." She watched him hurry away. *I should get word to John about what has happened.* She went to the reception desk, where a young man was attending to the admittance duties. "Excuse me, sir, I need to get a wire out."

He opened a drawer in the desk and took out a pad with a telegraph form on it. "Where is this going to?" He poised the pencil over the paper.

"Dr. John Mallory, 235 Maple Avenue, Waukesha, Wisconsin. Will shot stop At Michigan Street Hospital stop Nora." She opened her reticule and paid for the telegram, then went back to the lobby to wait.

The padded wicker chair felt good as Nora put her head back and closed her eyes for a few minutes. It felt like a lifetime since she'd left Waukesha. Her mind drifted back to what Will had said. She liked Will as a friend and had entertained the thought of a relationship when he took her to the ball at Fountain Spring. But he'd pulled back from her in that respect. What made him confess to her now? She drifted off and was awakened by Dr. Reynolds.

He patted her hand. "I'm sorry to wake you, Miss La Rue, but Mr. Canton is in the ward now, if you'd like to see him."

Nora blinked the sleep out of her eyes and rose. "Yes, I would." She followed him down the hallway to a large open double door showing whitewashed walls and rows of beds and curtains. The doctor stopped in front of one of the beds and pulled aside its curtains. Will was in the bed, his upper body bandaged tightly. Nora brought a chair over and sat beside him. Sun filtered in from the frosted windows behind them, and dust floated lazily on the light beams. She leaned forward and put her hand on his. "Will?"

He opened his eyes. "Nora? What are you—" His glance traveled to Dr. Reynolds, standing behind her. "Oh, yes. I remember. I got shot. Excuse me, Nora, but stupid damn luck."

Dr. Reynolds went to the other side of the bed. "Mr. Canton, we removed the bullet. It had broken your clavicle, or collarbone. We set it, and it should be mended in a month or so."

Will's eyebrows rose. "Do I have to spend all that time in the hospital?"

"We'd like you to stay for a couple of days. Just to see that there are no complications."

Will turned to Nora. "I'm sorry for all this."

She shook her head. "It wasn't your fault."

He paused. "If you hadn't knocked the gun out of Leaver's hand—Where did you learn to use a whip like that?"

She gave a quick glance at Dr. Reynolds. "I was taught a long time ago."

A young man appeared at the foot of the bed. "Is Miss La Rue here?"

"I am she."

He handed her an envelope. "Here's the reply to your wire."

She gave him a quarter. "Thank you very much." She opened the telegram after the man left and read it aloud. "Nora stop Coming with Cantons stop John."

The doctor patted her on the shoulder. "They probably won't arrive here until tomorrow. I can arrange for someone to escort you back to the hotel."

Nora glanced at Will. He nodded. "Yes, why don't you go. I'll be all right, and I need some rest."

Nora hesitated. She wanted to ask Will if he remembered what he had said to her. Will's eyes closed. Maybe it could wait until tomorrow. She sighed and turned to the doctor. "I'm ready."

Back in the hotel, she paced the floor. She didn't

know why this bothered her so much. She had never thought of Will as anything beyond a friend. John was the one she was in love with. She smiled at the tingling it brought when she pictured him. Her gaze fixed on the gilded plants on the green wallpaper in the room and made images out of the patterns. She blew out a slow breath. *I might as well go to bed. Nothing will get resolved tonight anyway.* She turned in and closed her eyes to a long night of guns, horses, and crime.

Nora checked out the next morning and took the streetcar to the hospital. She hoped she could talk to Will before John and the Cantons arrived, but Will was being checked by Dr. Reynolds. Reluctantly, Nora went to the lobby to wait.

Chapter 16

John, accompanied by Will's parents, stepped off the streetcar in front of the hospital. Mrs. Canton had been distraught because there was no word on how bad Will was. John was happy that Will was alive. It could have been worse, and Nora was—No, he wouldn't let his mind wander there.

The morning sun poured through the large lobby windows as John held the door for the Cantons. He heard his name called from across the room, and then Nora was in front of him. John took his hat off and hugged her. "Oh, darling, this must have been terrible for you."

"More so for Will. Come, I'll take you to see him. Dr. Reynolds should be finished checking him over." She led the way to the ward and let the nurse know at the desk that his parents were here.

Will was propped in bed, reading the morning newspaper, and glanced up as the group came in. He set the paper aside. "You just missed the doctor. He told me there doesn't seem to be any infection. My, it's good to see all of you."

His mother squeezed his hand, and his father patted his arm. "Tell us what happened, son."

Will related the whole story while John stood with his arm around Nora. John had a hitch in his breathing when the part about Nora and the whip was revealed.

Mrs. Canton came over and gave Nora a hug. "That was very brave of you."

Nora shrugged. "I had to do something."

Will hesitated, then made a motion at John. "May I make a request of you?"

John nodded. "What is it?"

"Could you take Chance back with you and stable him with your carriage horse until I can get out of here?"

John glanced at Nora. "Why not at your uncle's again?"

"Just in case any of the thugs that work for Leaver try to get him back."

Nora looked at him with a plea. "I could work out the dye from his coat."

John paused. "Where is Chance now?"

Will breathed a sigh of relief. "He's at the police stables. I can give you the money for the rail transport, and a letter of permission."

John shook his head. "Pay me back when you get back home." He turned to Nora. "We should be getting back to Waukesha."

Nora pointed to a chair with a bag on it. "I checked out of the hotel this morning, but Will still has his room there."

John glanced at Will. "Do you want me to bring your things here?"

Mr. Canton spoke up. "I'll retrieve Will's things from the hotel. Thank you, John." He shook his hand.

After goodbyes, and with Will's letter of permission, John picked up Nora's bag and they went to the lobby to ask directions to the police station. They caught one of the streetcars, and John paid the fare. A fog from Lake Michigan was clinging stubbornly to the land, but they were able to find the station.

Going to the desk inside, Nora asked if Sgt. Finney was there. The young officer went back to the office area, then reappeared. "He asked me to show you to his office."

When they walked in, there was Finney thumping on a typewriter. He looked up and waved his hand toward two wooden chairs. "Have a seat." He pulled the paper out of the typewriter with a snap and set it down. He nodded at Nora. "Miss La Rue." He glanced at John. "And you are?"

"Dr. John Mallory. I'm a friend of Will Canton. Will asked me to take his horse home with us." John handed him the envelope with a permission letter signed by Will.

Finney picked up a folder and thumbed through the papers. "We have the bill of sale and a photograph of the horse. I don't think we'll need the actual animal for evidence. Wait a moment, and I'll go back to the stable with you." He filed the paper he had been working on and slipped on his coat as John and Nora rose.

They followed him down a dark hallway to an old wooden door around the corner. The cool spring air rushed in as he opened it, along with the scent of warm equine and hay. Down a couple of wooden plank steps to the stable where the horses and police wagons were kept, a young officer was hanging some of the harnesses on large pegs lined on the wall. He turned when Sgt. Finney entered. "You need something, sir?"

"Yes. Officer Brown, I want you to take the small wagon and escort Dr. John Mallory and Miss La Rue to the train station. They're going to take Mr. Canton's horse back to Wisconsin with them."

The young man acknowledged Finney and soon had a horse hitched to a wagon and brought over Chance. The horse was skittish, and Nora went over to quiet him. As soon as Chance eyed Nora, he whinnied and nickered as he nudged her with his nose. She cooed and crooned to the horse and before long he was quiet.

Sgt. Finney gave a low whistle. "Miss La Rue, you sure have a way with horses. If he was a dog, he would have wagged his tail."

She smiled. "I've been around them all my life." She tied Chance to the back of the wagon. John helped her into the back and climbed in beside her. Officer Brown hopped onto the driver's seat, and with goodbyes to Sgt. Finney, they were off to the train station.

When they arrived, John and Nora took their things out of the wagon, and Nora untied Chance. They thanked Officer Brown, and John hurried to the ticket office to purchase their fare and a stall for Chance.

Nora led the horse into the stable car and got him settled, and John met her outside the car. "Do you think he'll be all right in there?"

Nora nodded. "He's used to traveling with Will. I'm sure he will be fine." John offered his arm, and they strolled toward the chair car.

****

Nora stared out the window at the changing scenery, not really looking at it. It worried her that she had not gotten a chance to talk to Will privately, and his declaration of love still haunted her.

She felt fingers sliding over her hand. "Nora, something is wrong," came John's voice. "Tell me what's bothering you."

She gazed at John's face with the strong jawline and deep brown eyes and wanted to tell him everything. This was a man she trusted, but she would die if this caused a rift between friends. She took a deep breath, and went on her instincts. "When Will was under the influence of the drug, he told me he loved me." There, she'd said it.

John laughed. "Is that all? People tend to say strange things when they're drugged."

Nora felt her mouth going into a pout. "You mean, he couldn't possibly love me?"

He cupped her chin. "There's your self-pity coming around again. No, I didn't mean that. And I know you well enough that any explanation I give you now will only get me in more trouble."

Nora turned her gaze back out the window, not knowing if she should be grateful to him or flatten him with a heavy object. Their mundane fits and starts of conversation continued until they reached the Waukesha train station in mid-afternoon. He had wired Elinore from the hospital to meet them, when he found out he was going to bring Chance with them. She was waiting with her runabout carriage. John piled the bags on while Nora went to get Chance.

She found him nervous, but she soon calmed him and led him off the car. John tied the horse to the back of the carriage and helped Nora onto the seat. Nora greeted Elinore, and Elinore guided the carriage horse to the practice, with Chance prancing behind.

They turned into their drive, and Nora had never felt so glad to be home.

John untied Chance. "I'm going to bed him down

in the stable."

As Nora nodded and retrieved her bag from the carriage, Elinore came over and put her arm around Nora's shoulders. "Everything all right?"

Nora hesitated. "Yes—No. I don't know."

Elinore snorted. "Well, that covers all the bases. I noticed a faint wall between you and John. What happened?"

Nora told her what had taken place in Chicago. "I like Will and I love John. I don't want this to cause a rift between them."

John was on his way back, and Elinore waved her hand toward the cottage. "Why don't you unpack your bag, and I'll talk to him."

Nora nodded, went up the porch steps, and slid through the door. She set the bag down and peeked through the lace curtains at the two figures standing in the late-day sun, their shadows making an India rubber man to the main house. They both looked at the cottage, and Nora ducked, then opened her bag to unpack.

When she heard Nellie call from the house, Nora glanced outside and saw Elinore climbing into the carriage and John hurrying to the back porch where Nellie stood. Nora had just finished unpacking and storing away her things when Nellie came in. She gave Nora a hug. "I heard what happened. I'm so glad you're safe. I've fixed supper for you two."

Nora pulled back. "Aren't you going to have any?"

She shook her head. "We don't have any patients, and Elinore invited me over tonight." She pushed Nora toward the door. "Go. John is dishing up the stew, and it will get cold."

Nora squeezed her hand. "Thank you, Nellie."

Nora noticed Elinore was waiting in the drive, and Nellie went out to the carriage. She smiled and waved to them as the carriage went to the street.

The sun had gone down, and the chilly April wind ruffled her hair as she headed to the back porch. John was setting the plates on the table when she stepped into the kitchen. He took her cape and hung it on a peg by the door. Pulling out a chair by the table, he waved his hand. "Sit."

The rich savory aroma of the beef stew wrapped itself around her nose, and her stomach growled. She'd forgotten that she hadn't eaten since breakfast. John sat just around the corner next to her. She dipped her spoon into the brown gravy and let its warmth travel down her throat. "Mmm, that tastes good." She held up the bread bowl with the sliced loaf. "Bread?"

John hesitated. "Yes." He took a slice. "Nora? Remember we're getting married in a couple of weeks. We have to talk about this wall that's come up."

"Wall?"

"You've been stilted since the trip to Chicago. Talk to me."

She chased a bit of potato around the bowl with her spoon. "What Will said to me shook me to my core. What if he has fallen in love with me and I didn't know it? I was so aware of my feelings for you, but I muted them because of Thea. Has he done the same thing? I know nothing about love." Tears formed in her eyes. "John, nobody has ever loved me before. My family, Rico…the only love I received was from the people I performed for in the show, and they weren't a part of my life. That's why I'm so drawn to horses. They were the only ones who loved me back."

John brushed his fingers across the wet trails on her cheek. "Listen to me. For good or ill, I was attracted to you when I saw you perform at the circus. When I treated you at the hospital, I got too involved because I wanted to protect you. I never let myself do that before. I knew I never felt that way with Thea. She was a good friend and we had grown up together, but I realized I didn't love her." He rose and drew her up into an embrace. "I do love you. I realized this fully when your telegram came. There was not a thought except for your safety. I dropped everything to go to you."

Nora gazed into the deep brown eyes that reminded her of liquid chocolate. There was pain there. She pulled back and spread her hands on his chest and felt the rhythm of his heart.

He raised an eyebrow at her.

"John, if this is love, I want it."

His lips claimed hers, and she felt like she had downed a whole pint of champagne at one sitting. She pressed against his body and gave as good as she got. They hadn't made love since that one brief interlude after he moved in. He pulled back and grasped her hand. "Come with me."

They went down the back hall to a small room, which had been the maid's room, with simple furnishings: an iron bed, a desk, a washstand, and a wardrobe. John pulled the chain on the desk lamp and the amber glow softened the whitewashed walls. She knew exactly what he was doing. She took the combs from her hair, and it fell loosely down her back. Her fingers went to the buttons on her shirtwaist, and John put his hand on hers. "John?"

"Let me." He started unbuttoning her from the

neck, pausing sometimes as if to take her in. He reached her waist, unbuttoning the two fasteners on each side of her skirt, and it puddled to the floor. Finishing her shirtwaist, he edged it off her shoulders, and it joined the skirt. She stood in her petticoats and camisole while John kissed down her neck to her shoulder. A moan escaped her parted lips, and she could feel heat in her belly and between her thighs. John stroked his hands down her bare arms. "You're so beautiful, Nora." His voice was hoarse with need.

Nora hooked her fingers under the waistband of his trousers. "These have to go," she hissed in his ear. He growled and shed his outer clothing, which landed on top of hers. As she started to unhook her corset, he grabbed her to him, and she felt the heat of his erection next to her belly.

He traced his fingers between her breasts and cupped the twin globes. "Let me finish. Then we'll remove the limb. I want you as nature intended."

She paused. "Won't that repel you?"

He nipped the base of her neck. "Nothing about you repels me," he whispered.

Soon they were holding together skin to skin. She remembered when Rico took her inside the horse tent after a show. He was rough and set for his own pleasure, not thinking of hers. With John, it was different. He was gentle and went slowly, finding out what pleased her. John carried her to the bed and set her down, his hands getting to know the contours of her body. Teasing her nipples into tight peaks, he took a suckle of one. The heat tore through her body, causing her to gasp in a sharp breath.

Nora's fingers traveled from his shoulders to the

small pips on his chest, and she rubbed her thumbs over them, making John moan. She was happy she could give him the same sensations as he did her. A cry escaped his lips as she stroked the heavy shaft that was smooth as silk. He moved the tip against her hot, wet intimate part, and she shook with anticipation. With a thrust of his tongue in her mouth, he thrust his shaft into her sheath, and she delighted with the fullness.

He set a rhythm that tightened her like a watch spring. Her body was not her own. Her walls clamped around him, and she went willingly over the cliff, taking him with her. Seconds, minutes, hours went by, and they held each other, their skin slick with sweat.

John pulled out and was on his knees on the bed. Nora instantly felt like she had lost a part of herself and swung her stump around to sit at the edge. John leaned forward and cradled her body to his and kissed the top of her head. "I truly love you, Nora. Now and forever. I will do anything to keep and protect you. I pledge this on all that is sacred," he said in her hair. The walls and doubts she had entertained had come crashing down.

Chapter 17

A week before their wedding, Nora was busy balancing the ledger for that month. John was at the hospital that day, and Nellie took care of the simple injuries and sickness that came in the door. Hearing hoofbeats and carriage wheels on the drive, she went to the porch to see who it was. The driver of the carriage opened the door of the cab and helped a man out. It was Will. She went down the porch steps. "Will! It's good to see you."

Will looked around. "Where's John?"

"He's at the hospital today." She studied him as he stood with the bindings still around his upper chest and his right arm in a sling. "How are you doing?"

He grinned. "Mending nicely, thank you." He looked around. "I'm here to take Chance to my uncle's home."

A little sadness seeped through her. "He could stay here."

"My uncle has a large pasture there. Chance needs to stretch his muscles." He pointed south. "He lives about two miles from here. I'll be staying there for a week or so."

"Before you take him, would you like to have some coffee with me?"

Will turned to the driver and handed him some coins. "Would you wait for me?" The driver tipped his hat and nodded. Will followed Nora inside.

Nellie was heading upstairs with medicine for an ague patient. Nora stopped her. "I'll be in the kitchen for a bit if you need me." Nellie nodded and continued upstairs. In the kitchen, Nora waved her hand at a chair at the table. "Sit and tell me what's been happening."

While Nora poured the coffee, Will began, "It looks like there's enough evidence on Leaver to put him away for a long time. I'm not the first person he's stolen horses from, and others are coming forth. His trial is set for next week."

Nora set the steaming cups on the table. "I'm glad for you it's almost over." She didn't know how to approach the subject, but she had to have an answer. "Will, do you remember anything you said before they took you into surgery?"

He paused. "Bits and pieces, why?"

She leaned forward in her chair. "How do you feel about me?"

A parade of expressions crossed his face. "Why do you ask?"

"Honestly, are we going to have a conversation of questions?"

He chuckled a bit. "There has to be a reason for this."

"When you were going into surgery, you said you loved me."

He sighed. "That's because I do."

She inadvertently sucked in a gasp and started coughing. When she calmed her spasms down, Nora glanced at him in horror. "You never told me this before."

"I fell for you when I met you at my uncle's store."

He took a sip of coffee and tapped his fingers on the cup. "I tried, Nora, I really did, but you being a cripple was too much for me. I couldn't get past that. Then when we were with you and John at the ball, I saw he loved you without reservation. Apparently, Thea saw it, too. Under the influence of that drug at the hospital, I said I loved you. Otherwise I never would have told you. I'm sorry."

There was that hurt again for being different with an artificial limb, but she couldn't be angry with Will. She put her hand on his arm. "Don't be sorry. I hope you can still be friends with John. He loves you like a brother."

He kissed her on the forehead. "Sweet Nora, for being raised in the family you were, you have more of a heart than all of them put together." He finished off his cup. "Let's go get Chance."

She rose and slipped on her sweater against the cool spring air and led him out to the stable. "I've been working the dye out of his coat."

Nora opened the heavy wood door and let Will inside. Chance greeted Will with a loud whinny, then nuzzled him. Nora chuckled. "He missed you."

Will stood back and looked at her handiwork. "His coat is back to the copper color. Thank you."

Nora scratched Chance's nose and gave him a bit of carrot she had stowed in her pocket. As he munched happily, Nora picked the halter and lead off a peg. She strapped it on and scratched the horse's nose again. "I'm going to miss you, boy." She turned to Will. "I'll lead him out and tie the lead to the cab."

The corners of Will's mouth curled up. "For once, you seem more able than I."

When she was finished, she turned and looked deep into Will's eyes, imagining what might have happened if things were different, but she knew, down in her soul, she could never love Will like she did John. "Let us know when you go back to racing him." Nora held the carriage door open, and Will carefully climbed into the seat.

He leaned toward her. "Thank you and John for everything." She closed the door, and Will called for the driver to go.

As Nora watched the cab go into the street, a sense of peace settled over her. She was glad the air was cleared and they were still friends.

****

John yawned as he turned Mack, his carriage horse, into the practice's drive. The amber glow from the residential street lamp and the houses cast shadows in the backyard. Mack suddenly snorted and backed a couple of steps. John pulled on the reins. "What's wrong, boy?" Then he heard a rustle and the snap of a twig. A dark figure jumped the fence by the stable and ran. John was off the carriage and looking over the fence immediately, but the figure had disappeared into the night. He went to the carriage and calmed the nervous animal, then noticed the stable door was open. He led Mack to the entrance and gave him a final pat before he took the lantern from the outside peg and lit it. Blowing out a breath, he stepped inside and looked around. All seemed to be in order, nothing stolen, as far as he could see.

John unhitched Mack, bedded him in his stall, and brought some fresh water and oats. He pushed the carriage inside and closed the heavy door. Then he took a walk around the building with the lantern, but nothing was disturbed. He blew out the light, returned it to the peg, and headed to the house.

Nora came out to the porch of the cottage. "What happened? I thought I heard something."

He stood at the bottom of the steps. "Someone ran off as I was turning into the drive. What did you hear?"

"A few moments ago, I heard the stable door open. I thought you had come back, but I hadn't heard the carriage. Some dry leaves crackled, but I thought it could have been an animal."

His mouth went into a tight line. "That was no animal. I saw a dark figure jump the fence."

She leaned against the post. "Was anything taken from the stable?"

"Not that I could see." He paused. "I want you and Nellie to stay at the main house tonight."

"Nellie was going to because of the scarlet fever patient. I can stay in the maid's room."

He nodded. "If you hear anything, come and wake me."

She turned to go inside the cottage. "I'll need a few things. I'll be in soon."

He made his way to the main house, and Nellie was in the kitchen readying the nighttime medicine for the patient. John told her what had happened and gave her the same instructions he had given Nora.

He poured himself a brandy. *Maybe it was just a vagrant looking for a place to sleep.* He heard the back door close and saw Nora with her bag, heading to the maid's room.

When she saw him, she set the bag down and ran into his arms. "You're worried, aren't you?"

He paused, not wanting to scare her. "Just want to take precautions. It might be a vagrant from the railroad." A wave of tenderness and lust settled over him, but he knew, for propriety's sake, they couldn't stay together with others in the house. He leaned over and tasted her sweet lips, almost throwing caution to the wind. He gritted his teeth against the urges. "Good night, my love."

She settled her hand lightly on his cheek, and the corners of her mouth curled up slightly. "Sweet dreams, Doctor." Then she left to seclude herself.

The long day behind him started to take its toll. He took the brandy into the waiting room/parlor and sat on an overstuffed chair, putting his feet up on an ottoman. He took another sip and let the warm, sharp liquid roll around on his tongue. He sighed and set the snifter on the table. *I'll close my eyes for a few moments.*

John felt a hand patting him on his shoulder. "Dr. Mallory. Dr. Mallory! It's an hour before the practice opens!"

He opened his eyes to see Nellie standing over him. He rubbed his face and groaned. "I must have fallen asleep." Finally, he got his wits about him. "How's the patient?"

Nellie straightened and folded her hands. "He slept through the night and seems to be on the mend."

John rose and gave the snifter to Nellie. "Could you take this to the kitchen? I need to go upstairs and clean up. I'll take a look at Mr. Bailey before I come down."

He went to his bedroom, took off yesterday's clothing, and did his morning routine. Wiping the excess shaving cream off his face, he donned his practice coat and hurried to the patient guest room. Mr. Bailey was sitting up in bed looking wan, but there was definite color coming back into his cheeks. "How are you feeling today, Mr. Bailey?"

Mr. Bailey cleared his throat. "Still weak, but better."

John checked his temperature and pulse. "I think we can call your family to come and take you home. We'll do that after breakfast."

Mr. Bailey ran his fingers through his sparse gray hair. "Thank you, Doc."

John smiled. "You're welcome. I'll send Nellie up with a tray. She can lay your things out for you." At the patient's acknowledgment, John went downstairs. Nora was unlocking the front door and setting up the appointments for the day. Nellie passed by with the breakfast tray, and John told her about Mr. Bailey.

Nora glanced up. "Do you want me to call his family now?"

"Yes. Then join me in the kitchen."

John helped himself to the eggs, ham, and fruit compote Nellie had prepared. As he sat at the table, he heard Nora talking on the telephone. When she hung up, it rang again. It was going to be a busy day.

Nora came back and poured them each a cup of coffee. "Mr. Bailey's family will be here in a couple of hours, and Will called inviting us to dinner at his uncle's tonight." She joined him at the table and set the cups down.

He looked up. "Aren't you going to eat?"

"I did earlier. I checked in the back this morning, and nothing seemed to be disturbed. I think you were right. It was just a vagrant."

Nora looked like she had been in the cool morning air. Her cheeks were rosy, her eyes sparkling, and her long black hair, tied up in red ribbons, had small loose tendrils where the breeze had blown them. "You're staring at me." Her expression was teasing over the rim of her coffee cup.

"You're especially beautiful this morning."

The red in her cheeks deepened. She stood and took her cup. "Guess I'm susceptible to flattery. I'd better go and start the ledger."

She was out the door by the time Nellie came into the room. "I've put Mr. Bailey's clothes out for him. He'll call us if he needs any help. Did Nora reach his family?"

"Yes. They'll be here this morning. Nellie, Nora and I have been invited to the Cantons' for dinner. Could you stay in here until we get back, in case an emergency call comes in?"

Nellie agreed, and John finished his breakfast and headed to the office to wait for the first patients of the day.

The sun was casting long shadows when John turned the carriage into Bart Canton's drive on his small farm. Will came out of the house to greet them. "I'm glad you could get away this evening. I have a few things to discuss with you."

John stopped the horse in front of the barn and hopped down to help Nora off. He led Mack to the trough and tied the reins. "You didn't say what you wanted."

Will waved his hand toward the house. "Come in, and I'll tell you." They had just turned their backs to the barn and started walking toward the porch when a loud bang made them all jump. They whirled around and caught sight of a figure coming around the barn. Will shouted, "Leaver! What the hell are you doing here?"

Leveling a shotgun at all of them, Leaver sneered, "I got a deal for you, Canton."

Will's uncle came to the side door. "What's going on out here?"

Leaver fired a blast in the direction of the porch and the side of a post near the door splintered. Bart ducked. "Get back inside, and you won't get hurt."

Will took a step toward him. "How did you get out of jail?"

Leaver's eyes narrowed. "A good friend posted bail money."

"Not to cross the state line, I'll bet."

One of Leaver's men came out of the barn leading Chance. Leaver pointed to the drive. "Tie him to our wagon."

Will's hands shook. "Leaver, you're obsessed with that animal. I've won, and he's mine."

Leaver leveled the gun at Will's chest. "I don't like losing to anybody. This horse is one of the best racers I've seen. He should have been mine."

John was looking around for something he could do to stop this, but there was nothing that wouldn't put them all in grave danger. He glanced at Nora, and her eyes were telling him the same thing. The wagon came up the drive. Apparently it had been parked behind the copse of trees by the road.

The driver waved. "Ready to go, boss?"

Leaver started backing to the wagon. "I'm going to take some insurance with me. I'm taking the lame girl with us."

John's stomach dropped to the ground. "She stays here."

Leaver cocked the gun. "Then she's dead."

Nora put her hand on John's arm. "I'll go." She went to the wagon, and Leaver's man lifted her into the back.

"Tie her hands behind her, and tie her feet." When that was done, the other man picked up a rifle to cover Leaver, who climbed into the driver's seat. When Leaver's man sat down with his rifle still trained on Will and John, Leaver turned the horse down the drive.

John sprinted to the carriage. "Damn it! If he hurts her, he won't live to see tomorrow."

Bart Canton came running out of the house. "Will! John! I called the sheriff, and he's on his way. Don't do anything foolish or Nora could get shot."

John hit the hitching post with his hand. "I've never felt so helpless in my life."

Will patted his shoulder. "The sheriff will take care of it."

John wished he could be so sure. "Bart, may I saddle up one of your horses? I'm going after them."

Will turned to his uncle. "I'd like to go too."

Bart hesitated. "You don't have any guns with you. How will you protect yourselves?"

Will waved his hand to the house. "Let me have your rifle."

Bart stood in thought for a moment. "All right. You two saddle up, and I'll go get the rifle."

John and Will rode out of the barn and saw Bart at the end of the drive. The sheriff and two of his deputies had stopped and were talking to him. John pulled up alongside the sheriff. "We want to go with you."

The sheriff rubbed his hand across his mouth. "Only if you stay behind us and don't try any heroics."

Will took the rifle from his uncle. "We won't." He glanced at John. "Will we?"

John shook his head. "No. Sheriff, it's your call."

"Let's go."

John prayed the villains would let Nora go as soon as they got out of the area. He didn't let his mind go to what could happen.

****

Little rocks and dirt clods were dancing around her body as Nora lay bound on the floor of the wagon. She wished she could see where she was, but Leaver's man sat on a hay bale with the rifle in the crook of his arm. She knew if she moved it could be the last thing she ever did. She could smell the freshly plowed fields, so she was sure they were heading into farm country.

In a wooded area, Leaver stopped the horses. "Charlie, unbind her legs." While Leaver climbed down, Charlie took out his pocketknife and cut the rope. Leaver tied Chance to a branch of a small tree and opened the rear of the wagon. He took the rifle from Charlie and waved it from her to the side of the road. "Get out."

Nora twisted her body. "It's hard to do that with my hands bound."

He grabbed her left foot and yanked her around until she was sitting on the edge of the hinged plank. Charlie pushed her off, and she was standing in the road by the side of a ditch. Fear flowed quickly through her veins. "Walk over there." He indicated the edge of the ditch.

"What are you going to—" A blast cut off her

question. Nora felt like a horse had kicked her in the right leg. Wood crunched, and her left leg buckled. Grass, rocks, and branches pummeled her body as she rolled down into the ditch, landing in moldy water at the bottom. She heard a loud call from Chance and a scuffle on the road.

Leaver leaned over the edge of the ditch. "We don't need you anymore, Miss La Rue. By the time you work your way up, we'll be long gone." He sneered. "And if you don't, consider it a payback for the trouble you've caused me." He gave a short wave, then disappeared. Soon the horses' hoof beats and the rattle of the wagon faded.

Nora's first thought was to control her breathing and racing heart. Then she looked around, assessing her situation. She was on her left side, with her hands still bound behind her back. Carefully, she tested each part of her body to see if anything was broken. Then she felt a sharp pain through her right leg and foot. A stab of fear hit her. There wasn't a right leg or foot any longer. She gritted her teeth until the pain and the fear passed. Everything seemed to be moving all right, but she knew there would be many bumps and bruises.

Her hands and wrists were in the fetid water behind her back, and in the wet and slime, she felt her hand move through the bindings a bit. Working back and forth, she tried to make her hand as small as possible. Finally, she was able to force it free. She sat up and took the rope off the other wrist and rubbed her aching arms and shoulders.

A beat of horses' hooves came rumbling along the road, and she gave a shout as they came nearer, but they kept on going. She was on the brink of despair as they rode by. *I don't think they heard me.*

Nora knew she had to climb the side of the ditch somehow. She pulled the bottom of her soggy skirt up to check her wooden leg. Part of it had been blown away by the shotgun blast, and the rest was hanging by the outer knee hinge. Useless. She rolled onto her stomach and looked up. There were foot and hand holds, if she could manage to pull herself up. Her wet clothes weighed a ton, and the chilly spring breeze was making her shiver, but she removed her cape, then unbuttoned her wool skirt and kicked it off, which made her much lighter, but colder, too.

Slowly, she began to climb. Putting her left shoe on a rock, she pushed herself up out of the water, dragging her broken limb behind. She grabbed onto some of the shrubs, tested their root strength, and pulled up farther. Inching along, making some slips and missteps, she clamped her hand onto a tree root on the side of the road, swung her left leg over the rim of the ditch, and rolled to the side of the road. With the last bit of strength left in her body, she propped herself with her back against the tree. At least she could be seen now. *In case somebody comes along. Soon.*

Nora's breathing was labored, and she was lightheaded. She rested her head against the tree and closed her eyes. After what seemed like hours, she heard someone coming in the distance. She shaded her eyes and saw dust rising from the road, with the sound of hooves and wagon wheels.

As the sound drew closer, she heard a shout: "Nora! There she is!" Pounding horse hooves got rapidly closer. Then she was being held and lifted up. John had found her.

She buried her face in his neck. "My wooden leg is ruined. My skirt and cape are in the ditch. I couldn't climb with them on."

Will jumped off his horse from behind John. "I'll go down and get them." Will held on to a branch and took two steps to retrieve the items.

Nora shook her head. "It seemed like hours for me to get out of there. Thank you, Will."

John helped her balance on her left leg as he put the cape around her, but her skirt was too sodden, and Nora was beginning to shiver again. John called back to the sheriff. "She needs assistance to get back."

The sheriff rode to them. "The deputy is driving the wagon with the two prisoners in back. Would she be able to ride the deputy's horse? Mr. Canton's horse isn't saddled."

John nodded. "We can help her on." He turned to Nora. "Do you think you can do it?"

Nora paused. "I haven't been on a horse since—" She had trouble letting her mind go there.

Will brought over the deputy's horse. "I'll hold him."

Nora waved at the deputy on the wagon. "What's his name?"

"Rocky," the deputy replied.

Nora scratched the animal's nose. "How fitting, since he's a dapple gray." She whispered, "Calm and quiet," in the horse's ear.

John carried her to the steed's side while she ran her hand over Rocky's neck. "Ready?" he prompted. At her nod, he put her left foot into the stirrup, and Nora pulled herself straight with the saddle horn. John went around to the other side. "Now lean forward and move your right limb as best you can. I'll grab it from here."

Nora patted Rocky's neck when the horse took a couple of nervous steps to the side. She leaned forward and moved her thigh as well as possible. The useless wooden limb slid to the middle of the animal's back, where John grabbed it and pulled her onto the saddle, putting the limb into the other stirrup. "Can you hold with your thighs?"

Nora nodded and glanced up. She was no longer in the Waukesha countryside. Nora was on King, ready for her performance, in front of the entrance flap. "Where's the music? Why hasn't the band started?" She looked at the young man standing next to her. "Where's your clipboard? Aren't I on next?"

The young man gripped her thigh. "Nora, it's me, John Mallory."

"John Mallory?" The fog in her mind cleared, and she looked around. A wave of grief settled over her like a dark cloud, and deep sobs wracked her body for what seemed like hours.

She heard the sheriff ask, "Will she be all right?"

John gave her his handkerchief. "We'll talk about this later." To the sheriff, he said, "I think she's coming out of it now." He glanced at Nora. "Can you go on now?" He handed the folded skirt to her, and she put it in front of her on the saddle.

Nora dried her face. "I'm sorry. I don't know what came over me. Yes, I'm ready."

Will gave a concerned glance at John. "Maybe we should ride on either side of her."

They started back to Bart Canton's farm, and Nora's concern about her mental state grew. *What happened to me? And will I be able to fix it? Maybe cripples do become inferior. No. I can still think and function. This is my mind playing tricks on me.*

Soon they were back at the farm, and Bart came out to greet them when they turned into the drive. "I'm relieved to see all of you."

John helped Nora off the horse while Will untied Chance and took him to the barn. "I think we should get back home."

Bart's wife, Sadie, came off the porch. "Not without supper. I won't hear of it."

Nora felt her cheeks heat. "My skirt was in moldy water, and I can't be company in petticoats."

John lifted her up in his arms. "We thank you very much, Sadie, but Nora's wooden leg has been broken."

Sadie laid her hand on Nora's shoulder. "I'm sorry to hear that. I have to go back inside. Don't be long, Bart, Will."

John carried Nora to their carriage and set her on the seat. The sheriff rode over. "I'll have to take your statement, Miss La Rue, on what happened."

Nora nodded. "Of course." She told them what had happened to her when she was forced to go with Leaver.

The sheriff wrote it down on a pad, then flipped it shut and put it in his pocket. He tipped his hat. "I'll be in touch with both of you." He rode back to the wagon, tied the deputy's horse to the back, and they all went down the drive and turned toward town.

John climbed onto the driver's seat and was turning the horse to the drive just as Will came from the barn. John told him, "I'll let you know if plans change for this Saturday."

Will smiled. "Take care, both of you. I'll stay in

touch." He gave Mack a swat on the rump, and the horse took off.

Chapter 18

Nellie made a fuss over Nora and helped her out of her moldy clothes, checking her bumps and bruises as she did so. She helped Nora into her house dress, and when John came over, Nellie handed him Nora's broken limb. Nora wasn't happy to be back on crutches again.

Nellie had fixed a beef stew at the cottage and invited John over, since John and Nora had missed supper at the Canton's. Nora enjoyed the rich broth, dipping the fresh-made bread into it. Afterwards, Nellie served some hot apple cider, and they relaxed around the table.

Nellie turned to John. "Nora told me her side of what happened, but I'm curious about how you found her."

Nora watched John lean back in his chair like he was gathering his thoughts. "After Leaver left, Bart came out and told us he had called the sheriff. When the sheriff and deputy arrived, Will and I had saddled up to go with them. We knew what direction they took and that we could travel faster on horseback than they could in the wagon. We came to a crossroads and were trying to figure out if the wagon had turned, when we heard a gunshot straight ahead, about a half a mile distant. We urged the horses to a fast clip, and in a few minutes, we caught up with Leaver and his man. That's when we discovered they no longer had Nora with them. With the sheriff and his deputy having their rifles trained on them, they gave up without a fight." He paused and closed his eyes for a moment. "That's when I lost my temper and started toward them, shouting, 'Where is Nora?' Will and the sheriff stopped me, and the sheriff repeated my question. Leaver's man told him what they had done. When we turned back, after the sheriff had secured the vermin to the back of the wagon, we scoured the ditches until we saw Nora resting by the tree. I guess she told you the rest."

Nora glanced at him. "Do you know if there was any connection between Leaver and the man you saw by our stable?"

John nodded. "That was Leaver's man looking for Chance."

Nellie blew out a breath. "That's quite a story. I'm glad you all are safe." She got up to clear the table, and John rose also.

He checked his pocket watch. "It's getting late. I'm going back to the house."

Nora grabbed her crutches. "I'll walk out to the porch with you." She closed the cottage door behind them. John was so handsome, her own personal hero tonight. She laid her hands on either side of his face and felt the late-day whiskers. "I love you so much."

He moved his index finger over her lips. "When I heard that shot, I was so scared that I had lost you."

Her eyes became blurry with tears, and she threw her arms around his neck. He embraced her and moved his lips softly over hers, then claimed them. Either the kiss or the soft April breeze was starting to make her shiver, and she pulled back. "Goodnight, my John."

He smiled tenderly. "Until tomorrow, my love." He

put his hat on and headed toward the house as she turned to the door, emotion overflowing within her.

****

John settled in the parlor with a brandy to read the newspaper. He lit a cigar and started on the headlines. A few minutes into his reading, a knock came on the front door, and he laid the paper down and went to answer it, wondering who on earth it could be.

A man in a dark suit stood there and doffed his hat. "Dr. Mallory?" When John acknowledged, he went on, "I'm Asa Griffith from the Waukesha *Daily Freeman*. I was wondering if you could talk to me about the incident at Bart Canton's farm this afternoon."

John pressed his lips. "I'm sure you can get details from the sheriff."

"Oh, I did, but I wanted to know how the crippled girl is doing."

"Her name is Nora La Rue, and she's doing well. Now, I'm very tired, so I'll say goodnight." John closed the door on the reporter and went back to his easy chair.

The next morning, before heading to the hospital, he stopped by the local woodworker's shop with the shattered wooden leg. The smell of freshly cut wood wafted out from the back room. An older man with graying brown hair came out, wiping his hands on a dirty rag. "Yes, sir, may I help you?"

"I'm Dr. John Mallory. I was wondering if you could fix the hinge on this artificial limb." He handed it to him.

The man studied it. "This must be the leg of the crippled girl that was abducted from Bart Canton's farm yesterday."

John paused. "How did you know about that?"

"It's all over town this morning." He pointed at a chunk of wood that was missing. "I can probably use the lathe to fashion another leg to those dimensions and then connect the hinge to that."

"How long will that take? We'll need it before Saturday."

He checked his job sheet on the desk. "I can have it for you in two days. That will be seven dollars."

John paid the man, who put a numbered tag on the limb and gave John the receipt with the same number. "Who do I ask for when I come back?"

The man held out his hand. "Mr. Gaspar. Thank you, Dr. Mallory."

John left the shop knowing Nora wouldn't have to get married on crutches.

****

Nora was recording the appointments on their desk calendar when Elinore bustled in with her carpetbag. "I'm here for your final fitting."

Nora's hand went to her mouth. "Oh, no! I forgot about that. But can you do that while I'm on crutches?"

Nellie came downstairs and greeted Elinore. "If you're here for the fitting, why don't you go into the doctor's office, since he's at the hospital."

Elinore hustled Nora into the back office. "Let's see what we can do."

Nora glanced around. "I don't think it would work for me to lean against the wall."

Elinore tapped her lips with her index finger. "Maybe if we could find a stool, you could prop yourself up." They went back into the parlor. "How about that footstool?" she said, pointing to a padded one in front of the padded chairs.

Nora stood beside it. "It's a few inches too short." She looked around, then waved her hand to the couch. "We could pile a couple of the pillows on it."

Elinore brought over some of the fringed pillows and stacked them onto the stool. "That should work."

"I can take the pillows with me," Nora said. She grasped the fringes along with the holds on her crutches, and Elinore carried the footstool to the office. Nora removed her skirt and shirtwaist and stood in her camisole and petticoats. They put the pillows on the stool, and Nora made an indent with her fist, resting her stump on it. "There. I can stand straight." She looked down. "But the skirt won't fall right."

Elinore shook her head. "I only need to take tucks on the bodice, so it will do." She opened the carpetbag and carefully unrolled the white silk material out of the tissue paper, shook it out, and helped Nora put it over her head. The soft folds of the skirt fluttered as Nora felt the sleeves flow over her arms. Elinore fastened the buttons in back, then pinned the darts on the front and the side seams. "I'll sew it for you and bring it to Ben and Lillian's house on Friday. That way it can hang overnight."

Nora ran her hands over the mutton-chop sleeves. "It feels so soft. I'd love to see it on, but we don't have a mirror in here."

"Trust me, child, you're going to love it." Elinore rolled it in the paper again and laid it in the bag. Then she helped Nora dress in her everyday clothes and gave her the crutches, and they returned the stool and pillows to the parlor.

Nora checked in the hall. "There doesn't seem to be anyone here, and the telephone has been quiet.

Would you like some coffee before you go?"

Nellie was coming downstairs. "I heard that. Go, you two. I'll stay out here for awhile and take care of things."

Nora nodded. "Thank you. Come to the kitchen, Aunt Elinore." They went back, and Nora poured two cups from the pot on the stove. "Cream?"

"Thank you." Elinore poured from the small ewer on the table.

They sat, and Nora took a sip. "Can I talk to you about something?" At Elinore's yes, she went on. "I think I may be losing my sanity." She told Elinore about the pain in her missing foot, the hallucination, and her hysterics when she mounted the horse after her abduction. "That's never happened to me before, and it scared me."

"Have you talked to John about this?"

"I was afraid he would think I was going insane."

"Nora, you've gone through a lot of grief and changes in only a few short months. That would rattle anyone." She put her hand over Nora's. "I saw what you were like when you first came to the sanitarium. In some ways you were defiant. In others, you were scared and unsure of yourself. You have bloomed into a mature young woman who can run a practice efficiently. And that in quite a short time. I wouldn't worry about a few setbacks."

Nora set her cup down. "How do I know this won't happen again?"

"You can't be sure. John has been reading books by a European—Dr. Freud, I think his name is, who has written about the human mind. Some people claim it's bunk, but there might be some truth in it. Talk to John about your fears."

"Maybe he won't want to marry an insane person."

"Nora, stop that. You're not insane. I know John, and I know he cares very deeply for you. Trust me." She patted Nora's hand and rose. "I must be going so I can finish your dress."

Nora grabbed her crutches and stood. "Thank you for listening to me. You're a good friend." She walked Elinore to the door.

Elinore ran her fingers over Nora's cheek. "Next week, I'll be your aunt. You'll have a family who cares about you. Remember that." They said their goodbyes, and Nora attacked the ledger again.

****

John came out of the Knights of Pythias meeting to find Will waiting for him. "John, would you like a beer? I have a few things to discuss with you."

They made their way a few doors down to a cozy tavern with paneled walls and the smell of cigar smoke. They ordered their beers at the long bar and took them to sit at one of the tables.

John took a sip of his brew. "Did you pick up the rings from Goldstein's?"

Will nodded. "I gave them to your father for safekeeping." He paused. "How is Nora?"

"She has some melancholy about what happened to her. I think the stress from the incident shook something loose in her mind. That scared her and made her fear she was insane, but from what I've read in the Freud book, that must be her mind healing itself."

Will stared into his glass. "I never should have gotten the both of you involved in this. I'm sorry, John."

John waved him off. "We stopped a criminal before he could hurt someone else. I would do it again for you."

"It's just that Nora—" Will's voice trailed off.

John put his glass down and studied Will's face. "You care for her, don't you?"

Will glanced at him in surprise. "How did you guess?"

"It wasn't difficult. But you didn't pursue her when you had the chance."

Will sighed. "That's because I was scared of her. I never knew a cripple before, and I didn't know how to handle my feeling of—it sounds terrible—revulsion. Nora is a beautiful and intelligent girl, but I couldn't handle looking at her mangled body." He blew out a breath. "That's why I'm happy you fell in love with her. I enjoy her company. And don't worry, I'm not physically attracted to her."

John quirked an eyebrow. "That's quite a confession for a best man to make to a groom. I'm not upset."

Will took another sip of beer. "On another subject, I ran into Thea at the courthouse in Milwaukee when I was there to sign the papers on the complaint about Leaver. She and a Lawrence Baxter were there purchasing a marriage license."

"Lawrence Baxter?"

"He's a lawyer downtown. He's handling the finances for her and her mother. She told me to give you and Nora her best and to tell you she doesn't hold a grudge against you. She said Lawrence loves her the way it should be and she understands the difference now."

John felt some relief at hearing that. What had happened with Thea still brought on feelings of guilt about how they'd ended their relationship. "At least she's found happiness. For that I'm grateful. Thank you for telling me that." He checked his watch and finished the glass of beer. "I'd better be getting home. I have some early appointments tomorrow."

Will rose with John. "If I don't see you before, I'll see you Saturday." The friends shook hands, and John went out to his carriage and turned the horse back to the house.

Chapter 19

Nora was never so pleased to receive anything in her life as she was when John brought the new leg back. She kissed him and headed out to the cottage immediately to put it on. Almost a half hour later, she returned sans crutches. She threw her arms up and announced, "I feel so free!"

Both John and Nellie shared her joy and raised their coffee cups to her. Nellie exclaimed, "It's so good to see you without crutches again!"

The telephone pealed from the front of the house, and Nora went to answer it. It was one of the men from John's lodge. She called him to the telephone and set to work on the monthly accounts.

John turned to her as he hung up the receiver. "We're invited to the anniversary celebration of Bethesda Park a week from Saturday. He said to dress in our best."

A wave of doubt went into Nora's bones. "John, I don't think I have anything fancy except the ball gown, and that won't do."

He pulled her into a standing position and embraced her. "You're going to be my wife. Buy anything you want next week." As he kissed her, she heard someone coming up the porch steps.

She gently pushed him away. "Your patient is here." She smiled and touched his cheek as the door opened.

John took the patient into an examining room, and Nora finished her bookwork. She told Nellie she would be in the cottage and headed out to pack her case for the weekend.

Her heart raced to think she wouldn't have to worry about where she was going to get the money for things. Here she was, rich most of her life, but now, with a painful interlude nearly over, she found she wouldn't trade any of it to have her past life back again. The accident and its aftermath had made her grow and mature in a way she never would have if she'd stayed with the circus. Maybe it was a blessing in a strange way. Nora was not sure Rico would have treated her as well as John did. He was too consumed with himself. John was a compassionate doctor, but he had dropped everything to come to her rescue in Chicago. That must be love.

She closed the case and put it by the door. Fare-thee-well, Miss Lenora La Rue, circus bareback rider. Hello to Mrs. John Mallory, a woman who can do anything.

She went back to the house to finish arranging her things in John's—their room.

****

John hopped off the train and waved at his brother, who was there to meet them. John helped Nora down, and they made their way to the carriage where Robert and Julia waited for them. Robert climbed down and slapped John on the back. "Well, brother, it's your turn to put on the shackles."

John laughed. "You look no worse for wear. Have you two settled into the new home yet?"

Robert picked up one of the cases and put it in the back of the carriage. "We still have a few things to work on, but we moved in a week ago." Robert swung into the driver's seat, and John sat with Nora. Julia was up front next to Robert.

Julia turned to them. "You'll have to come and visit us one of these days, when we're finished with it."

Nora nodded. "We'd love to."

John sat back and watched the late afternoon Friday bustle in the city as they went by. The air certainly didn't smell as sweet as Waukesha's. He'd forgotten how rank the river was, with its floating oil and debris. The coal smoke made gray smudges on the blue sky. He almost welcomed the yeasty aroma of the breweries.

Finally, they were in the east side residential section, with the homes sequestered in the trees, shutting out the dirty city. They turned into the drive of his father's immaculate home. His mother's spring garden was blooming happily with sunny daffodils, tulips of many hues, and deep purple hyacinths that gave a rich perfume to the air.

John climbed down and helped Nora out while Robert did the same for Julia. John and Robert took the bags to the house, and Bess met them at the door.

John hugged his mother, who came out of the parlor to greet them. "I see you've been busy in the garden again. Your prize bulbs from Holland are beautiful."

His mother glowed with pride. "Thank you, John." She turned to Bess. "Take the bags to their rooms."

John stopped Bess. "I'll take mine up."

"Yes, sir." She took Nora's bag and started up the

stairs.

Elinore appeared at the top. "You're rooming with me tonight, Nora. I'll help you with your hair and clothes."

John watched them go with nothing but love and pride in his heart. And, yes, there was some lust there, too.

His father's voice came from behind him. "You should be proud of her. And yourself, too. The irony is if she had stayed with her family, she may have had money but no character. You gave her that. For that, I am very proud of you, son." He clapped John on the shoulder.

John inclined his head at his father. "Thank you, Father." He picked up his bag. "I'll be down as soon as I settle in."

He went to his old room and set the bag on the bed. Opening the window, he gazed over the backyard, where the spring leaves and buds were making their appearance. The wrought iron garden benches had been painted a few weeks before, to prevent rusting, as had the lattice arbor and gazebo. It looked like his mother had had the gardener clear out the branches and leaves from last fall. Plank benches and folding chairs were set up in front of the arbor. He could smell the aroma of freshly cut grass, and that took him back to his boyhood when he and Robert used to climb the old apple tree and steal the fruit his mother had staked a claim on for her pies and preserves.

He stepped back and checked in the wardrobe. His mother had his morning suit hung, waiting, and his top hat was cleaned. He unpacked and stored his things, then stopped at the washstand, where there was a fresh pitcher of water.

After cleaning up from his journey, he joined the others in the parlor. Nora was there with Elinore, talking to his mother and Franny. The latter jumped up and gave him a hug.

"It's so exciting…two weddings in one year! I'm so happy for my brothers."

John laughed. "Poor Franny! No one to tease or torment you anymore. Well, don't worry. I shall tease and torment every time I see you."

"As will I," Robert called from the other side of the room.

Franny grabbed one of the pillows off the couch, and John shielded himself from being a target of the fringed missile. "There are a few things I won't miss," she pouted.

They heard a knock at the front door, and Bess announced that Reverend Nolan had arrived. A jovial white-haired man entered, and John and his father went to greet him. He warmly shook John's hand. "Well, my son, I've been told the second brother has decided to take the big step. Congratulations! Was it the girl I saw you with at Robert's wedding?"

John nodded. "Yes, sir. Miss Nora La Rue."

Nora was beside John. "Pleased to see you again, Reverend."

John's mother stood and waved her hand toward the tea tray on the table. "Would you have some tea?"

"Delighted," the reverend said with a smile. As he poured, he asked, "Is everyone here for the rehearsal?"

John shook his head. "Not yet. We're still waiting on…" There was a knock on the door. "On Will." John went to the door, and Will bounded in.

"Sorry I'm late." Bess took his hat and coat.

John's father took the lead. "Shall we all go out back?" He led the way through the kitchen to the back porch.

Reverend Nolan turned to Nora. "Ben tells me your family isn't coming."

Nora glanced down. "No, sir. They're too busy for me."

The reverend's lips pressed together. "I'm so sorry, my dear. Who's going to give you away?"

"I'll do it myself, sir. I'm the one who agreed to marry John, not my father."

"So everyone who is going to be here is from the Mallorys' side?"

A trace of a smile skimmed her lips. "They all have become my family and friends too."

John put his arm around her shoulders and gave her a squeeze. He was so proud of her, and pure love swelled in his heart.

They spent the better part of an hour going through the whole ceremony. Since it was a garden wedding, there wasn't too much pageantry to it, and for the music, his mother had hired a violinist and singer to stand on the back porch. After the rehearsal was declared finished, they went back inside for refreshments.

At the buffet table, Bess had set sandwiches, finger food, and desserts of various kinds. John was getting some for himself and Nora when Will put an arm around his shoulder. "Can I see you and Nora in the library for a few minutes?"

John called Nora over, then asked his father, "May we three be excused for a bit?" At the affirmative nod, they retired to the library. John and Will sat in the two leather chairs, and Nora sat on the couch, setting their refreshments on the table.

John picked up his cucumber sandwich. "What did you want to see us about?"

Will leaned forward. "I was late because I was talking to Uncle Bart about a business. He and my aunt want to move into town, and he wanted me to take over the farmland. He said it would be perfect for a breed farm for standard-bred horses." He turned to Nora. "I know your magic with them and wondered if you'd like to be one of the trainers?"

She set her plate down, and a sad expression crossed her face. "I don't know, with the way I am now, if I could handle that."

"You helped with the show horses, didn't you?"

"Yes. But I could get up and down from them then. I can't get on a horse without help now."

"You won't be there by yourself." A light glowed from Will's eyes. "I had a thought. Why couldn't we train show horses, as well? There's a lot of call for them."

She shook her head. "You give them commands with your feet, and I—"

John stood and put both hands on Nora's shoulders. "You could find a way to do it."

She wavered. "I would love to try."

Will grinned. "That's all I ask. For your help, I'll give you a cut of what I sell the horses for. Say thirty percent?" He held his hand out.

Nora paused, then shook it. "Deal."

"I won't be ready to start for a few months. I'll let you know."

"John! Reverend Nolan is about to leave," he heard his mother call from the parlor.

The three went out to bid the reverend farewell, and Will retrieved his hat and coat as well. "I think I'll go, too." He slapped John on the back. "Don't worry. I won't be late tomorrow." He quirked his eyebrow. "What time is it again?"

John slugged his good friend on the arm. "Don't make me come looking for you."

John and Nora walked Will to the edge of the porch and waved goodbye as he took off on his horse. John put his arm around Nora and waved his other hand toward the porch swing. "Sit." Nora leaned in and put her head on his shoulder. His fingers lifted her chin to look at him. "Are you happy, Nora?"

She smiled slightly. "A complicated question. There are many things I'm unhappy about, but being married to you is an easy answer." Her eyes softened. "Yes. I'm very happy. For someone who thought she would never find love, you showed me what true love is. Not ever having it in my life, I didn't know what it was until you showed me."

A slight spring breeze riffled through her raven hair. Her luminous brown eyes made his heart swell with a love he didn't know he had. His groin stiffened, and he sat back, fighting the lust. This would never do at his father's home on the eve of their wedding. He slowly blew out a breath. "You realize we both have challenges ahead of us. It won't be smooth sailing for either of us."

She stroked his cheek. "I've found that is what life is all about. We've got each other to face whatever is in the future. I love you, John, and I trust you."

As an answer, his mouth went over hers in an all-consuming kiss. He had to catch his breath when he pulled back. He rose and put out his hand. "Will the soon-to-be Mrs. John Mallory please accompany me into the house?"

She raised an eyebrow. "With pleasure, Dr. John." They walked back to the family in the parlor.

****

Nora awakened to the sun streaming through the lace curtains. She looked around and saw that Elinore had risen earlier. She glanced at the clock ticking away on the dresser. *Just six more hours and I will no longer be a La Rue.* That revelation made her smile. *I guess, in a strange way, I can thank the cyclone for taking my leg.* She grabbed her crutches and got out of bed.

She poured water from the pitcher on the washstand into the matching basin with its bunches of red roses and blue ribbons. Splashing the water on her face, she reached for the cake of lavender soap on the dish. As she was drying her face, there was a knock at the door. "It's Elinore, dear. I've brought your breakfast."

Nora opened the door to the robed figure, who set the tray on the bedside table. "Thank you, but I could have gone down."

Elinore tsked. "It's traditional for the groom to not see his bride on the day of the wedding until the ceremony." She checked out the door. "They all seem to be downstairs now. You may use the washroom."

After Nora's morning routine, she joined Elinore back in the bedroom. Nora poured the hot tea into the cup and added two sugar lumps, then picked up a slice of buttered toast. Elinore had opened the window, and a cool morning breeze freshened the room. Nora found her in the chair by the window, watching the activity in the yard. She leaned against the sill, peeking at the people putting up flowers and trim around the gazebo. Nora turned and finished the toast, then sat on the edge of the bed and sipped the tea. She sighed. "Six hours of being confined up here. It's going to seem like six days."

Elinore laughed. "Come, come. This is supposed to be the happiest day of your life."

"I just hope I can find something to keep me occupied."

Elinore rose. "We can start by getting your leg on." She helped put Nora together until she was clothed up to her petticoats and chemise. Nora put her dressing gown over that. Elinore hung the wedding dress by the window to let the wrinkles settle out.

Nora sat on the bed again. "Well, that's an hour gone." She warmed her tea from the pot that was still lukewarm.

Elinore gathered up the breakfast tray. "I'll see what mischief I can stir up." She swept out of the room and came back only minutes later with Franny, in her house dress, carrying a box.

Franny set the box on the table by the chair. "Do you like to play Lotto?"

Nora was intrigued. "I've never played it. Could you teach me?"

Franny beamed. "I certainly can." She opened the box and removed all the playing cards, and in the next couple of hours Nora learned the popular matching game.

All too soon they heard Lillian Mallory calling

Franny: "Time to change clothes."

Franny put the playing cards back in the box, then sang out, "Coming, Mother."

When she left, there was a knock at the door. Elinore opened it, and Bess stood there with a tray of refreshments. "The missus thought both of you should have something to eat before the ceremony." She entered and placed the tray on the table. Elinore thanked her, and Bess left.

Nora wavered. "I'm too nervous to eat."

Elinore handed her a cheese-and-watercress sandwich. "You don't want to pass out from hunger during your wedding, do you?" She took one of the jam ones for herself.

Nora nibbled her sandwich, then took a drink of the iced water that had been sent up. "I feel more anxious now than I ever did before a performance."

Elinore smiled. "Performing wasn't a life-changing experience. This is. I'll get dressed first, and then I'll help you." She took off the robe and put on her spring suit, of pale blue silk, that had also been hung by the window.

When Elinore had finished, Nora stood and admired her, saying, "That looks wonderful on you!"

Elinore gave her a slight bow of her head. "Thank you, my dear. Now sit at the vanity and let me fix your hair." She coaxed Nora's thick hair into a bun at the top of her head, with a few ringlet wisps flowing free. Lillian and Franny came in to help with the dress, and Franny set a basket of spring flowers on the table.

Nora rose to smooth her petticoats and chemise in front of the full-length mirror. Lillian and Franny had the entire back of the dress unbuttoned, holding it open while Elinore raised the back of the skirt over Nora's head so it wouldn't disturb her hair. Nora slipped her arms through the unbuttoned sleeves. The dress flowed into place, and the women did up all the pearl buttons.

Franny stepped back and clapped her hands. "Both of you did a beautiful job on that."

Nora studied herself in the mirror. The skirt and the shoulder part of the mutton sleeves were plain white silk, but the bodice and the sleeves from wrists to elbows were covered with a cream-colored lace. Nora had sewn seed pearls vertically a few inches apart on the front of the bodice, and the lace on the bodice was gathered at the neck with a dark blue velvet ribbon.

Lillian went to the door. "Oh, I almost forgot." She disappeared and returned with a jewelry box. "When my mother passed on, she willed her jewelry to be distributed to the family. Julia received her wedding rings. To John's bride, she willed this pendant." She removed a scalloped double chain of pearls with a pendant ruby rose and two green emerald leaves. She fastened the necklace around Nora's neck. "That looks wonderful with your coloring, dear."

Nora fingered the rose. "It's absolutely beautiful! Thank you, Mrs. Mallory."

Lillian glanced at her tenderly. "You may call me ' Mother.'"

Nora had no words, and her tears threatened. She took Lillian into an embrace. "Thank you, Mother." If only her own mother would have treated her so.

Elinore picked up the white netting. "Franny, bring the basket of flowers." Nora sat at the vanity again, and Elinore put combs in her hair to hold the netting, with hair pins for some of the flowers. Franny tied the rest together with a dark blue velvet ribbon for a bouquet.

Nora rose, and Franny gave her the flowers. In the mirror Nora saw an elegant lady now, not a circus performer or a poor working girl. So many changes in less than a year! But all of them were her, and she knew now that she could survive anything.

Lillian glanced out the window. "It looks like they're ready down there. Franny, come with me."

As they left, Elinore took a turn in front of the mirror and picked up her small bouquet of flowers. "All set?"

Nora felt her stomach climbing to her throat. "Yes." She wound the netting around her arm.

Elinore helped her down the steps, so she wouldn't get her artificial limb caught in the skirt. Lillian and Franny were waiting for them on the back porch. Nora heard the violin and the singer doing "Oh, Promise Me" as they came down the stairs, and then Lillian signaled the musicians, who waited until she and Franny were seated with the other guests before the violinist started playing Lohengrin's "Wedding March."

Elinore helped Nora on the porch steps, stopping to stretch the netting behind Nora, then went about twenty paces in front of her. Nora glanced at the sea of Mallory family friends and relatives as she walked to the gazebo. Some she had met and others she was seeing for the first time.

Her gaze traveled to the gazebo, where John was waiting with Will. John's eyes connected with hers, and Nora's heart swelled with love for this man who had drawn her from the precipice of despair into a life of love. He looked so handsome in his gray morning coat and top hat. There was joy in his face as he stretched out his hand to her. His warm clasp sent tingles up her arm.

They stood in front of Reverend Nolan, saying the proper things and exchanging rings. Finally, Nolan announced to the gathered, "May I present Dr. and Mrs. John Mallory?"

The couple turned toward the seats, and then John took her in his arms and gave her a kiss that electrified her entire being, while everyone applauded. "I love you," he murmured in her ear.

When they pulled back, Will slapped John on the back and gave Nora a kiss on her cheek. "My two dear friends. May your marriage be always happy."

Family and friends converged on the young couple and enveloped them in a web of love. Nora, for the first time, felt like she had a real family. The heartbreaks of the past faded in the attic of her mind, where she shoved them away in a trunk. She was no longer a La Rue.

Wine was passed around, and Ben raised his glass. "I want to make a toast on this happy occasion. Having two of my sons wed within months of each other makes it a proud year for me. John's bride, Nora, surprises me all the time. A very brave young lady. It makes me happy that John didn't listen to my advice that he not get too involved with his patients. Here's to many happy years ahead for them both."

John glanced at Nora and gave her a wink as they raised their glasses and took a drink. Nora soon learned who was who among all the family and friends, making idle chit-chat along the way. If they had any reservations about her, they didn't express it, for which she was grateful.

At the end of the evening, Robert brought the carriage, and Will took John and Nora's bags to be placed in the back. Will hit John on the arm. "Time for you to go. Robert and I arranged a suite at the Pfister tonight. Robert will pick you up in the morning to take you to the train station."

Nora turned to Elinore. "Could you help me take the netting off?"

Elinore drew her to a chair and undid the combs holding it. Bess brought Nora's hat, and Elinore pinned it in place. John held the cape for her.

Nora and John thanked everyone and went to the porch steps, where they were met with a shower of rice before they climbed into the carriage and Robert slapped the reins. After waving goodbye, Nora watched the sun swimming on the crest of the hills as everything was bathed in a late afternoon gold.

Robert stopped the horse in front of a huge building, and a doorman came over to them. "May I help you, sir?"

Robert made a motion to indicate his passengers. "Dr. and Mrs. John Mallory have a reservation for tonight. Their bags are in the back."

The doorman tipped his hat. "Very good." He retrieved the bags and said to John and Nora, "Please follow me."

John and Nora thanked Robert and wished him farewell, then accompanied the doorman to the front desk. Nora was awed by the columned lobby with its carvings and paintings even on the high lobby ceiling. John checked in at the desk, and a bellboy took their bags up to the suite. Even the elevator was the latest in style. It moved smoothly from floor to floor.

Nora was enchanted with their suite and its rich materials and gilding. They even had a marble bath that glowed in the light. A complimentary bottle of Champagne and a bowl of fruit graced the table. John tipped the bellboy before the lad left, then took Nora into his arms. "I'm so happy you're mine, my love." They kissed, and Nora seemed to melt in his embrace.

Nora pulled back. "This is more than I ever thought I'd have. I love you so."

John picked up the chilled bottle and opened it. "Here. A private toast to the both of us." He poured the bubbly liquid into the stemmed glasses, and they saluted each other. Then he set both of their glasses down and turned Nora around, unclasping his grandmother's necklace. "We don't want to lose this," he said, as he tucked it inside her case pocket. He pulled the combs from her hair, and it cascaded past her shoulders.

As they started undressing, Nora suddenly cried, "Oh, no! I forgot my crutches."

John gave her a wicked grin. "Don't worry. You won't need them." He undid her artificial limb, swept her up in his arms, and with a laugh, dropped her on the large bed with its red velvet spread. "And there you will stay for a while."

The air felt chilly against her bare skin, and she was grateful when John was next to her. The heat from his body radiated as he traced the contours of hers. He claimed her lips with his own, and she felt his love pulsing against her thighs. She surrendered her whole being to him.

The night was timeless: Periods of sleep; Periods of being swept into ecstasy. The quick trysts from before were nothing like feeling his warm flesh next to her for hours.

She woke to the sun streaming across the bed. John was next to her, holding her in an embrace in his sleep. He looked so young and handsome. She touched his cheek and felt the roughness of the early morning beard there. He stirred and broke into a beaming smile as she fingered his hair out of his eyes. "Good morning, husband."

He nuzzled her neck. "Good morning, wife." He heaved a sigh as he looked at the clock on the end table. "I'd like to linger here a bit longer, but we slept in late. Robert should be here soon to take us to the station." With a quick warm kiss, they set about their morning routines and removed their traveling clothes from their cases.

Nora carefully rolled her wedding dress in tissue paper and laid it in her case. John did likewise with his formal suit and flattened his top hat into his case. Nora took one more look around the magnificent suite before they left. "I want to remember this for the rest of my life…such riches."

John nodded. "It is beautiful, isn't it?" He kissed her nose. "So are you." He rang for the bellboy, who showed up in a few minutes. He flipped him a quarter. "Take our bags down."

The boy tipped his hat. "Yes, sir."

Nora and John went down in the elevator and saw Robert waiting in one of the lobby's elegant chairs with the carved wood and blue velvet trim. John waved, and Robert came over. "Robert, do we have some time for breakfast before we go?"

Robert checked his watch. "Coffee and toast,

perhaps. I'll have a cup with you."

John picked up their bags from the bellboy, and they entered the dining room, where John ordered coffee, toast, and jam from the waiter.

When the order came, Robert poured some cream in his coffee and smirked at John. "You two look calm and refreshed this morning."

John hit his brother on the arm. "Best vacation ever."

Nora's cheeks heated. "John! Really!" The brothers laughed.

Robert set his cup down. "Tsk, Nora. Being in a family, you have to be able to take some jesting."

She pursed her lips. "Our family never jested. My brother hardly ever spoke to me."

John shook his head. "Another thing you'll have to get used to."

They finished their quick meal, packed the carriage, and headed to the station. Nora was determined that her new life wouldn't be anything like her old one. She hadn't realize how much she had missed.

Chapter 20

Nora's next few days were filled with moving the rest of her things from the cottage to their room in the house. John gave her permission to add feminine touches to his masculine ones. Since the weather was warming up, she took down the heavy drapes and installed lace curtains and added freshly cut flowers on the dresser.

They hired a maid and a cook, Calista Meyers and Bertha Thomas, to free up Nora for her office work and Nellie with her nursing. Callie moved into the cottage with Nellie, and Bertha moved into the back maid's room. The practice was doing well and bursting with efficiency.

With the social outing coming up on Saturday, Nora was getting increasingly nervous. Outside of being with John's family, social situations never went well when people found out she was a cripple.

She hung her new garden party gown and hat next to the wardrobe. She had found the pretty green organdy with the dark green velvet sash at one of the women's clothiers downtown, along with a wide-brimmed hat with a dyed ostrich feather and red flowers. John had pronounced it a capital outfit. This was the first real purchase she had made of clothes for herself.

She went downstairs to greet John's next patient,

but instead of Mrs. Thompson, a man in a business suit stood in the lobby. He removed his hat. "I need to see Dr. and Mrs. Mallory. My name is Halcourt Leslie."

She paused. "I'm Mrs. Mallory. What business do you have with us?"

"I need to see you both together."

"The doctor is with a patient now. Can you wait a few minutes?" The man nodded and sat on one of the chairs.

After a while, John came out with Mr. Percy, his patient, and Nora called him over. At the same time, Mrs. Thompson walked in.

"John, this is Mr. Leslie. He says he has some business with us both."

John pursed his lips. "Will this take long?"

Mr. Leslie shook his head. "Very quick."

John called to Nellie, "Will you take Mrs. Thompson to the examining room?"

Nellie nodded and waved her hand, saying to Mrs. Thompson, "Please come with me."

"Now, what is it?"

Mr. Leslie handed John and Nora each an envelope. "This is a summons to appear in Federal court in Chicago next month, on Friday the seventeenth at ten o'clock, for the trial of Frederick Leaver."

Nora felt a cramp in her stomach. She had thought all that was behind her. Mr. Leslie tipped his hat and left. "John?"

John slapped the envelope against his hand. "I had a feeling this was going to happen. We were in it too deep." He glanced at her and patted her arm. "Don't worry. We'll be all right. We just have to tell what happened." He gave her a quick kiss and went to see his patient.

Nora went to her bookwork, but a feeling of dread didn't leave her.

****

"Nora! Are you ready, my dear?" John called up the stairs.

Nora appeared at the top in her new garden party outfit and took a deep breath. "I'm still nervous about this."

He held out his hand as she reached the bottom step. "Nonsense. You look beautiful." He put her arm through his. "Are you sure you want to walk the three blocks to Bethesda?"

She nodded. "It's a sunny, warm day. I walked much farther when I worked at Canton's."

The air smelled sweet after the rain the day before, and the scent of spring flowers wafted on the soft breeze. Many people were taking advantage of the warm sunshine and walking, too. There were carriages crowded along Dunbar, and John was happy they hadn't taken theirs. He paid the fare at the gate, and they strolled into the tree-lined paths and carriage roads

Nora squeezed his arm. "Have you ever been here before?"

He shook his head. "I haven't visited the pleasure parks in Waukesha. This is a beautiful one on the banks of the river." They heard a train going over the bridge near the entrance. "That must be the excursion train to Waukesha Beach."

Surprise crossed her face. "They have a beach in Waukesha?"

"It's actually on Pewaukee Lake, northwest of here. We'll have to visit it sometime. Wirt Jones told me about all the amusements there."

John stopped for a moment and turned to Nora. "My dear, you're going to be meeting some of my friends and their wives. I want you to promise that, if they ask about your background, you will tell them the truth."

Nora paused and sighed. "You're taking a chance that they won't be your friends anymore."

He grasped her shoulders. "If they are too shallow to accept you for who you are, they will never be true friends."

"I already have the stigma of being a cripple."

John nodded. "And that you can't hide."

Nora slipped her arm through his again. "I shall try it your way."

They arrived in a clearing around a pond lined with colorful flowers. People were gathering near a magnificent domed and pillared spring house. On the hill behind it, white letters spelled "Bethesda." A huge oak was decorated with American flags, and a picture of a gentleman hung on the trunk. Nora waved her hand toward the picture. "Who is that, I wonder?"

"That must be the Dunbar Oak that Wirt was telling me about. The gentleman must be Colonel Dunbar, who discovered the spring."

They joined the crowd at the spring, and one of the "dipper boys" ladled the spring water into a glass for each of them. The water was cool and sweet. John noticed Wirt Jones and several of the lodge members and their wives. He nodded to them, and the couples came over to join them. Introductions were made, and John could feel Nora tensing up.

Mrs. Parker gave her a slight smile. "Lovely gown,

Mrs. Mallory."

John hoped she'd remember the social manners she was taught. She replied, "Thank you, Mrs. Parker. You look nice, too." So far, so good. John noticed the slight nudge Wirt gave his wife.

Mrs. Jones put her gloved fingers on Nora's hand. "Mrs. Mallory, I want to invite you to a meeting of the Sisters of Pythias. We're a sorority of the lodge. I can send an invitation with the time and place of the meetings. We do much charity work."

Nora took a deep breath. "Thank you. I'd be interested."

The group followed the Joneses to benches that had been set up near the orchestra stand, and John noticed Nora was beginning to relax with the small talk among the couples. Then Mrs. Parker asked Nora where she was from.

Nora set her jaw and looked directly at Mrs. Parker. "My family lives in Peru, Indiana." The predictable pattern of questions followed, and John knew what was coming next.

"What does your father do?"

Without a beat, Nora replied, "He owns a circus."

There was a moment of silence before Mrs. Parker said, "Well, isn't that interesting?"

John closed his eyes for a minute, hoping the advice he'd given Nora was right. Then he heard Mrs. Jones ask, "Are you the girl who lost her leg in the cyclone last summer?"

At Nora's acknowledgment, the group was asking her questions without being judgmental. John was grateful to his friends and proud of Nora's courage.

The day was splendid, and John and Nora enjoyed

the concert in the afternoon. Nora seemed happy when they started for home. As they walked, Mr. and Mrs. Parker joined them. "Do you mind if we join you?" he asked. "We live a few doors down."

John shook his head. "No, of course not."

Mrs. Parker glanced at Nora. "Mrs. Mallory, do you happen to follow the serial stories in *Harper's Monthly*?"

Nora nodded. "We have them in our waiting room. Yes, I do."

"A group of us girls are forming a club to discuss those and other articles. Would you be interested in joining us? We meet at each other's homes."

Nora smiled. "I would be delighted to join your discussions."

John enjoyed the Parkers' company. He knew Parker because he owned a pharmacy downtown where John sent many of his patients. He was relieved that his friends were finally accepting his wife into their circle. They would see what a delightful person Nora was.

They waved to the Parkers and bade them goodbye after arriving at the practice, which was now their home, too. John could see Nora was relaxed and happier than he'd seen her in any social situations before. He squeezed her arm. "You did well today, my love."

Nora beamed at him. "I'm getting them to look past my artificial leg, and they are seeing me." They went into their room for a night of sweet contentment.

****

Nora turned from the telephone and stopped John as he was coming back from seeing a patient. "Will just called, and he said he needed to talk to us. Since you're off tomorrow night, I invited him to dinner. He said he's bringing a guest."

John wrinkled his brows. "I wonder if it has something to do with the trial in a couple of weeks."

She shook her head. "He didn't say exactly what he wanted, but I guess we'll find out."

The next evening, a knock came on the front door just as Nora and Callie were setting the table. John came in from the parlor. "I'll get the door." He came back a few minutes later with Will and a young lady Nora had never met.

Nora came around the table to greet them. She called back, "Callie, could you take Mr. Canton's hat?"

Callie did so, and Will turned to Nora. "Mrs. Nora Mallory, may I introduce Miss Phoebe Proctor?" Phoebe was fashionably dressed and had beautiful green eyes and reddish-brown hair done in ringlets.

Nora smiled. "How do you do, Miss Proctor?" She gave her a slight bow. "Callie, could you bring refreshments into the parlor?"

They made their way to the front room, and when Callie brought in the tray, John waved his hand toward the table. "Please help yourself."

Nora set her cup of tea on the end table of the couch. "Where did you meet Will, Phoebe?"

A smile played around her lips. "He came to my father's breed farm in Delafield to find brood mares."

John quirked his eyebrow at Will. "Oh?"

Will reddened slightly. "For my new venture on my uncle's land. Mr. Proctor has some of the best standard bred stock in the Midwest. And a very interesting daughter that I have much in common with."

Phoebe blushed at that. "Will, please."

Will continued, "We've been seeing each other for a couple of weeks now."

John laughed. "So that's where you've been."

Callie appeared at the door. "Dinner is ready." They all rose and went to the table in the dining room. Through the meal, Will told them how his business was shaping up, and John and Nora told about the event at Bethesda Park.

"Since you are going to be living in the area, I'll see if you can join the Knights of Pythias. It would be nice to be at the lodge together," John mentioned to Will.

The conversation turned to the coming trial, and they all filled Phoebe in on their adventures. Will was telling about what took place when the police arrested Leaver, including the trick Nora used with the whip to dislodge Leaver's gun. He turned to Nora. "You never did tell me where you learned a thing like that with the whip."

Nora grinned. "There was a man with us in the circus for several seasons, Texas Rhodes, who was an expert with the rope, knives, and whip. He taught me several tricks with each. I got pretty good with them."

Will chuckled. "I saw your expertise with the whip. I wouldn't want to be on the wrong end of a knife with you, however."

John glanced at her. "I'm sure I will be very careful not to anger you in the kitchen." Nora reddened, and everyone laughed.

Phoebe nodded. "Working with a lasso will help you with the horses. I didn't realize you could learn so much at the circus. I envy you."

Nora paused. "Don't envy me. There's much I

didn't learn and probably never would have if I had stayed."

The evening ended on a happy note, and Nora felt she was going to be seeing a lot of Phoebe in the coming years, the way Will gazed at her. She felt relieved that he'd found a girl who seemed worthy of him. Yes, she still cared for him, but John she loved with all her heart.

Chapter 21

The morning before Fredrick Leaver's trial in Chicago found Nora, John, and Will waiting for the train in the Milwaukee station. The warmth of early summer was pleasant outside, but the steam being hissed out of the engines made it feel like a Turkish bath.

Finally, their train came huffing and puffing into the passenger area, and they boarded the coach. The rich red-brown mahogany walls with the small chandeliers hung along the aisle made a suitable backdrop to the blue-cushioned seats that were filling up rapidly. The three seated themselves in a group facing each other.

As the train pulled out of the station, Will leaned forward. "I hope you didn't have difficulty in finding doctors to cover for you."

John shook his head. "We are going into the resort season full blast now, but we're all ready to cover when some need a rest. I'll have my days in the future to help out someone else."

Nora placed her fingers on Will's wrist. "How is the farm coming along? I haven't had a chance to get out there yet."

Will beamed with pride. "Splendidly! If you remember my driver, Trenton Casper, he's in charge of training the racers. I'll give you warning when we purchase the show horses."

Nora felt more excitement at the thought than she'd expected. "I'm so looking forward to it!"

Will smiled. "I even constructed a set of steps for you, so you can get on and off the horses yourself."

She clapped her gloved hands. "Wonderful!"

They continued the small talk as the fields and towns passed by. Big white fluffy clouds grazed like sheep in the deep blue sky, cutting patterns on the landscape. When they reached the Dearborn Street Station in Chicago, they took a streetcar to their hotel just a few blocks from the courthouse.

The next morning, the streets were alive with people, horses, and a few of the new horseless carriages chugging down the avenue. They decided to take the streetcar to the Federal courthouse to avoid the dust and the coal soot coming from the factories. The mighty edifice loomed in front of them as they stepped off the streetcar. In the lobby, Will asked the clerk where the courtroom was for the Fredrick Leaver trial. They found the room, and Sgt. Finney spotted them, tipping his hat.

Nora's heart begin to pound, and her stomach tightened. It seemed that John could sense that, and he took her hand and squeezed it. Will was blotting his temples with his handkerchief. The courtroom was full. Apparently there were many people Leaver had hurt. After what seemed an eternity, guards brought Leaver in and seated him next to his lawyer, who leaned over to talk to him.

The judge entered, and the curtain opened on the drama. Will was the first called to the stand, because his was the main complaint. Will set his jaw and was sworn in. The prosecutor had him give the history of Leaver's claiming that the horse in question was his. The bill of sale and photograph of Chance was entered as evidence. When the prosecution rested, Leaver's attorney rose and faced Will.

The lawyer closed in like a hungry lion. "Isn't it true, Mr. Canton, that you and Mr. Aaron Blake conspired to manipulate the sale of said horse away from Mr. Leaver, who was promised the horse first?"

Will coolly sat back in the chair. "Where it was true that Mr. Leaver put in a bid for the horse first, Mr. Blake didn't want to sell to him. There was no conspiracy."

"Every time he tried to talk to you about the horse, you harassed him."

Will's jaw dropped. "He was the one who was harassing me! The man sent his employee to Waukesha and stole the horse, murdered Dan, and burned my uncle's stable down in the process."

The lawyer slapped the wood on the witness stand. "You can't prove he knew about it."

"Then why did he disguise the horse and change the name?" Will snapped.

The lawyer whirled around. "No further questions."

Aaron Blake testified the same as Will when he was called to the stand. Nora followed Aaron, and she went up with a big knot in her gut. She told about her and John's deception to find Chance and her stained handkerchief was put into evidence by the prosecutor. There was a deep sense of relief when the defense waved her off with, "No questions."

The other plaintiffs were called in turn to the stand,

and they gave similar stories. Then the jury was retired to the chambers after the lawyers gave their final pleas. Will herded John and Nora out. "Let's get something to eat while we're waiting."

They went to the small diner next door to the courthouse, and after consuming a hasty lunch, went back to wait for the jury. The twelve men came in an hour later, and everyone assembled into the stuffy courtroom. A wave of anticipation rumbled through the crowd, and the judge banged his gavel. "Will the defendant please rise?" To the twelve men, he asked, "Has the jury reached a verdict?"

The foreman rose. "We have, your honor."

"What say you?"

"We the gentlemen of the jury find the defendant, Frederick Leaver, guilty of horse theft, murder, and fraud."

Leaver leaned forward and slapped his hand on the table with a whack. "Damn you all to hell!"

The judge used the gavel again. "Order! Mr. Leaver, you have been found guilty. Your sentence will be entered on the fifteenth of July. Guards, remove Mr. Leaver from the court."

Leaver shot murderous daggers from his eyes at Will as Leaver was being escorted from the court to the jailhouse. Finney approached the group and slapped Will on the shoulder. "Thank you, my boy. We finally got Leaver off the street. Unfortunately, there's more where he came from."

Will grinned. "Well, at least there's one less."

Finney laughed and wished them a safe trip home. Nora was exhausted, and she held onto John's arm on the walk to the streetcar that took them to the hotel. The next morning, they checked out and picked up their bags for the train home.

At the station, Nora sat on one of the wooden benches in the outdoor passenger section while John and Will purchased the tickets. The two returned just as their train came huffing and puffing into the station with a steamy blast from its whistle and a clang of the bell.

John gave a hand to Nora, and they walked to one of the coaches. She heard a small voice behind them. "Look, Mama, she's a cripple."

"Hush, child. Don't stare at the poor unfortunate."

John frowned and made a move to turn around, but Nora squeezed his arm. "Let it go, John. I know now you won't change their minds."

He relaxed and leaned toward her. "I'm proud of you, you know."

Nora smiled, and he helped her up the steps into the car.

Chapter 22
Six years later

Nora held tight to the lead of the big white gelding, Caesar. He lifted his head and snorted impatiently. She scratched his ears. "Yes, I know you want to get to your work, but you have to learn to wait."

Will and Trenton strolled to the outside of the gate to the show horse ring. "Are you really going to let Cal ride Caesar?" Will nodded to the small boy standing at the top of the steps at the edge of the ring.

"I was five years old when I mounted my first full-sized horse. I think he's ready." She led the horse to stand beside the steps.

Cal put his hands on the horse's back. "Will you give me a boost, Mama?" Nora helped him swing his foot over, and he landed firmly. "He's bigger than Pokey." The boy gulped, glancing down.

"You can do this, Cal. Just follow my instructions and do as I showed you." Nora walked the horse to the center of the ring and unhooked the lead. She patted the horse's neck and whispered, "That's my son up there. Be calm." Nora stepped to the center. "Now, make Caesar go right."

Cal held up his right hand. "Is this right?" At Nora's nod, the big horse turned and walked around the ring to the right.

"Now turn him and go left." The horse did so with

no visible cues from Cal. "Very good! Now make him prance." The horse arched his neck, lifted his tail, and danced in a circle. "Stop and turn him to face Uncle Will and Trenton." As the boy did so, the two men gave them a round of applause. She saw Cal's left foot lightly touch the horse's ribs. She gasped. "No, Cal! Don't make him—"

The horse's front legs nearly kneed the ground, and Caesar's head went into a graceful bow. Cal did a somersault over the horse's neck and landed on his back in the sawdust. Will and Trenton were over the gate in a split second, and the three adults landed by Cal at the same time.

The boy lay stunned for a moment or so, then his chest started heaving. Trenton stood up. "Looks like the boy just got the wind knocked out of him."

Nora checked him over. "Seems nothing is broken. Can you stand up?" The boy stood, and Nora brushed the sawdust from his clothes. "Cal, that was wrong. You could have been badly hurt. Your balance isn't good enough yet for bowing."

His lower lip went into a pout and a tear rolled down his cheek. "Sorry, Mama." Then his arms went around her neck. She could never stay mad at him.

Trenton held his hand out. "I'll take Caesar back to his stall for you, Mrs. Mallory."

Nora handed him the lead. "Thank you, Trenton."

Will helped Nora up. "Caesar seems ready to be sold. You did capital work on him."

"Thank you. I've enjoyed working with your show horses. Have you gotten word about the filly team yet?" She brushed her denims off.

"We should be getting word about those two next

week."

Nora checked the horizon. "Sun's getting low. I'd better be heading back."

Will put Cal on his shoulders, and they all headed to the house, where Nora's horse Ellie was by the trough. Will's wife, Phoebe, came out on the porch. "Nora! Remember you and John are invited to supper Saturday evening."

"I remember, Phoebe. You're sure it won't be any trouble? You're getting on now." Nora glanced at her hostess's blossoming figure.

"No, I'm fine."

Will put Cal down and helped Nora onto the horse, then deposited Cal behind her. The boy leaned in and took a hold on her shirt. They said their goodbyes, and Nora turned Ellie toward the road. The warm late June breeze blew through the woven straw of her summer hat. The scent of freshly cut grass mingled with that of the last of the spring flowers, and she took a deep breath of the promise of summer.

They headed into town and had just passed by Carroll College when Nora felt a small tug on her shirt. "Mama, what's that train car over there?"

Nora glanced at the railroad siding and saw a colorful red, blue, and yellow car. She turned Ellie to go around the side of it. "It looks like an advance car for a circus."

"What's an advance car?"

"It's a car that arrives a couple of weeks before a circus comes, to arrange for the grounds and to advertise."

She felt Cal moving up and down behind her. "Can we go to the circus, Mama? What do those words say?"

She read the side of the car. "Stupendous show of shows—" The words caught in her throat and she coughed. The rest of the words on the side were "The La Rue Family Circus."

"Let's go on home, Cal." The boy was asking questions all the way back, but Nora just gave one-word answers. She was shaken to the core. They turned into the drive and went back to the stable. John had built steps similar to the ones Will had to help Nora get on and off horses. She reached back and got Cal off. "Why don't you feed and water Pokey?" she told him and pointed to his pony in the stall.

"What about the circus, Mama?"

"We'll talk about it." As the boy left, she put her foot on the step and swung her leg over Ellie's back. Numbly, she climbed down and led the horse into the stall. While she was taking care of Ellie, Cal finished with Pokey. "Cal, go see what Bertha is cooking in the kitchen. I'll be in after I feed and water Ellie."

The boy happily skipped to the house. "All right, Mama!"

Nora did the necessary chores, but a great wave of sorrow had come over her. Closing the lower stable door, she sat on one of the hay bales and put her face in her hands. For years, she had pushed the way her family abandoned her back into the recesses of her mind. It was too much for her to deal with. She had stayed away from circuses coming to Waukesha because Cal had been too young to notice. Now he wasn't. Why, oh, why did it have to be her family's? She heard the screen door on the back porch slam, and she glanced up. John was walking toward her. She took her hat off and rested her head against the wood frame. "Don't you have patients?"

He stood over her. "I've just finished for the day. And I talked to Cal. What happened?"

She paused. "We saw a circus advance car on the siding by the college, and Cal asked me what it was. It turned out to be for the La Rue Family Circus." Tears started plowing their way down her cheeks.

He took her hand and pulled her up. Taking her into an embrace, he said, "I'm so sorry."

She pulled back. "Now that Cal is old enough to notice, why did it have to be my family?" She swallowed another sob.

He dried her cheeks with his handkerchief. "Maybe this is a good thing."

"What? Why?"

"You haven't been dealing with their callousness. Maybe providence stepped in so you can clear the air. You can't run away forever, Nora."

"I hate this." She put her hat on again, and they walked to the house.

Nora's chest had a tightness for the next few days. During the day on Saturday, summer thunder growled in the skies. The clouds had cleared when she and John took off in the carriage for Will's place. The evening sun cast sparkles over the wet ground, and the air smelled clean and fresh. If she hadn't been in such a state of mind, she would have enjoyed it.

Will came out to welcome them and helped Nora down from the carriage. She sensed an air of seriousness about him.

John noticed it, too. "Something wrong?" he asked as they went inside.

Will paused and glanced at Nora. "I received a

letter about interest in purchasing a show horse yesterday." He turned to Phoebe, who came up to welcome them. "Where is the letter that came in the mail?"

Phoebe disappeared and returned with a colorful envelope. "Here it is." She handed to to Nora.

Nora shuddered as she recognized her father's elaborately printed stationery. She opened it and read silently.

John nudged her. "What does it say?"

She pursed her lips, then revealed, "My father wants to stop here when they get into town. They need another horse for bareback riding." She paused. "He has heard ours are some of the best ever trained."

Will put his hand on her shoulder. "You don't have to be here when they come."

Something inside her steeled. "I want to be here. I have to be here. I need to face my father."

Will turned to John. "Do you think that's wise?"

John nodded. "She won't get over this until she faces her problem head on. She will be haunted for the rest of her life if she doesn't."

Will shook his head. "I think you've been reading too much Freud, but I'll leave that up to you."

For some reason, the tension in her chest eased a bit. Maybe getting a bit of resolve was the beginning of the end.

****

Caesar nickered contentedly as Nora brushed his coat until he gleamed. She buckled the straps in place and tugged to see if they were tight enough. She had dressed today in her denims and white shirt, borrowing one of John's hats to disguise herself a bit. She wanted her father to see what she could do before he judged her on who or what she was.

She drew out a bit of carrot from her pocket, and Caesar happily crunched on it. She scratched his nose while he swished his elegant tail in a graceful arc to disturb the flies. Will and Cal were raking the practice ring to smooth out the sawdust.

The warm breeze stirred her hair as she shaded her eyes to peer down the road. A distant bang was heard in the direction of town, and a motor grinding closer. Caesar shuffled his hoofs, and the whites of his eyes shone while Nora calmed him.

With a chug-chug and sputter, a horseless carriage turned into the drive, and then the motor died. Two men got out of it. They were dressed in tails and top hats, and Nora recognized her father and her brother Rene. Will said something to Cal, and the boy headed for her while Will went to greet the men.

"Are you going to show the men Caesar, Mama?" Cal raised his eyes to her.

Nora was climbing up the steps. "Yes. Will you hold Caesar, please?"

Cal took the reins and led the horse by the steps. "Are they going to buy him?"

Nora set her artificial limb and swung it over the horse's back. "We have to show him first. Cal, stay here by the steps, all right?"

"Yes, Mama." The boy dutifully sat on the top step to watch.

Will brought the men to the fence, and Nora pulled her hat down. Will gave her the signal to start, and Nora put Caesar through his paces. Her thigh and left foot movements were almost imperceptible, and the horse flowed from one pace and direction to another. Finally, she held the strap, placing her right hand on his withers, and Caesar rose on his hind legs and pawed the air. When he came down, she touched her left toe on his ribs and he gave a graceful bow to the applauding audience.

Jacques La Rue turned to Will. "Bravo! I must meet your trainer."

Nora sidled Caesar to the fence. "My name is Nora Mallory." She pushed her hat back and watched astonishment cross both her father's and her brother's faces.

"Lenora? You?" her father sputtered.

"But how do you do this? You're a cripple!" said Rene after he had gaped at her.

Nora felt the corners of her mouth curl up. "I come from a circus family. I can do almost anything I put my mind to."

Cal ran to them. "Do you know these men, Mama?"

"Calvin Mallory, may I introduce you to your grandfather and your uncle?"

He wrinkled his nose. "That's not my grandfather and my uncle. We were just at their house last month."

"That's Papa's family. These are mine. Your Grandfather Jacques La Rue and Uncle Rene."

Jacques smiled at Cal. "That's quite a boy you have there. Does he ride?"

"As well as I did at his age."

Will opened the gate and put his hand on Cal's shoulder. "Let's you and me take Caesar back to his stall." Will took the lead and led the horse to the steps so Nora could climb down. "I'll be back in a few minutes," he said to the La Rues. Nora went out the gate and stood in front of her father.

Jacques' mouth was in a straight line. "You know, Lenora, you owe me a trained horse."

Nora seethed. "Caesar is not mine to give. He belongs to Will Canton. I just train for him. In fact, if you purchase Caesar, I'll have to show your riders the signals, since they are different. I use my thighs, my left foot, and my hands to direct him." She paused. "I don't owe you anything, Father. You abandoned me."

"You're the one who never came home."

She dug her fingernails into her palms. "At the time I needed my family the most, you packed up and left." She poked her finger for emphasis. "Where were you when I got out of the hospital? When I needed a place to stay? Needed money to live on? If I remember correctly, when John asked for my hand in marriage, you told him you had washed your hands of me. You were invited to our wedding and you didn't respond. *Now* you tell me I owe you a horse? No, Father, I don't." Tears threatened but didn't flow.

Jacques and Rene stood there stunned. Jacques took a deep breath. "I didn't think you had it in you, girl. I have to say, you've grown." He took off his hat. "Hearing all that, I'm so sorry, Lenora, for the way we treated you."

Shaken in her anger, Nora was struck speechless. "You're apologizing for ruining my life?" she finally said.

"For being blind. This had been bothering me the past few years, but I didn't know what to say to you. I challenged you to see how I'd harmed you, and I find you have a spine." He held out his hand. "I know what

I've done to you doesn't deserve forgiveness, but may I have a truce?"

Nora didn't know if this was flim-flam on her father's part, but she gave him the benefit of the doubt. "Truce." She shook his hand.

Will and Cal came back from the stable, and Jacques slapped Will on the back. "Now, let's go talk about the horse." They all walked to the house and sat around the kitchen table, with Phoebe joining them. Will negotiated a price with Jacques and Rene. The men signed the agreement that Phoebe had drawn up.

Jacques turned to Nora. "Can you come early in the morning to show our bareback riders how to control Caesar?"

Nora wavered slightly. She didn't know how she would handle being in a circus environment again. Going to see the show was one thing, but working? "Yes, I'll be there."

Rene leaned in. "Bring Cal and your husband with you. We might be able to find something for the boy to do."

Nora glanced at Will. "I'll ride Caesar home tonight and then take him to the grounds in the morning." To Rene, she said, "John has patients to see, but he will be there for the show."

The men rose and shook hands to seal the agreement. Nora found she was dreading the next day but excited about it as well.

Chapter 23

John helped Nora and Cal onto a saddled Caesar for the ride to the riverside site where the circus had set up the night before. "I'll bring the carriage with me this afternoon." With a concerned face, he added, "Are you sure you're ready for this?"

Nora took a deep breath to settle her nerves. "No. But I have to face this hurdle and take it."

The summer air was damp and warming in the early morning sun. People were milling about downtown, and there was anticipation in the air for the welcomed diversion. In the middle of the resort season, most of the hotels were full of vacationers looking for excitement.

A lump hardened in Nora's throat as she saw tents and colorful flags and banners lining the river. She hadn't realized how much she missed this. There were a lot of bad memories connected to the circus, but many happy ones, too. She heard the calliope hissing out its music to lure people to the grounds. "What's that noise, Mama?"

"That's the steam-driven calliope. It's a type of pipe organ."

As she rode up, a gray-haired, leathery man in overalls turned and shaded his eyes. "I'll be hornswaggled! That can't be Miss La Rue!"

Nora laughed. "It isn't. I'm Mrs. Mallory now. And

behind me is my son, Cal. Cal, this is Old Bob, the head roustabout."

Bob patted Cal's leg. "Well, isn't he a fine fellow!"

Cal wiggled behind her. "Hello, Old Bob!"

Nora tightened the reins as Caesar danced a few steps. "Where should I take the horse? My father just purchased him."

He pointed. "The equine tent is over there."

"Could you find my father or Rene, please?"

"Sure will, miss—er, ma'am." He hurried in the direction of the main tent.

She turned Caesar toward the equine tent and passed by the food stands with the warm aroma of popcorn thick in the air. Cal wiggled again. "Mama, that smells good!"

"We shall get some later." As they approached the tent, a muscular, dark-haired man in riding breeches came out to greet them.

In his clipped British accent, he said, "Lenora! I was surprised when Jacques told me you'd be bringing the new horse. I didn't think you'd ever ride again."

"It's good to see you, Niles. This is Cal, my son."

"What a fine little chap. A rider, too, I see."

"Niles, could you bring over the steps for me?" He disappeared inside and brought out the booster steps. Nora helped Cal down, then dismounted herself.

Niles was getting acquainted with Caesar, who was snorting and doing a dance step. "Spirited fellow, isn't he?"

"And well trained," came a voice from behind. Jacques strode to them. "Tell Stella and Catrine they have to learn the commands for Caesar."

Nora took the reins. "Father, if you could bring the

bareback harness, I'll put it on Caesar. May I store the saddle in the tent?" At his nod, she pulled it off, and Jacques brought the harness, then stored the saddle. Nora and Cal had just finished buckling the harness when Niles came back with the girls.

The slight girl with henna-soaked hair turned to Niles and pointed at Nora. "You're going to have a cripple show us how to handle a horse?"

Niles frowned. "Stella, may I introduce to you Mr. La Rue's daughter, Lenora?"

Her mouth banged shut, and she turned a nervous eye on Jacques. "I didn't know you had a daughter."

He looked at her coldly. "Before she lost her leg, she was the best rider in the business. Now she's a superb trainer."

Nora was overwhelmed by the praise from her father. She had never received any before. She mounted Caesar and showed the girls the subtle commands from her hands, thighs, and left foot, then had them try in turn. Once Caesar was used to them, he worked like a well-oiled engine.

The little blonde, Catrine, happily clapped her hands when she got off his back. "I absolutely love this horse."

Out of the corner of her eye, Nora noticed Jacques and Rene with their heads together in conversation. Nora took hold of the horse's lead, ready to take him into the equine tent, but her father came over, hat in hand. "Lenora, we were discussing letting you ride Caesar in the show tonight. Would you be interested?"

Nora paused. There was a slight ping of fear in her stomach, remembering the last time. She swallowed. "I don't know. I haven't practiced any routine with Caesar.

And no costume—"

"Annie is still here. You know how fast she can whip up a costume. As for a routine, just do what you normally do with him, only with music."

Then she remembered the excitement of being in front of a crowd and performing. A catch came into her throat. "I'll do it," she said with a rasp. She saw John walking to them and ran into his arms. "Oh, John, they want me to ride Caesar in the show tonight!"

Jacques gave a tilt of his head. "Of course, with your permission. I assume you're her husband."

John put out his hand. "Dr. John Mallory. We met before."

Jacques shook it. "Ah, yes, you're the young surgeon who was so upset with me."

John studied Nora. "Do you want to do this?"

She felt the elation. "Yes, yes. I want this one more time."

He smiled. "Then do this." He looked around. "Where's Cal?"

She glanced at the hay bale the boy had been sitting on and felt her heart fall. "He was right there. *Cal!*"

John ran around the side of the tent. "I see him!"

Nora hurried the best she could after him and saw Cal by the river watching the two elephants wading and spraying water over their backs. John scooped him up. Nora put her hand on her chest. "Cal, never run off like that without telling anyone!"

Cal buried his face on John's shoulder. "I'm sorry, Papa. I never saw elephants before, outside of picture books."

The handler glanced over and gasped. "Miss

Lenora, is that you?"

"Yes, Samuel, only it's Mrs. Mallory now." She introduced her family.

Samuel smiled, showing his tobacco-stained teeth. "We've missed you around here."

Jacques appeared next to Nora. "I see you found the boy. Lenora, the band is practicing. Would you try a routine on Caesar with them in the ring?"

Nora took a deep breath and pushed down the trembling. "Yes, of course." John put a hand on her arm. She gazed at him lovingly. "I'm fine."

He kissed her on the forehead. "Then go."

She went to Caesar and took his lead. Scratching his nose, she whispered, "Let's show them what we can do." He threw his head up and snorted. After she mounted him from the steps, she saw Major Sands at the entrance of the main tent.

He gave a slight bow. "Lenora, I'm happy to see you again. Your father tells me you're going to be performing this evening. What piece of music do you want?"

Nora thought for a moment. "How about the "Radetzky March?"

"We can do that. Give me a few minutes, and I'll start the cue." He disappeared into the tent.

Nora guided Caesar to the entrance flap. A wave of panic washed over her, and she shut her mind against it. "I'm going to be fine," she murmured. Caesar shuffled, and she knew she was transmitting her anxiety to the horse. She stroked his neck and took a deep breath. "Sorry, boy. Let's do what we do best."

She heard the cue, and the flap was opened for her. The horse performed like a champ to the private audience. At the end, Caesar swept around and pawed the air, then went into his graceful bow. Many of her old friends gave her a standing ovation, and Cal cheered from John's shoulder. Her father helped her dismount, and she hugged Caesar's neck and buried her face in his mane to hide her tears.

Jacques wiped his eyes. "You'll be superb, Lenora."

Nora heard her name called from the entrance, and there was Skinny Annie, the costume mistress, smoking her corncob pipe. "Have I got a costume for you!"

Nora followed Annie to the costume wagon. "I know you do wonderful work."

Inside, Annie studied her critically. "I can hide your leg."

Nora shook her head. "No. I want everyone to see what I can do."

Annie searched for a pair of tights and handed Nora white ones. Nora stripped down to her corset, and Annie helped to put them on. Annie went to the costume rack and pulled out a red-sequined riding jacket with a short filmy blue skirt. She shook it out. "This should fit. It doesn't look like your size has changed much."

Nora stood in front of the full-length mirror and watched as Annie secured the skirt and put the tight-fitting jacket over it. The neckline was very low, and every curve was emphasized. "Oh, my," she whispered.

Annie checked her pocket watch. "We have a half hour before show time. I'll heat the curling irons in the kitchen." She handed Nora a small red-sequined top hat with blue and white ostrich feathers. "Let your hair down and secure this hat." When Annie returned with the irons, she pinned Nora's hair in a cascade of curls down her back, then applied the stage makeup. Nora stood and gazed at the old Lenora La Rue, Bareback Rider Extraordinaire, in the mirror.

"I think this is a bad idea," came a voice from behind them. Nora hadn't noticed her mother's entrance.

Nora frowned. "Don't worry, Mother. After tonight, I'll never darken your door again."

Margarete's face turned into a sneer. "Rico married an aerialist and is with Ringling Brothers now."

Nora pursed her lips. "I'm married, too, and couldn't care less."

Margarete turned on her heel and slammed the wagon door. Annie tapped the pipe stem against her teeth. "Unpleasant woman."

Nora had to get some air. She went to the equine tent, where all the horses were getting fitted for their acts. Caesar shone like new snow, with red and blue ribbons in his mane and tail. He nickered as soon as he saw her. She scratched his nose. "Sorry I don't have a carrot for you."

Nora saw Aunt Elinore with Frank in a wheelchair by the corner of the main tent. She went to greet them. Putting her hand on the old soldier's arm, she said, "Thank you, for all the advice when I needed it."

He patted her hand. "You've come a long way, Nora. We're all proud of you."

Elinore kissed her on the cheek. "Our whole family is inside. John told them yesterday." She turned Frank around. "We have to go get our seat. We'll be cheering for you."

Nora checked the roster of acts and saw she was

fourth in line, so she went to the food tables and picked up a sandwich. Butterflies were doing a cotillion in her stomach, but she didn't want to faint from hunger, either. The time neared, and Niles helped Nora onto Caesar.

Niles' eyes started to water. "I never believed I would see you riding again. You look as beautiful as you ever did."

Nora's eyes were misty as well. "Thank you, Niles." She reached out and squeezed his hand. Turning Caesar toward the entrance flap, she felt an earthquake start in the core of her being, and her hands trembled so badly she could barely hold on. Caesar danced sideways, and she stroked his neck to calm him—and herself.

She heard Lyman, the ringmaster, as he announced her. "Ladies and gentlemen, we have a treat for you tonight. For this one time, Lenora La Rue, now Mallory, who was injured dreadfully in a cyclone several years ago, will perform for you tonight. May I present the former Lenora La Rue on the magnificent steed Caesar!"

The music cue started, and she rode in to thunderous applause and cheers. She ate it up. It was almost like the last few years had disappeared in a dream. Caesar cavorted gracefully to the music and, at the end, gave a masterful bow. How heady this was! She had forgotten what it was like to be a star. At the finale, she rode in to a standing ovation. Her father helped her down and drew her to the platform beside him, where they took a bow. She walked out of the tent beside her father, leading Caesar with his halter.

All of her circus family were hugging her and

congratulating her. Her father quieted them down. "Lenora, would you like to travel with us for the rest of the season?"

She gasped. She wanted to be a star again. She missed this. Nora took in all the colorful characters standing around her, but then she saw another group of people standing by the corner of the tent. They also were waiting for her answer... Elinore and Frank. The friends from Waukesha she had made. Ben and Lillian. Robert, Julia, and their children. Franny and her intended, Douglas. Will and Phoebe. John. Cal, who was running to her. She caught him up in her arms. She felt John put his arms around her.

"We're all waiting for you to answer," John said softly.

Nora looked into John's loving eyes and then turned to her father. "I'm sorry, Father, but I can see it on your face: I'm a way to make more money. These people took me into their hearts and lives. The answer is no." Her chosen family and friends closed around her.

A word about the author...

Ilona Fridl resides in southeast Wisconsin with her loving husband, Mark. This is her eighth book for The Wild Rose Press.

You can find her at her web site:
http://www.ilonafridl.com
and look her up on Facebook.

Thank you for purchasing
this publication of The Wild Rose Press, Inc.

If you enjoyed the story, we would appreciate your
letting others know by leaving a review.

For other wonderful stories,
please visit our on-line bookstore at
www.thewildrosepress.com.

For questions or more information
contact us at
info@thewildrosepress.com.

The Wild Rose Press, Inc.
www.thewildrosepress.com

Stay current with The Wild Rose Press, Inc.

Like us on Facebook

https://www.facebook.com/TheWildRosePress

And Follow us on Twitter
https://twitter.com/WildRosePress